ANNIE MELVILLE

The enthralling saga of Annie Pepper's search for love and romance continues

Sandra Savage

ISBN-13: 978-1503281240
ISBN-10: 1503281248

To all the women who have taken on the worst that fate could throw at them and survived.

We never know the depth of our love, till we are faced with separation.

CONTENTS

Chapter 1

"Oh, Annie," whispered Mary, pulling back the curtain to let in the sunlight. "What a lovely day for a wedding."

Annie lay on her back, gazing at the low ceiling above her and tried to picture Alex. Today would be the happiest day of her life. At two o'clock on 3 June 1913, she would become Mrs Annie Melville.

"What time is it?" she asked her sister softly, not wishing to wake up Nancy, her niece, who was to be her little flower girl.

Mary squinted at the mantelpiece clock. "Ten past seven."

"Time for a nice cup of tea, I think," replied Annie, rising quickly from the warm bed in the single room she'd shared with Mary since her sister's return from Edinburgh six months ago.

Annie busied herself about the kitchen, filling the kettle from the cold tap and hooking it over the coals to boil. The range was the main source of energy in their tiny home in William Lane in Dundee and was kept burning day and night, no matter the time of year. But being Scotland, even in June, it seldom got too hot.

The two sisters sipped their tea and relished the day ahead.

Annie's husband to be, Alexander Melville, was a Police Sergeant in the Dundee Constabulary and had met Annie, a flax weaver, when Mary's marriage had broken up. It seemed a lot longer than six months ago since Annie and Alex had gone through to Edinburgh with Alex's sister, Isabella, to persuade Mary to come back and to reunite Isabella with her errant husband,

John Anderson. Annie still couldn't understand how Mary could have left her beautiful daughter, Nancy, to run away to Edinburgh with John Anderson, but she could understand her fear of her husband, Billy Dawson.

She handed Mary her tea. "Are you sure you want to be my bridesmaid?" she asked, aware that it may bring back unhappy memories for her sister of her own marriage.

Mary smiled. "I wouldn't miss it for the world, Annie Pepper. Me and Nancy'll be the best bridesmaid and flower girl a sister ever had. I just wish Mammy and Daddy could've been here to see it."

Both women's eyes misted over at the memory of their parents, now both dead and buried in their homeland of Ireland.

"If the good Lord's anything to do with it," said Annie. "They'll be watching it from somewhere up there and grinning all over."

Mary sniffed and rubbed her bare arms. "I hope so," she replied, suddenly feeling chilly. "To be sure my marriage would have been a big disappointment to them, not to mention me and John's infidelity..." Mary's voice trailed off at the memory of how she'd deserted her daughter and run off to Edinburgh with John Anderson, a Captain in the Salvation Army, and the man she'd fallen in love with. She shook her head to disperse the thoughts and went to waken Nancy.

Annie watched her go. The last four years, since Billy Dawson had first arrived at their farm in Ireland to help with the flax gathering, had been hard on both of them. Annie had fallen hard for Billy and he, it had seemed, had felt the same, but before he left for Scotland at the end of the harvest, both Mary and herself were pregnant by him.

But it was Mary who had followed him to Scotland and it was Mary who he'd married, leaving Annie alone with her ailing mother to fend for herself. She had borne a son, John, who had been taken at birth by the nuns at the poorhouse and whom Billy had never seen, nor even knew about. A pang of pain stabbed at her heart at the memory of her firstborn son. Somewhere in Ireland, he was alive and growing into a boy. He would be four now, the same age as Nancy.

Mary came through carrying her yawning child.

"Now then, little one," cooed her mother. "You and me are going to make ourselves pretty, so Auntie Annie can be proud of us both at her wedding to Uncle Alex." She placed the child on the wooden coal bunker beside the small sink and ran the cold tap. "Now, be a good girl while mummy fills the kettle and we'll get you nice and scrubbed."

Nancy sat obediently, her legs dangling over the wooden edge. "Nancy hungry," she announced loudly. "Toast!"

Annie smiled and lifted her niece into her arms. "Is it toast you're wanting young lady?" She grinned, tickling the child's tummy. "For a hungry girl."

Nancy squirmed and giggled.

"I'll get her some," called Mary, already putting a slice of bread on the toasting fork and holding it to the flames.

"Make some for all of us, why don't you," suggested Annie. "It'll keep the butterflies from attacking the lining of my stomach."

Mary bent to the task as the kettle boiled and the sun rose higher.

Suddenly, into this gentle morning, there came a loud banging at the door. In an instant, their happiness was replaced by fear. Instinctively, each knew there was only one person who would be knocking at their door at this hour of the morning and that was Billy.

"I'll go," said Annie, handing Nancy back to her mother.

Mary and her daughter moved to the back of the room as Annie opened the door.

It had been six months since Mary's return and, amazingly, he had stayed away from them. Annie knew it was something to do with Alex, but she didn't know what, but now her worst fears were being realised as Billy's figure stood before her leaning casually against the wall outside her house.

For a moment, neither of them spoke, as they got used to seeing one another again.

It was Billy who breached the silence. "I believe congratulations are in order," he said coldly.

Annie's eyes levelled with his. "They are," she replied, trying to keep the anxiety out of her voice.

Billy inhaled and exhaled deeply before speaking again. "So, Sergeant Melville's got his wicked way with you, has he?" he continued. "Now, there's the power of the police for you."

Annie's eyes held his. "What do you want, Billy?" she asked quietly.

"What do I want?" he repeated sarcastically. "What indeed." He folded his arms across his chest and raised his eyes skywards. "I want," he began. "I want to turn the clock back four years. That's what I want. Can you do that, Annie?" His eyes were bleak and Annie felt a chill round her heart. There was a time when she'd wished for nothing more than to be with Billy, but so much had happened since their first encounter, that the love she had felt for him then had long since died.

"No, Billy," Annie replied. "I can't."

Billy dropped his eyes to the ground. "Can I see my little girl then," he asked, "My little Nancy?"

Annie tensed. "This isn't the time, Billy. She's still asleep. Tomorrow, come and see her tomorrow."

"Sure, sure. And you'll make certain Sergeant Melville's around when I arrive."

"No," insisted Annie. "There'll just be me and Nancy."

Billy's eyes narrowed. "And Mary?" he asked, "Will she be here too?"

Annie flinched. "No," she replied quickly, "She won't be."

Billy's eyes narrowed even further. "Perhaps she's here now," he said, the menace in his voice becoming apparent, as he tried to look past her into the dimness of the kitchen. "Maybe she's here for the wedding!"

Annie backed into the room and slammed the door shut, turning the key quickly in the lock as Billy's anger boiled over.

"Let me see the bitch," he roared. "Let me see the whore who's the mother of my child."

Annie leaned against the door, her heart pounding.

"Go away, Billy," she shouted. "Alex's going to be here at any minute and you'll end up in jail again."

The banging stopped.

"I'll be back, Annie Pepper," Billy told her icily through the door. "Don't think you and that tart that's your sister'll get away with humiliating Billy Dawson."

Annie heard his feet move away and her breathing steadied.

Mary was clutching Nancy, both their faces pale and drawn.

"He's gone," Annie told them shakily. "He's gone."

Mary began to cry with despair. "Oh, Annie, I'm so sorry," she began. "And on your wedding day."

"Sssshhhh," Annie consoled her. "Everything'll be alright once Alex and me are wed and we all go to live with him. Billy won't be able to touch either of us then. Alex'll see to that."

Mary nodded, her eyes still full of fear.

"Now, c'mon you two. We've a wedding to go to."

As the day's activity increased, the fear of their encounter with Billy diminished and by the afternoon it was replaced by the excitement of the coming nuptials.

"You look beautiful, Annie," said Mary, smoothing the folds of the cream skirt. Annie flicked the ruffle of lace at her neck and patted a stray curl back into place under the circle of silk roses which held her small cream veil in place. She picked up her gloves and her bible and smiled in thanks.

"And you, too, have never looked lovelier." Mary blushed, adding to the glow of happiness around her.

Nancy tugged at Annie's skirt, and raised her arms to be lifted. Annie bent down to her.

"Auntie Annie can't lift you today," she told her. "But how about a hug?"

Nancy threw her arms around her and pressed her cheek to Annie's. "Happy birthday," she exclaimed, unable to fully understand the occasion, but realising it was special.

Annie and Mary laughed in merriment.

"Happy birthday, Nancy," giggled Annie. "Now be a good girl and later on, you can eat as much cake as you like."

The clock chimed two o'clock.

"We're late!" exclaimed Mary, ushering Nancy through the door. "Alex'll think you've left him up at the altar."

"The church is only over the road in King Street," Annie reminded her. "And anyway, the bride's supposed to keep her groom waiting. Just a little while."

A clutch of neighbours had gathered at the end of the close to wish Annie well as she and Mary emerged into William Lane to gasps of delight. Two of Alex's constables were also waiting to escort them the short distance to the small vestry of Wishart Church and cleared a way through for them amidst the excitement.

The whole of William Lane seemed to have taken on a special brightness despite the grey of the tenement homes and Annie felt a wave of gratitude to the hard-working people she now shared her life with.

"Ah the best, Annie," called a voice. It was Jessie Greig, Annie's constant support since befriending her on her first day at Baxters Mill.

Annie waved happily back to her as the parade moved down the lane and across King Street to the red stone church where Alex was waiting anxiously.

They entered into the arched vestibule together and, after taking their vows, Alex placed the gold wedding ring on Annie's finger.

"I now pronounce you man and wife," intoned the Minister as Annie fought back tears of happiness. "And I hope you will both be very happy."

Chapter 2

The hunched figure of Billy Dawson watched from the railings around the stone walkway above the close, till Annie had disappeared from sight and the excitement had died down. Neighbours gradually returned to their chores until only he remained, gazing at the white clouds blowing in the June breeze and clenching his fists till the nails bit into his palms.

He'd lost and Alex Melville had won.

He closed the door behind him and slumped into his chair. His life was a mess. The only good thing which had come out of the whole sorry business was his daughter, Nancy, and he could now see even her slipping from his grasp. It had been six months since Mary had returned and, at Annie's insistence, Billy had handed back his daughter again to her mother, hoping it would somehow raise him up in Annie's eyes.

The fire he felt for her still burned within him and, no matter how much he drank, he couldn't put it out. He cursed Alex Melville again, but at the same time, knew he was beaten.

Annie would be moving away soon to Maryfield, in the North of the city, where Alex had his house, and she'd already given up her job as a weaver at Baxters. He'd never see her again. Billy reached for his whiskey bottle to fill the emptiness he felt and closed his eyes as the warmth of the liquid ran through him. The alcohol numbed his brain and his emotions took over as dreams of Annie filled his head and his heart.

His decision, four years ago, to do the right thing and marry Mary had been so wrong. But it seemed at the time that there was no other way, not with Mary six months pregnant with his child. At first, he'd felt he could make it work, forget Annie and do his duty, but when Mrs Pepper had died and Mary had asked if Annie could come over from Ireland to live with them, Billy had too easily agreed. The consequences of this decision had been dire, catapulting him into the depression which had twisted his mind and ended in his losing everything, including the thing he loved most, Annie.

The whiskey shimmered before his eyes, catching the light of the fire as it swirled in its glass with every movement to his lips. Real tears were forming in his eyes and he squeezed his lashes tight to prevent them from rolling down onto his face, but to no avail. The whiskey spilled from the glass onto the hearth as Billy reached for his tobacco, but he only succeeded in pushing the jar further away from him.

He lay back in his chair and allowed the tiredness to take over. He'd be asleep soon. The coals settled and turned grey as the fire burned lower and in their movement, an ember fell onto the spilled whiskey setting it alight. The alcohol blazed instantly igniting a newspaper which had been lying near the hearth and before long, the fire spread and acrid smoke began to fill the room. Billy slept.

It was the sound of breaking glass and the voice of Andy Kennedy that saved his life.

"Billy," he shouted. "FIRE!"

From somewhere in the depth of his soul, Billy roused himself to the realisation that he was in danger.

"This way!" screamed Andy, making his way towards Billy as he tried to shield his face from the heat. Billy staggered and stumbled after Andy and finally fell on his knees on the landing outside, coughing and gasping for breath. The rush of air through the open door had driven the blaze out of control and all they could do was raise the alarm. The two men rushed from door to door, banging loudly and shouting "FIRE!" Doors opened and panic gripped the occupants as they saw the flames and smoke belching from Billy's door and window.

"Somebody git the brigade," Andy shouted. "Afore the whole buildin' gaes up."

"Bring buckets!" yelled Billy. "Fill them up at Jimmy Burnie's."

Before long there was a snake of householders passing buckets of water to one another up the stairwells and onto the landing where Billy and Andy Kennedy poured them in desperation at the flames and smoke.

A street urchin ran into the close from the Lane. "The fire-eeze ir cumin'!" he shouted as loud as his small voice would let him. The fire cart struggled up the narrow lane and disgorged firefighters with stirrup pumps and hoses.

"Clear a space," ordered their chief. "Let the men through." The crowd of watchers parted and scrambled up onto to dykes and railings to get a better view of the drama.

"Is there anybody inside?" shouted a fireman to Billy, on reaching the blaze.

"No," he shouted back. "I was in alone."

The fireman nodded and drew his axe from his belt.

"Stand back," he ordered, breaking the remains of the glass in the window and directing the water into the smoke-black room. "We'll soon have this ane oot."

Billy and Andy stood back, as the firemen fought to control the blaze. The chief went from door to door ensuring everyone was out of the tenement and instructed one of his men to keep an eye on the residents, especially the young ones who were jumping up and down to try to get a better view, too young to understand the danger.

Within an hour of their arrival, the fire brigade had succeeded in quelling the fire.

"Mr Dawson?" enquired the chief. "I'm told this is your house."

Billy nodded. "Was, you mean."

Water dripped everywhere and black ash coated every surface. Charred wood and burnt fabric mixed with the smell of smoke and white-faced women peered through the window, gasping at the destruction.

Billy's temper flared. "Clear off, you old hags," he shouted at them. "Have you nothin' better to do that gawp at another's misfortune?" The white faces disappeared.

"Have you anywhere you can go?" asked the fire chief. "It'll be a long time before this place is habitable again."

Billy shook his head. "No, but, I'll manage," he said. "Somehow."

"You can bide wi' us, Billy, till yi get soarted."

"Thanks Andy," replied Billy, experiencing a surge of warmth towards his neighbour. "But you and your wife have enough on your plate with the twins and another one on the way, but your offer's appreciated."

Andy Kennedy nodded and returned to his family. "Richt yi' are, Billy."

The firemen left and a strange stillness settled on Billy and his black dwelling. He picked through the charred remains of his life and wondered why he'd been spared. Death would not have been a bad thing at that minute, removing him as it would have done from all the hurt and pain that was his lot. He wandered through into the back-room. In the corner, badly charred but still recognisable, was Nancy's cot. He'd often drunk himself to sleep as she'd lain in slumber in her cot and Mary had been at the Salvation Army Hall, and the realisation suddenly hit him of what could have happened if Nancy had been with him. He fell to his knees clutching the blackened wood as great sobs wracked his body.

"Dear God," he muttered in desperation, his despair gripping him in its pincers. "What's happened to me?"

The wedding party was in full swing at Alex's house when a policeman brought them the news. They listened in stunned silence as he told them of the fire and how Billy could have been killed and how he was sorry to have interrupted their enjoyment.

"Thanks for letting us know, Ewan," Alex murmured solemnly, guiding Constable MacPherson to the door before returning to his bride and their guests.

Annie had her arm around Mary, her eyes full of unanswered questions.

"I think perhaps, given the news we've just had, that it's best we end the evening now," Alex told the guests. "Mrs Melville and I thank you all for coming and I'm sure there'll be times, in the months to come, when we'll meet again under happier circumstances."

The assembled guests nodded in agreement and began donning coats and dispersing.

"Good night, Annie," whispered Isabella Anderson, who'd come alone from Edinburgh for the wedding. "If there's anything I can do for you or Mary, please let me know."

Annie marvelled at Isabella's charity. Mary had been the cause of so much unhappiness for her when she'd ran away with her husband, John, but here she was, offering her help.

Annie hugged her. "I'm so glad to have you for my sister-in-law," she said. "Thank you and please visit any time. Alex and me will always be glad of your company."

"And Mary?" enquired Isabella. "I believe she's going to be living with you and Alex."

Annie nodded. "Mary too, will be glad to see you," replied Annie, truthfully. "Her only concern now is her daughter."

Mary took Nancy up to bed, leaving Annie and Alex alone in the parlour.

"You don't think it was deliberate, do you?" she ventured to Alex, fearful of the answer. She knew how much Billy had endured these last months and, even although she no longer loved him, she couldn't help but feel deep concern.

"Who knows!" responded Alex, conscious of the part he'd recently played in Billy's life. Everything Alex had done since falling in love with Annie, he'd done with her best interest at heart and it was up to Billy to deal with his life like a man.

Mary quietly returned to the room and sat beside Annie on the settee. "I've decided to go back," she announced simply. "To Billy."

It was Alex who broke the silence that followed the announcement. "It's been a shock to us all, Mary," he began. "And we're all concerned for Billy, but going back might not be a good idea."

Annie had never seen Mary so calm. "I know what you're saying Alex, but I've made up my mind, me and Nancy are going back."

"From what Constable MacPherson said, Mary," continued Alex gently, "There's no home to go back to."

Mary turned to Annie. "Could me and Nancy live at the single-end till things get sorted?" she asked matter-of-factly.

"If that's what you want Mary," she replied, knowing her sister's determination when she had a mind to.

"And Billy too… if he'll come!"

"Billy too." Annie nodded.

"It's settled then," she affirmed, standing up and straightening her bridesmaid's dress. "We'll go tomorrow."

Annie and Alex sat in silent thought for some time before Alex finally crossed the room and took her hands in his.

"Come to bed?" he asked quietly. "Mrs Melville."

Annie felt her heart beat faster in her breast. "There's nothing I want more," she replied, smiling at her new husband. "Mr Melville."

"Not exactly the wedding day we'd planned," he whispered as they mounted the stairs. "Do you love me, Annie Melville?"

Annie felt her whole body relax. She was home at last. "I love you," she replied simply and honestly. "With all my heart."

Chapter 3

The following day, Mary was met by Grannie Ogilvie at the end of the close.

"An awful bizness," she exclaimed blackly. "Nearly killt, he waz."

Mary held Nancy closer to her. "Do you know where he is, Mrs Ogilvie?" asked Mary, hoping she might.

The crone leant closer and lowered her voice to a whisper. "Nobody kens where he is, Mrs Da'son. Nobody."

Mary fought back the urge to run up the stairs and shout out Billy's name.

"He waz last seen ga'in up Todburn Lane towards the Mill. But, since then… *nuthin'*."

Mary nodded her head. "Thanks anyway, Mrs Ogilvie. If you should see him, will you tell him, me and Nancy's living at the single-end, if he wants to see us."

Grannie Ogilvie raised a quizical eyebrow. "Annie's place?"

"That's right, Mrs Ogilvie. Now she's married, she's no need of it."

The neighbour folded her arms defensively across her large frontage. "And does the factor ken?"

Mary felt herself panicking. "Not yet, Mrs Ogilvie, but I'll be seeing him on Monday."

Mrs Ogilvie seemed to be satisfied with the answer and, on spying Mrs

Kennedy and her twins, moved away to pass on the 'latest news.'

The sight of her burned-out home reduced Mary to tears. There was nothing left to salvage and she quietly returned to the single-end.

"We'll be fine here, Nancy," she told her child. "Till your daddy comes for us."

Billy's brush with death had affected Mary more than she had imagined it would. She remembered how it had been when she and Billy had first married and Nancy had been born. It was only when Annie came to live with them, it had all gone wrong, and now she was married, maybe, just maybe, things could be sorted between her and Billy.

She tucked Nancy up in the small bed for the night. "We'll go and find daddy tomorrow," she promised her daughter. "When he finishes work at the Mill, we'll wait for him and bring him home."

Nancy sighed as her eyes closed.

"Not a care in the world," whispered Mary. "Oh, to be a child again."

The sun was still warm in the summer sky as Mary waited with Nancy at the gate of Baxters Mill. Long shadows stretched across the yard and the smell of jute hung in the air. She saw Billy emerge from the door of the weaving flat long before he saw her. He was still a handsome man, tall and dark, although his hair now had begun showing signs of grey. Mary squeezed Nancy's hand.

"There's daddy now," she whispered. "Go and say hello."

The child squealed in delight at the sight of Billy and toddled towards him. "Da da," she called. "Da da."

Billy looked up, his eyes filling with light at the sight of his daughter. He picked her up and swung her above his head. "Nancy," he grinned. "How's my darlin' girl?"

"She's fine, Billy," answered Mary from the shadows.

Billy's face hardened.

"Bad news travels fast," he said, placing Nancy back on her feet.

"Are you alright?"

Billy's defences began to form around him. "What's it to you if I'm alright or not?" he asked, not really wanting an answer.

"I was worried."

Billy threw his head back and laughed sarcastically. "*Worried*," he repeated. "Since when have you - or that sister of yours - worried about anyone but yourselves."

Mary recoiled. "Please, Billy," she whispered. "Don't be like that."

Billy closed in on her and the fear she had managed to dismiss from her heart, returned.

"I don't want your pity, Mary *Pepper*, and I don't want *you*. Now, clear off and leave me alone. They only thing you've got that I want is Nancy."

Mary tried to control her panic. "We're living at Annie's single-end now," she rushed. "You can visit Nancy there… if you want."

Billy eyed her suspiciously. "And why would you be saying that, after all the trouble you've taken to keep me away from her."

Mary pulled herself up straight. "I was wrong, Billy," she told him shakily. "I was *wrong*. And that's what I've come to say. If you'll forgive me, maybe, for Nancy's sake, we could try again."

Billy placed his hands on his hips and looked heavenward. "Oh, no, Mary Pepper. No more. I'll always love my daughter and do everything I can to make sure she doesn't suffer at your hands, but to go back to living with a woman who gives herself to the highest bidder… oh, no, not Billy Dawson."

Mary felt tears of humiliation start to trickle down her face. "It wasn't like that," she whispered. "Please understand."

Billy picked up Nancy and kissed her on both cheeks. "Daddy'll see you soon," he told her. "So you be a good girl." He turned to Mary. "And as for you, don't even consider that you and me could have a life together. Don't even consider it."

Mary watched him through tears as he went through the mill gate and turned up Princes Street. "C'mon Nancy," she whispered. "Let's go home."

Quickly, Billy walked away, breathing deeply to calm his ragged emotions. He could do with a drink but, after his lucky escape from the fire that could have cost him his life, he had taken a vow not to touch the liquor again. He continued his brisk pace up the steepness of Albert Street till it joined Mains Loan, Forfar Road and Pitkerro Road at Stobswell. Turning at the top into Morgan Street, he entered the first close of the tall tenement buildings which ran either side of the road and climbed the three flights of stairs up to his lodgings.

His mood had finally evened with the walk and he greeted his landlady, Mrs MacIntyre with a nod and a 'good evening.'

Mrs MacIntyre had recently been made a widow at the age of thirty-six. Her husband had been taken with Tuberculosis and shortage of money had forced her to advertise for a lodger to supplement the meagre income she got from tutoring English to paying pupils from the nearby Morgan Academy.

"Good evening, Mr Dawson," she replied in her precise and refined voice, which was in sharp contrast to the mill workers tongues that Billy heard every day in his job as overseer at Baxters Mill. "Will you be wishing your tea?"

Billy nodded. "I'll just freshen up a bit first, Mrs MacIntyre, if that's alright." He'd picked up some second-hand clothing at the flea market on the Sunday, which he'd washed and hung to dry that night and was thankful, at last, to discard the smoky clothes he'd arrived in.

"It'll be on the table in ten minutes," she replied. "I've a pupil coming at seven o'clock, so you'll have to eat in the kitchen, if that's alright."

Billy was glad he would be eating alone that night. He'd been in a state of some agitation since the fire and Mary turning up had unsettled him again, especially with her suggestion they should 'give their marriage another try'. Memories of her abortion of his child and her adultery with John Anderson flooded his mind and his appetite deserted him. He badly wanted a drink.

He lay down on his bed and stared at the glass shade of the oil lamp as it cast its soft glow into the room. He'd seen Mrs MacIntyre's advert for a lodger in Maryfield Post Office on the day of the fire. Blindly, he'd made his way to Maryfield that day, perhaps sub-consciously wanting to see where Annie and Alex Melville would be living, or perhaps just to walk as far away as he could from William Lane. He didn't know why, but he'd found himself gazing at the small postcard in the shop window. "Single room accommodation offered to working man. Must be clean and temperate." It gave Mrs MacIntyre's address in Morgan Street.

He'd knocked on her door that evening and explained about his need for lodgings due to the fire. The fact he was an over-seer at Baxters allowed Mrs MacIntyre the confidence to offer him the room and he'd moved in the next day with nothing but the clothes he stood up in.

A gentle knock at the door disturbed his thoughts. "Tea, Mr Dawson!"

Billy swung his legs over the edge of the bed and stood up. "Just coming, Mrs MacIntyre," he replied. "Thanks."

Her footsteps receded back to the parlour where her pupil was now waiting for English instruction and he heard the door close behind her.

The smell of beef stew and potatoes encouraged Billy's appetite to return and he soon cleared the plate. Mrs MacIntyre's cooking was tasty and nourishing and filled the empty space inside him. The thought of returning to his room was not a welcome one and he decided to take a walk instead. The summer light was still in the sky as he made his way up Pitkerro Road to Baxters Park. A few strollers were still taking the evening air and a group of young lads were playing kick-about with a ball as Billy made his way along the paths between the beds of roses and expanses of green grass. The low sun dappled patterns through the trees and Billy sat down beneath one of them, allowing the rustle of their leaves to fill his tired soul. He closed his eyes and once again, he was in Ireland on the flax farm with Annie. He could almost taste the flax flowers on the air, hear the birds and the sound of the river as Annie lay in his arms.

His muscles tensed as he tried to hold her tighter and kiss her lips, but his eyes opened with a jolt as a dog barked near him, bringing him back to reality.

A sadness swept over him. Annie had married another. Just as he had.

"Poetic justice," he murmured to himself and for the first time, realised how unhappy he must have made her when he and Mary had wed. No wonder she'd never forgiven him.

Chapter 4

Annie was writing a letter when Alex returned from shift duty at Bell Street Jail.

A month had passed since their wedding day and she was settling in to the routine of wife to Alex and minding Nancy, while Mary earned some money cleaning the offices at Baxters East Port Works in King Street. He bent over her and kissed the top of her head, sliding his hands down her arms and covering her hands with his.

"Thank you letters?" he asked. Annie shook her head.

"It's a letter to my friend in Belfast," she explained. "When me and mammie were in the Poorhouse, after we had to leave the farm, Bella was kindness itself to me, although to be sure she had enough troubles of her own. I'm just letting her know I'm married now and our address, so she can keep in touch."

Alex removed the pen from her fingers and lifted her to her feet to face him.

"Do you really want reminders of those days Annie?" he asked. "You've a new life now, with me. You're the wife of a police sergeant living in Maryfield. Isn't that enough for you?"

Annie wasn't sure what Alex wanted to hear. "Of course, I love my new life," she assured him. "But Bella was special to me. She's not an unhappy memory, Alex, she's a joyous one."

Alex's eyes clouded. "It's just that I want to protect you from the past my love. I'm sorry you still feel the need of it."

"But I don't," Annie protested. "Bella's just a friend from the past, that's all. I just want to tell her how happy and lucky I am to have you and..." Alex held a finger to her lips.

"Sssssshhhhhh, now," he murmured. "I'm just being foolish, of course you must keep in touch with Bella." He pulled her toward him and kissed her with an urgency that brooked no resistance. "Let me love you," he whispered. "Now." Annie felt herself being lifted in his arms and carried through to their bedroom. "Bella can wait."

It was some weeks before Annie finished the letter to Bella and by that time, she had some more news for her. She was pregnant.

Annie though Alex would burst with pride when she told him. "Now you won't have to look after your sister's child," he told her. "You'll have your own."

"But I don't mind looking after Nancy," she responded. "She's no trouble and Mary's got no one else to look after her while she does her cleaning job."

Alex sighed and tipped his head towards her. "Mary, Mary, Mary," he repeated. "Haven't you done enough for your sister yet? You've looked after her like a baby since you've been in Scotland, even when she didn't deserve your help. Isn't it time she looked after herself?"

Annie felt herself stiffen at the criticism of her sister. "I know you've more to reproach Mary for than most," she began. "But she *is* my sister Alex, no matter what she's done."

Alex sensed he'd touched a nerve and drew back. "Fine, fine," he smoothed. "But don't blame me when you're exhausted and tetchy with her demands on your time."

Annie felt deflated. "Nancy'll be going to school soon," she said, "and I won't be needed so much. So perhaps your concern isn't necessary."

"I'm only thinking of you, Annie," he assured her. "Especially now you're having our child."

Annie nodded, but a twinge of unease had formed somewhere in her heart.

Mary was overjoyed at the news of Annie's pregnancy. "You must tell Jessie," she squealed. "She'll be wanting to get started on knitting coats and bonnets for the babe. Oh, Annie, let's go and tell her." She looked at the mantelpiece clock. "It's nearly dinner-time, she'll be having her dinner in the yard in this sunshine."

Annie agreed and the sisters and Nancy made their way to where Annie used to share her troubles and jam pieces with Jessie when they worked together as weavers at the mill.

"There she is," called Mary, spying Jessie sitting on a pile of sacks by the wall. "Jessie." she waved. "Look who's here."

Jessie's face broke into a toothless grin. "Annie," she beamed. "Whit brings you back?" Her eyes took in every detail of Annie's appearance. "And in sic a fine frock too!"

"Oh, Jessie," she smiled. "I've something to tell you."

"Well, it certainly looks like guid news, judgin' by the glow on you."

Annie laughed. "I'm going to have a baby."

Jessie hugged her tightly. "Oh, Annie, I'm that pleased for ye. After all you've been thru." She could see tears glistening in her friend's eyes.

"I only got through thanks to you, Jessie. And when the baby's born, if it's a girl, she'll have your name."

Jessie Greig smiled the smile of angels. "I could want for nuthin' more, Annie. Thank you."

The one o'clock bummer sounded shrill in their ears.

"Time I waz back at the toil lassies," Jessie announced. "Some oh us have to keep the looms runnin'."

"Come and see me Jessie," Annie asked her. "At Maryfield. I miss our chats."

"At Maryfield," Jessie repeated. "Goad Annie, I'm no' good enough for up there."

Annie took her friend's hand. "Then neither am I. Please say you'll come."

Jessie glanced at Mary. "Will you come as well?" she asked worriedly.

"We'll all go," affirmed Mary. "It'll be just like old times."

"Come on Sunday," Annie grinned happily. "For tea, at four o'clock."

Jessie clasped her hand tightly. "Four o'clock it is then on Sunday."

The sisters watched as Jessie disappeared through the mill door into the weaving flat.

"Do you miss it, Annie?" asked Mary.

Annie sighed. "I miss Jessie, and the friends I made, but I don't miss getting up at six o'clock on a winter's morning."

They both laughed as they made their way back through the yard to the iron gate which led into Princes Street. "Who'd be a Dundee weaver?"

It was Mary who heard the footsteps hurrying up behind them first and turned to see Billy bearing down on them.

She clasped Nancy's hand tightly and pulled at Annie's arm.

"It's Billy," she whispered urgently. "Keep walking."

"Where?" asked Annie, taken aback by the change in tone of her sister's voice.

"Stop. Wait."

Mary and Annie froze as Billy drew alongside them. He'd lost weight and the leanness was back in his angular face.

He never took his eyes off Annie. "I saw you from Campbell's window," he said. "I thought I was seeing things." Mary pulled Nancy close to her, remembering their last meeting.

"Are you coming back to work at the mill?" he asked Annie, hope apparent in his voice. He was different. Not just the weight loss, Billy's whole being was different. He was almost as Annie had remembered him that first day at the farm when she'd came into the kitchen to find him sitting at the table.

"No, Billy," Annie replied quietly. "I'm not."

His face fell. "Then why are you here?"

"To speak to Jessie," Annie answered. "To tell her my news."

Billy's eyes narrowed as he waited for Annie to elaborate. He didn't have to wait long.

"I'm going to have a baby," she said.

Billy took the blow to his dreams full in the stomach.

"Pregnant are you!" he grimaced.

Memories of the birth of her first child, Billy's child, filled her mind as she watched him, but the memory was too painful for her to bear.

"C'mon Mary," she said, linking her arm into her sister's. "It's time we were going." Annie's legs trembled slightly as she walked away from Billy and it wasn't until she was sipping tea at the single-end that she felt herself steady. She blamed it on being pregnant, but something about Billy had unnerved her and she didn't like the feeling.

She finished her tea. "I'll just take a walk into town," she told Mary. "Meet Alex at the Station. He's due off his shift at three o'clock."

Mary nodded and helped her on with her coat.

"Billy didn't have much to say to you," Annie noted. "Is there no hope you and he will get back together?"

Mary shook her head. "None," she stated flatly, a finality in her voice. "There's just me and Nancy now."

Annie took a deep breath. "And me, Mary," she added. "There's always me."

The sisters hugged. "I'll see you both on Sunday." Annie smiled, kissing Nancy on the top of her head. "And don't forget to bring Jessie."

"I won't," Mary replied, following her sister to the door. "See you Sunday."

Mary closed the door of her small home and stroked Nancy's hair.

"One day," she said. "A handsome prince will come along and take you to his castle in the sky."

"When?" Nancy asked in delight, thinking a story was beginning.

"Someday, Nancy," replied Mary sadly. "Someday."

Chapter 5

Annie had just turned into the cobbled yard of the jail when Alex emerged from the door of the jailhouse.

"Alex," she called, waving her arm to attract his attention. "Over here."

Alex hurried towards her. "This is a surprise," he smiled. "Are you alright?"

"Fine," Annie assured him. "I've been visiting with Mary and Jessie Greig and…"

"Jessie Greig!" Alex interrupted her, the smile suddenly disappearing from his lips.

"What was she doing at Mary's?"

Annie fell into step beside him as they turned into Bell Street and headed for home.

"She wasn't at Mary's," Annie began. "She was at the mill. We went to tell her my good news."

Alex's mouth had now set in a straight line.

"Is anything wrong?" Annie asked, feeling the same unease she'd experienced a few weeks ago when Alex had interrupted her letter-writing to Bella.

His response was to quicken his pace and fix his eyes on the road ahead.

Annie hurried to keep up with him. "I've invited her and Mary to tea on Sunday and…"

Alex stopped walking and swung her round to face him. "You've done what!"

"Invited Jessie and Mary to tea," Annie stammered. "This Sunday."

"Without asking my permission," Alex retorted angrily.

Annie felt herself panicking, without being sure why. "I didn't think you'd mind," she began to explain, her mind now racing to understand Alex's anger. "I miss Jessie's company, sometimes, and I wanted to share…"

"I don't want to hear any more, Annie," Alex stated coldly. "You obviously have more consideration for your friends than for your husband."

The rest of the journey home was taken in stony silence. Once inside their home, Annie busied herself in the kitchen preparing the evening meal while Alex closeted himself in their bedroom. Try as she could, she couldn't understand Alex's anger but decided to let sleeping dogs lie and felt sure he would be his old self again by the evening. But it wasn't to be.

Annie carefully laid the table and brought through the meal.

"Alex," she called from the foot of the stair. "Supper's ready."

There was no response. Worried now, she went upstairs to the bedroom and knocked softly on the door. "Alex," she called again. "Are you alright?"

There was the sound of movement inside and Alex appeared at the door. To Annie's shock she could see he'd been crying.

"Alex," she said, concern and confusion in her voice. "What's wrong?"

His eyes looked empty and distant. "Aren't I enough?" he asked quietly.

Annie's concern deepened. "Enough?" she queried.

"I've given you my name, a beautiful home to live in, the life of a lady and now, a child of your own, but all you seem to want…" He turned away from her. "Are your friends."

Annie moved around in front of him and put her arms around his neck. "Alex," she began, real fear in her heart. "How can you say that…?"

He removed her hands from his shoulders. "Because it's true."

Annie felt frustration replacing the fear. "It's *not.*"

Alex looked at her, his eyes full of pain. "Then tell Jessie and your sister they can't come on Sunday."

Annie felt herself backed into a corner. "But, Alex," she whispered. "They're only coming for a little while. I promise they won't stay long."

He shrugged his shoulders. "Do you hear what you're saying?" he asked. "You prefer to be with them than with me."

Annie couldn't believe her ears. "*Alright,*" she said, her voice rising in panic. "They won't come. I'll tell Mary tomorrow."

She could see his shoulders relax and his eyes brighten.

"I love you," he said quietly. "And I want you and I to grow old together."

Annie nodded in agreement. "So do I," she whispered, moving towards him, sensing the return of the Alex she knew. "So do I."

"Then let's have no more talk of your so-called friends, shall we?"

Annie felt herself rearrange her thoughts. "If that's what you want, Alex," she replied, relieved and confused at the same time.

"Do you love me, Annie Melville?"

"I love you."

"Good. Now, what've you made for supper? Something special, I hope."

That night, Alex made love to Annie with such intensity that she feared for her baby and the following day, after Alex had left for the station, she went to see Mary to tell her about the cancelled treat.

"It's alright," assured Mary. "If you're not feeling too well, of course, Jessie and me won't come."

Annie felt guilty about the lie, but didn't understand Alex's objection herself, never mind try to explain it to Mary.

"And will you tell Jessie?" she asked anxiously. "Tell her I'm sorry."

Mary looked at her sister quizzically. "I told you, Annie, it's alright. Now stop worrying, or you'll make yourself really ill."

"Alright, Mary, I'll stop."

Annie stood up and turned to go. "And I won't be able to look after Nancy anymore," she added, unable to meet her sister's eyes. "I really don't feel too well at all."

Mary put her hand on her sister's shoulder. "It's alright, Annie," she replied. "Grannie Ogilvie'll look out for her." She guided her to the door of the single-end. "Billy may not have been the perfect husband but he's a good provider and he'll make sure Nancy's looked after alright."

Annie nodded and stepped out over the doorstep. "I'll see you later then," she told Mary nervously. "When I feel a bit better."

Mary nodded and watched her sister walk along the close and turn into William Lane. She didn't know what exactly it was she was sensing about Annie, but whatever it was, she didn't like it.

Annie hurried down the lane and into King Street. It was a long walk up Princes Street and Albert Street to Maryfield and she didn't want to be late for Alex's tea. She had caused him enough anguish.

"Annie!" a voice called out to her, but she was so intent on getting home, she never heard.

"What's up with her?" asked Joe Cassiday of his brother Charlie.

Charlie shrugged his shoulders. "Search me, Joe. Somebody said she doesn't work at the mill any longer, but I don't know any more than that."

Joe straightened the Black Watch jacket of his soldier's uniform and gazed after the disappearing figure of the woman he almost married and felt a pang of longing for her.

"Maybe I'll just stop by at the single-end and see how she is later on."

"Not a wise move, Joe," cautioned his brother. "I know you've been away for a while, but some things never change, and morals is one of them."

Joe grinned. "Gi'way with you," he scolded mockingly. "You're a right auld Holy Joe, so you are."

Joe had walked out on Annie when he found out that Billy had bedded her before him and he'd regretted doing so ever since. 'Maybe too much water has gone under the bridge,' he thought to himself. 'But then again… maybe I should visit Annie. For old times' sake.'

"C'mon, Charlie," he grinned, slapping his older brother on the back. "I'll buy you a pint of Dundee's finest ale and you can confess all your sins to me."

It was late in the evening before Joe had consumed enough alcohol to pluck up the courage to knock on Annie's door. Not that he was drunk, mind, far from it. His first year in the Black Watch had hardened his constitution as well as his muscles and he could drink most men under the table.

But despite himself, he felt nervous as he approached the door of the single-end. The last time he'd stood there, he'd felt only Annie's wrath as their dreams of happiness together had crumbled under the weight of Annie's sin with Billy. Joe frowned at the memory. How sanctimonious he must have seemed with his insistence that only a virgin bride would do for the great Joe Cassiday.

Taking a deep breath, Joe knocked at the door. A candle flickered past the window and a female voice asked tentatively, "Who's there?"

"It's me, Annie. Joe Cassiday."

The key turned in the lock and a hand bearing the flickering candle followed by a small face, framed with auburn hair, appeared around the corner of the lintel.

Joe leant forward towards the light. "It's Joe," he repeated. "Come to see you."

"She's not here Mr Cassiday, she's moved."

Joe squinted past the flame, at once realising the female in front of him wasn't Annie. "You know me?" he asked, surprised at being called Mr Cassiday.

"I'm Annie's sister, Mary!"

"*Mary*," Joe exclaimed. "Billy's wife!"

Mary put her finger to her lips. "Ssssshhhhhh," she told him. "The neighbours'll hear you."

"I don't understand…" Joe began, but was interrupted by Mary's invitation to come inside.

"Hurry," she urged him. "Before you wake up the whole land."

Joe stepped into the shadows of the small candlelit room and seemed to fill it with his presence. "Do you mind if I sit down?" he asked, conscious of his height. Mary indicated a wooden chair by the fire.

"We've never met, but Annie's told me of you. I'm sorry things went wrong for you and her."

Joe acknowledged the apology. "More my fault than anyone else's," he replied. "Never did know when to shut up."

"Can I get you some tea?"

Joe nodded and watched as Mary raked the coals and swung the iron kettle over the heat.

"It won't be a moment."

Joe leant back in the chair and looked around the small abode. "How long've you been living here then?" he asked.

Mary spooned some tea into the kettle. "Since December of last year."

Joe nodded, taking in the information. "And, Annie," he added. "Where's she then?"

The hot tea splattered from the kettle into the two cups.

"You've not heard then?" Mary asked cautiously.

"No."

"She's married."

Joe's eyes widened. "Not to... Billy?" he asked, painfully aware that Mary was now living alone.

Mary shook her head. "No. She's married Alex Melville."

Joe indicated ignorance.

"He's a police sergeant at Bell Street," Mary continued. "They met round about the time I was having difficulties in my own marriage..." Mary sunk onto the end of the bed, disturbing her sleeping daughter, who turned and sighed back into slumber.

Joe strained to see into the gloom.

"Who's that?" he asked.

"My daughter, Nancy."

Joe stood up and crossed the room to look at the child.

"Is that the same Nancy that Annie used to take for walks in her pram?"

Mary nodded. "The same."

"How old is she now?"

"She'll be five next birthday."

Joe sat down again and cupped his hands round the cup of tea, his eyes fixed on the steaming liquid as the memory of his first meeting with Annie returned. How happy he'd been then. He shook himself back to the present and looked at the woman before him. She was smaller than Annie. Thinner and almost childlike. He could see she'd been through some hard times by the sadness that dwelt in her eyes.

"Can I ask how you've ended up here, living alone with your daughter?"

Mary hung her head. "It's a long story, Mr Cassiday and it doesn't get better by repeating it. Let's just say if it hadn't been for Annie, I wouldn't be here today."

Joe leant forward to question her further, but she held up her hand. "Please, Mr Cassiday, no more questions. I'm sorry I was the one who had to tell you about Annie's marriage and if you want me to convey your regards to her, I will, but it's late and..."

Joe stood up quickly and drained the cup placing it on the mantelpiece. "Of course," he responded. "I'll be on my way. Sorry to have bothered you."

Mary picked up the candle and led the way to the door. “It’s no bother, Mr Cassiday,” she replied. “I’m sorry I’m not Annie.”

Joe’s eyes watched her open the door, her slender body somehow elegant in its poverty. “Thanks,” he told her. “And please… call me Joe.”

Chapter 6

Annie recognised Bella's small, neat handwriting immediately the letter dropped through the letter box. She slipped it into her apron pocket to savour and read later, once Alex had gone on duty.

"Was that the post?" asked Alex coming into the hall in search of his tunic.

Annie felt herself colour. "No," she lied. "Just me being clumsy. I knocked the umbrella off the hall-stand."

She felt the need to lie to Alex often these days. Concealing her visits to Mary had just been the beginning, now it seemed that Alex checked her every move. Questioning… forever questioning. She was sure the letter from Bella would have been met with disapproval.

"And what will my wife be up to today?" Alex asked, almost as if he'd read Annie's thoughts.

"The weather's getting colder," Annie responded. "So I'll probably stay indoors."

Alex kissed her on the forehead. "Love you."

Annie smiled weakly. "Love you too," she responded.

She listened till the sound of his footsteps faded into nothing and hurried through to the kitchen. Placing the envelope against the sugar bowl, Annie poured herself a cup of tea and gazed in anticipation at the envelope as she sipped it.

She slipped the end of her teaspoon under the flap and unfolded the single page of the letter.

Dear Annie, it read.

How wunderful to heer of your marrage to Mr Melville. He sounds so good. Now you are such a fine lady, you must eat cakes all day and sew fine hems.

I am happy to, and getting on fine and I have sumthing to tell you that will gladden your heart, specially now you're going to get a new babe of your own. Mother Superior visited the master some weeks ago and I heard her speak of the master's son. He's to go for scooling soon and she had papers for the master to sign. Annie, the boy is not theirs after all. He was given to them by the nuns to look after and luv till he was grown. I don't know for sure, Annie, but I think he's your very child that you bore in the poorhouse. I'll try to find out more but you shood no he's a hansum lad and very fine.

Pleese rite agen soon. Your luving frend, Bella.

Annie read the page again, her brain memorising every word and her mind racing. She tried to recall the events at the time of the birth but couldn't. Misery had blocked out the days following the delivery of her child. Billy's child. Annie's fingers froze and a chill surged through her heart. No one knew of her firstborn, except Bella, not even Billy and if Alex were to find out… Annie felt sick.

Her agitation grew all that morning despite trying to keep herself busy about the house, till eventually she had to get out and walk and walk to calm herself down. It wouldn't do if Alex found her in this state. She pulled on her coat and bonnet and grasping the letter tightly in her hand, she ran downstairs and out into the cold, autumn sunshine. She crossed the Forfar Road, rounded Morgan Academy and walked up Pitkerro Road to where it joined Clepington Road. The view dipped away towards Linlathen and the rolling farmlands on the edge of the town and Annie breathed in the fresh air wafting off the newly ploughed earth.

She tried to picture the son she'd called John. He'd be handsome alright, like Billy was. All dark hair and deep brown eyes. He'd be tall too, she reckoned. Annie wrapped her arms around herself to keep the cold out and felt her baby move inside her. She was instantly back in the poorhouse, remembering Billy's letter. *Me and Mary are married. She's pregnant with my child.* Tears began to flow unchecked down her face, the heaviness of her secret forcing them out as the fields of Linlathen blurred before her.

"C'mon Annie Pepper," she told herself feebly. "Enough of this self-pity." She sniffed miserably as gradually control returned to her emotions and she was able to retrace her footsteps back to Maryfield. She didn't know how long she'd been away but on her return Alex was waiting.

With panic rising she quickly moved past the open parlour door and upstairs to the bedroom, shrugging off her coat as she went. "Won't be a minute," she called over her shoulder. "You're early."

Annie scrutinised her complexion in the dressing table mirror. Her eyes were red-rimmed and her cheeks flushed. She dabbed some powder over her face and took a deep breath before descending downstairs to face Alex.

A smile forced itself across her husband's face as he watched her cross the room and take her seat opposite his.

"Where were you?" Alex asked looking at his pocket watch. "It's nearly four o'clock."

"Is it?" Annie responded.

Alex's eyes narrowed. "What's wrong with your face?"

Annie jumped up and looked at her reflection in the mirror above the fireplace, fearful that she'd missed some indication of her guilt.

"Nothing I can see."

"Your eyes are red," Alex continued, one question, as always, leading to another.

"Cold wind I expect, always makes my eyes red." Annie sat down again, clasping her hands together to keep them still.

"Well?" Alex intoned.

Annie looked up questioningly. "Well what?"

The newspaper Alex had been reading flew across the room, making Annie jump.

"I demand respect in my own house," he shouted. "And I demand an answer. Where have you been?"

Annie felt the blood drain from her face as her heart began to thump. "I went for a walk, Alex," she rushed. "That's all. I felt like a walk."

His eyes bored into her. "Liar," he muttered under his breath. "You've been to see that sister of yours, haven't you?"

Annie tried to steady her breathing. "No," she replied shakily. "I've told you, I've been for a walk."

"Stand up," he ordered her. Annie stood.

"I'll ask you again. Where have you been?"

Annie felt faint. "For a walk, Alex, that's all. Why won't you believe me?"

"Because you lie to me, Annie," he replied. "How can I believe you when you persist in lying to me?"

Annie closed her eyes and tried to stop the tears from beginning again.

"Stop snivelling."

Annie clenched her jaw and held her breath.

"What was in the post this morning?" Alex's voice was low and monotone.

Annie felt sheer panic overwhelming her. "There was no post," she stammered. "I told you this morning."

A knowing smile began to form at the corner of Alex's mouth. "That's not what the postman told me."

Annie's eyes widened in horror.

"He said he delivered a letter here, addressed to you."

The tension was tangible.

"Oh, yes,"' Annie whispered. "I forgot, there was a letter, more of a note really, from Bella."

"Show me."

Annie was shaking now. "I've lost it."

The slap, when it came, caught Annie full on the cheek.

"Show me." The anger in Alex's voice had been replaced by something more sinister. Ice.

Annie slowly withdrew the small envelope from her skirt pocket and handed it to him.

"That's better," he told her. "Now you can sit down."

It seemed that an eternity had passed before Alex finally folded the page and dangled it over the flames of the fire till it caught and burned.

"Who's the father?" he asked through clenched teeth. "And I warn you, Annie Melville, don't lie to me."

Annie's heart was pounding so loudly, she could hardly speak. There was no way out. She would have to tell him and suffer the consequences, which she knew now would be dire.

"Billy Dawson."

"Go to your room," Alex instructed, his voice menacing and barely audible. "And wait for me."

Annie's legs were shaking as she climbed the stairs. "Please God," she prayed. "Help me."

Darkness fell before she heard his footsteps climbing the stairs. The door opened and the shadow of his bulk fell across her.

"Take your clothes off," he ordered, as he drew the leather belt from around his waist. Annie's eyes widened in terror and disbelief as she backed into the furthest corner of the room.

"Alex," she begged. "I'm carrying your child… please, please, don't hit me."

"How can I forgive you unless you've been punished?" he breathed. "I knew I was right not to trust you. And now…"

The leather lashed across Annie's arm as she tried to protect herself. "Alex," she screamed. "NO!"

The belt whipped across her again and again, driving Annie further into a corner until, finally, his anger seemingly spent, Alex stopped. The belt fell from his hand and he dropped to his knees, as tears began coursing down his cheeks.

"Why did you make me do it?" he implored to Annie, crawling across to where she lay bruised and shocked. "You shouldn't have made me do it. Forgive me as I forgive you."

Annie tried to gather her wits. "Don't hurt me again," she begged, her voice shaking in her head.

Alex's hand reached up and stroked her hair. "I love you Annie, I didn't want to hurt you. You made me."

Annie tried to move away from him, but he pulled her in closer. "You're my wife Annie," he murmured. "Let me love you."

A wave of revulsion washed over her as she realised Alex's intentions. "Please don't Alex," she pleaded, staring into the darkness above his head, all of her senses now alert to the new danger. But her plea was ignored as he penetrated her. Annie clenched her fists and submitted in silence.

All that night Annie lay motionless, willing the shock to leave her body and fearing the morning, but the following day, Alex rose early and without a word, brought Annie tea.

"Have a rest today, dearest," he said calmly, the previous night's horror seemingly wiped from his mind. "Remember, I love you."

Annie winced as she turned on her back, the weals of the belt marks now purple on her skin.

After he'd gone, she carefully swung her legs over the edge of the bed and her baby flickered its presence inside her.

"You're alive," she murmured tearfully, stroking the womb which held her unborn child. "But what am I bringing you into?" Annie's fear increased when she saw the extent of the bruising on her back reflected in the mirror.

"God help us, my child," she whispered. "God help us."

Chapter 7

"More tea, Mr Dawson?"

Billy smiled at the woman opposite him. "Thanks, Mrs MacIntyre, I don't mind if I do." He'd settled into his lodgings with Josephine MacIntyre quite nicely now. After the fire three months ago, it had only been a refuge from the misery of his life but now, he had come to regard the house in Morgan Street as home.

"Are things going well for you at the mill?"

Billy nodded. "As well as can be expected, I suppose. What with all these rumours of war going around, the weavers are forever gossiping instead of getting on with their work."

Mrs MacIntyre reached for a scone and delicately sliced it open before spreading it with raspberry jam. Billy watched her smooth white hands manoeuvre around the crockery and cutlery with precision and expertise and felt clumsy.

He pushed his chair back from the table. "Delicious, as usual Mrs MacIntyre." He nodded.

Josephine MacIntyre smiled. "It's nice to have a man about the place who appreciates his food, Mr Dawson."

Billy smiled. "No trouble, Mrs MacIntyre. Now if you'll excuse me, I'll be off to my room now, leave you in peace."

Josephine rose quickly from the table. "Before you go, Mr Dawson… I was just wondering… do you read much?"

Billy stopped and turned. "Don't really have much time to read Mrs MacIntyre, but even if I did, I don't have any books."

"Exactly!"

Billy hesitated, not sure now whether to go or stay.

"But I have. Come with me."

Josephine led the way to a door at the end of the corridor hidden behind a blue, velvet curtain. She pulled it aside and, taking a key from a hook on the lintel, she turned it in the lock. The door creaked as it opened into the darkness of the room.

Josephine disappeared into the gloom while Billy waited at the door, not sure if he was meant to follow or not. He heard the scrape of a match and the smell of paraffin as a lamp flamed into life.

"Come away in, Mr Dawson," Josephine called softly.

Billy entered the small room. Every wall was lined with shelves filled with books. There was a heavy wooden desk below the window and a deep buttoned leather armchair was positioned beside the lamp.

Everything seemed to glow in the soft light as Billy walked around the walls, carefully touching the spine of a book here and there and breathing in the scent of leather and tobacco which seemed to pervade every inch of the walls.

"It was my husband's study, when he was alive."

Billy nodded. "He must have been a very clever man, Mrs MacIntyre."

"Oh, he was," she whispered. "Very clever."

Billy watched her as she moved around the room, lovingly patting the back of the leather chair as she passed it. He'd always seen her as strong and capable, busying herself with her young pupils as they struggled to learn their grammar, or in the kitchen about her chores but in this room, she somehow had become suddenly vulnerable.

"Are you alright, Mrs MacIntyre?" he asked, his voice almost a whisper.

Josephine nodded. "Please," she said. "Can't you call me Josephine?"

"Are you alright, Josephine?"

She smiled. "I'm fine, Billy. Quite fine."

For some reason Billy suddenly felt scared and anxious not to appear callow.

"Do you miss him still?" he asked.

"Mr MacIntyre, do you mean?"

Billy nodded.

Josephine smiled softly. "When he died of Tuberculosis, I wanted to die with him.

But it wasn't God's will that we go together." She hung her head. "I come here when I want to be close to him. This was his special place and it's here that he'll always remain for me."

Billy felt close to tears as he listened to her words. Pictures of Annie flashed through his mind. They had had a special place, down by the river at the flax farm in Ireland, but he knew he'd never see that again.

Josephine's voice interrupted his thoughts. "So, if you'd like to read sometime… I'm sure Mr MacIntyre wouldn't mind."

Words failed to come and Billy nodded.

Josephine MacIntyre seemed pleased. "That's settled then," she said. "You know where the key is." She turned the lamp down till the light was extinguished and the darkness once more enveloped them. "I think the door's to your right," she indicated to Billy. "We should have brought a candle."

Billy felt for the door handle. "Got it," he said. "Here, this way." He reached for her hand.

It felt small and soft in his as he guided her to the door.

"Thanks, Billy." She hung the key back on its hook and closed the curtain. "I'm glad you found your way here," she told him.

Billy smiled, his eyes adjusting to the light in the hallway. "So am I."

Mary was becoming more and more concerned about Annie. She had barely seen her since their meeting with Jessie at the mill and, when she did, she always seemed withdrawn and thoughtful, not like herself at all.

New Year was coming soon and she felt sure she and Nancy would be invited to join Annie and Alex for the celebrations, but no invitation came.

"Your Auntie Annie's not been very well," she told Nancy. "And she can't come to see us as often as she used to… So… we'll go and see her."

It was Saturday and there was no school for Nancy that day. She held her coat up as Nancy slipped her arms into the sleeves. "Fetch your hat and gloves," she told her daughter. "It's going to snow today."

Mary wrapped a thick scarf round her head and neck and fastened her coat up to the neck. She checked her boots. They were in need of repair but would have to do.

Mother and daughter held hands as they made their way through the Saturday morning shoppers in King Street. Brussels sprouts and carrots were piled in boxes outside the greengrocers at the top of St Roques Lane, and vied for space with cabbages and potatoes.

"Morning Mr McQueen," called Nancy to the shopkeeper. Mr McQueen put his hands on his hips as he surveyed Mary's little girl.

"An' how would ye like a bonnie wee orange?" he asked her. Nancy nodded gleefully as Mr McQueen rubbed the mandarin against his apron before handing it to the child.

"You spoil her, Mr McQueen," laughed Mary.

"An' she's well worth it."

Nancy thanked him nicely and clutched the juicy orange with both hands.

As they continued on their way, Mary became aware of the figure in front of her. There was no mistaking the swing of Joe Cassiday's kilt as he strode up Princes Street.

She quickened her step. "Mr Cassiday," she called. "Joe."

The kilt stopped swinging as Joe turned to see Mary hurrying towards him.

"It's me, Mary Dawson."

Joe grinned. "And little Miss Dawson too, I believe," he replied, ruffling Nancy's curls. "And where might you two lovely ladies be going this frosty morning?"

Nancy giggled and hid her face behind Mary's skirt.

"To visit Annie," Mary told him. "She's not been very well. I think it's just the pregnancy, but…"

"*Pregnancy*?" Joe echoed. "You didn't tell me she was pregnant."

Mary hesitated. "I did tell you she was married, didn't I…?"

Joe let out a deep breath. "You did, yes, you did, but *pregnant*…"

Mary felt deflated. She had liked Joe Cassiday, but it was obvious now where his feelings lay.

She grasped Nancy's hand. "C'mon Nancy," she murmured. "We need to be going."

Joe stepped in front of her, barring her way forward. "I'm sorry," he said. "I didn't mean to shout, it wasn't your fault… I just felt…" His voice trailed off. In truth, he didn't know how he felt.

Mary's feisty spirit took over. "Well, if you'll excuse us," she said in clipped tones. "Me and Nancy are in a hurry." Joe was left bewildered in her wake, his emotions jangling and any thoughts of a reconciliation with Annie firmly quashed.

Mary's face was flushed with the exertion of the climb up Albert Street to Maryfield as she and Nancy arrived finally at Annie's home. The close leading to the varnished wooden front door was hushed and pristine and Mary was conscious of their footsteps insulting the silence. She began to tiptoe up the flight of stairs. A stained-glass window cast its colours onto the steps as they wound round the central pillar.

"Now you be a good girl," she warned Nancy. "And only speak when you're spoken to."

Nancy's eyes widened as her mother's mood began to affect her. Mary tapped softly on Annie's door. There was no reply.

"Perhaps she's gone for the messages," she whispered to Nancy.

A noise from behind the door indicated that she had not.

"Who is it?" said Annie's voice.

Mary brightened. "It's me… Mary. Open the door."

There was silence.

"Annie," she called again. "It's Mary and Nancy. Come to see you."

The key turned in the lock and the door slowly opened.

"You'd better come in."

Mary ushered Nancy inside the dimness of the hallway and closed the door behind her. "It's bitter out there," she announced, removing Nancy's hat and gloves. "They say it'll be snowing before the day's out." She removed her own outdoor things and hung her coat and scarf on the hall stand. "I hope I hear you putting the kettle on," she called through to the kitchen into which Annie had disappeared. She steered Nancy towards the door.

Annie was sitting with her back to them as they entered the warm room.

"And how's my favourite sister?" Mary asked, kissing the top of her head and squeezing her shoulders. A twinge of concern formed in Mary's mind as Annie failed to respond. She walked round in front of her and bent down to see her face.

"Annie," she queried. "Is something wrong?"

The bruising on Annie's face could not be hidden as she raised her head to face her sister.

For a moment, Mary froze as she surveyed Annie's damaged features. "Annie! What's happened?" She took her hands and held them tightly as Annie's chin began to quiver.

"It's nothing," she managed to whisper. "I fell."

"*Fell*?" Mary echoed. "*When*?"

Annie tried to control her distress. "Last night," she murmured. "I fell out of bed."

Mary's concern was heightened as she realised Annie wasn't telling the truth. She pulled up a chair beside her. "Tell me the truth, Annie Pepper. What happened?"

Annie gave in to the tears. "Oh, Mary," she sobbed. "It was Alex. He's been beating me."

Mary felt a wave of disbelief and anger wash over her. "*Alex* did this?"

Annie nodded.

Mary looked anxiously at her sister. "But *why*?"

"Cause, I made him do it," Annie answered, her voice barely audible.

Mary squeezed her hands. "I'll make you some tea." She hurried to the kettle and filled it with water at the sink. "Nancy," she called. "Fetch some cups and get the milk and sugar."

The child responded without question, sensing the urgency in her mother's voice.

"Drink it all," she urged Annie. "I've made it sweet for you."

Annie gulped down the liquid between quiet sobs.

"Tell me what's wrong," she asked Annie softly. "And don't tell me you made Alex beat you like this, 'cause I don't believe you."

Annie's eyes were almost lifeless as she met those of her sister. "I'm a liar, Mary," she begun. "You don't know the half of it."

Mary stroked her hand. "Then tell me," she repeated. "Tell me the truth."

Annie felt tears begin to burn the rim of her eyes again. "You'll hate me too, if I tell you."

"No I won't. I'd never hate you, Annie, never."

Annie took as deep a breath as her emotions would allow. "The baby I'm carrying," she said, "Isn't my first." She gripped Mary's hands, fearful that if she let them go, she'd lose her sister forever. "You weren't the only one to give birth to Billy's child."

Mary's eyes sought to understand the statement.

"Before he left for Scotland," she continued. "I too was with child to him."

Mary allowed the words to sink into her brain. "I don't understand..." she began.

Annie held a finger to her lips. "Sshhhhh, let me go on."

Mary pulled Nancy closer to her as she listened to Annie's tale.

"And since Bella's letter..."

"And Billy doesn't know?" Mary asked, incredulity over-riding all other emotions. "That he has a son, in Ireland?"

Annie shook her head. "And he mustn't know Mary, not ever."

"He loves you still, Annie," Mary stated sadly. "He should be told."

Annie leapt to her feet, panic and fear taking over. "Please, Mary, Alex would kill me if Billy ever found out about his son. He blames me for everything that's happened and I don't know what to do..." Her body folded into the chair.

Mary's heart filled with pity for her sister. All the time she'd kept her secret, never showing her pain and now, the one man she thought she could trust was doing this to her.

"Annie," she whispered gently. "You can't stay here, not now."

Annie looked bleak. "I can do no else," she said woodenly. "It's all my fault. Alex loves me so much and I've failed him."

"Perhaps, if I talked to him..."

"*No*," Annie wailed. "He mustn't know I've spoken to you. Please, Mary..."

Mary soothed her sister's fears. "It's alright, I won't say anything."

Annie looked at the clock ticking above the mantelpiece. "You must *go*," she urged quickly. "He'll be home soon and he mustn't know you've seen me like this."

Mary gripped Annie's shoulders. "I'll go Annie," she said firmly. "But I'll be back. You stood by me when no one else was there for me and I'll not desert you now. It doesn't matter about Billy or what's gone on in the past, I'm your sister and I'll always care for you and you for me." She pulled the silent Nancy behind her into the hall and donned her coat and hat before fastening on her own. She hugged her sister to her. "Remember there's a place at the single-end always for you. We've coped before and we'll cope again."

Annie forced a weak smile and nodded. "Hurry now," she whispered. "And thanks, Mary, for being my sister."

The door closed quietly and Annie returned to her prison.

Chapter 8

Joe Cassiday was brooding.

"Penny for them," asked his brother quietly.

Joe looked up. "What?"

"Your thoughts," added Charlie. "I'll give you a penny for them."

Joe grunted. "They're not worth that much." He lit a cigarette and exhaled the smoke slowly into the air around him.

"Not still hankering after that Pepper woman are you?"

"If you mean, Annie, then the answer's no." He threw the cigarette end onto the coals. "And your information about her is out of date."

Charlie sat down on his chair opposite Joe. "Maybe you should tell me the rest then, Joe."

"She's married."

Charlie pursed his lips. "And who's the lucky man?" he asked, emphasising *lucky*.

"A bobby, called Melville. Alex Melville."

Charlie let the information settle. "So, that's that then."

"She's also pregnant to him," Joe added.

"Fancy that now," observed Charlie thoughtfully. "And I wonder how long it'll be before *he* finds out about her lack of morals then?"

"For Christ's sake Charlie, its nearly 1914 and they say there's another war coming and you're still preaching morals..." Joe shook his head.

"Sorry," said Charlie, feeling offended by his brother's dismissive tone. "I didn't realise that the year made any difference to the way good women behaved themselves."

"I need a drink," Joe announced sullenly. "I'll be glad when this leave's over and I get back to the *real* world." He donned his tunic and Black Watch cap and opened the door. "I'll be at the Thrums Bar if you want a pint," he called over his shoulder to Charlie, feeling sorry that he'd been so harsh to him. It wasn't his fault that the Catholic in him saw everything as a sin.

"Sure," came the reply from the kitchen. "If I feel like it."

Joe closed the door and sighed. He wished he'd never taken his leave. At least at the Barracks with the rest of the lads, there were no reminders of the past.

The door of the pub beckoned to him as he approached and, once inside, he became caught up in the atmosphere of men together.

"Joe," someone called. "The first pint's on me."

Joe squinted through the haze of smoke. Billy Dawson was smiling at him from the end of the bar. The last time they'd met, they had come to blows over Annie and now, he was being offered a pint! Joe pressed his way through the crowd of mill workers at the bar till he came alongside Billy.

"Ale?" he asked.

Joe nodded. "Pint of Ale for Joe Cassiday," called Billy to the barman. "And a glass of lemonade for me."

Joe's eyes widened. "Lemonade?"

Billy smiled. "Been off the drink for a while now, Joe, but I miss the company now and then, so..." He shrugged his shoulders.

The barman deposited the creamy beer in front of Joe.

He raised his glass to Billy. "Water under the bridge?" he said.

Billy lifted his lemonade. "Water under the bridge."

The two men fell silent and it was Joe who broached the subject of Annie.

"I hear she's married now," he began. Billy nodded.

"So neither of us won."

"Nope."

"Pregnant too," Joe added.

Billy nodded again.

"Do you know him then?"

Billy exhaled through his nostrils. "Just a bit," he said. Joe waited for more details, but none came.

"So how's the Black Watch treating you?" asked Billy, changing the subject off Annie.

Joe grinned. "It's a great life, Billy. Wish I'd joined younger. Another lemonade?"

Billy shook his head. "No thanks, Joe. I'm expected for my supper."

"I thought…"

Billy interrupted him. "That me and Mary had parted company? You're right."

"So where are you living?"

Billy patted his broad shoulder. "You're an awful man for questions." He smiled. "Let's just say, I'm happier than I've ever been." Billy drained his glass and waved to the barman. "G'night Davie."

The barman placed a second pint in front of Joe.

"Never thought I'd see the day you and him would be on speaking terms," he stated flatly.

Joe swallowed an inch of beer.

"What happened to him and his wife then? Mary, wasn't it?"

The barman shrugged. "There was some funny business went on there," he whispered hoarsely. "She ran off wi' some bloke from the Sally Army."

Joe drank some more. "So, her and Billy… are finished?"

The barman's eyebrows raised in arcs above his eyes. "*Feenished*," he repeated. "Would you no' be?" The barman moved away, shaking his head and turned his attention to his other customers.

Joe finished his pint. "Be seein' you," he called to no one in particular.

Outside in the cold air, Joe buttoned his tunic to the neck and turned to go home but, somehow, he found himself at the single end.

Mary opened the door to his knock.

Joe removed his cap. "I've come to apologise," he said. "For upsetting you on Saturday."

Mary crossed her arms. "You didn't upset me," she retorted defensively. "So you needn't bother apologising."

Joe was taken aback by her hostility. "Can I come in… for a minute?"

"What for?" demanded Mary.

Joe shuffled his feet. He wasn't sure himself why he was there. "Do I have to have a reason?" he asked. "It's bloody freezin' standing here."

Mary suddenly saw the funny side of the situation. "I thought these kilts were supposed to keep you warm." she smiled. "Or is that just a story put out by the kilt makers?" She stood back and indicated he could enter. Joe rubbed his hands together, pretending to be even colder.

"Thanks Mary," he grinned. Remembering Nancy may be asleep, Joe tiptoed towards the fire and stood with his back to it. A look of intense pleasure crossed his face as the heat of the coals penetrated the material of his kilt.

"Tea?" asked Mary. Joe nodded.

"Well, if you'll move out of the way for a minute, I'll boil the kettle."

Joe jumped aside. "Sorry," he said. "Can I help?"

Mary smiled and shook her head. "Sit," she ordered. Joe obeyed. "I see the Black Watch has taught you to do as you're told at least," she joshed, beginning to relax in Joe's company.

In the firelight, he was the handsomest man Mary had ever seen. She could understand why Annie had been captivated by him and wondered where it had all gone wrong.

"What made you join the regiment then?" she asked, handing him a mug of tea.

"Crossed in love," he grinned, nearer the truth than he cared to admit now.

Mary eyed him quizzically. "Annie?" she asked.

Joe sat back in his chair. He wasn't sure how much Mary knew of Billy's part in the breakup but this wasn't the time to elaborate.

"Annie, Jeanie, Lizzie," he responded, rolling his eyes in mock pain. "There were sooooo many."

Mary giggled. "You're a rogue, Joe Cassiday." She sipped her tea. The light from the fire sparkled in her eyes. "Do you like music, Joe?"

Joe leant forward. "Love it," he replied.

Mary put down her cup and crossed to the bed. She bent down and reached underneath, withdrawing a battered black instrument case.

"What's that?" asked Joe.

Mary opened the case and took out her banjo.

"Do you play?"

Mary nodded. "Would you like to hear me?"

Joe sat back and lit a cigarette. "I would indeed, Mary."

Mary began softly plucking the strings until a tune emerged. The notes rang fast and clear and Joe's feet tapped the beat. Mary played an Irish jig followed by a Scottish Lament and ended with 'The Black Bear'.

Joe sat astonished at her expertise and when she finished, he clapped spontaneously.

"Ssshhhhh," she urged. "You'll wake Nancy."

"I'm awake," called a small, sleepy voice from the bed. "What's all that noise?"

Mary handed Joe the banjo and went over to her daughter. "Hush now, Nancy. Go back to sleep. It's only your mammy enjoying herself for a change."

The child smiled and closed her eyes. "Night, night mammy," she whispered dreamily.

Joe had poured them more tea and handed Mary her cup as she sat down again.

"My God, Mary," he exclaimed. "That was wonderful."

Mary blushed. "I used to play for my daddy, long ago in Ireland…" her voice softened at the memory. "He used to love it."

Joe had a sudden urge to hold her to him. Just like a child. He could see what had attracted Billy… and the Sally Army!

"Maybe, I could call again," he asked gently. "And you could play for me instead?"

Mary searched his face for understanding. "Maybe."

Joe's eyes held hers. "I'll look forward to it," he said.

"It's getting late," Mary blushed. "Time you were going."

Joe nodded. "Will you see me to the door?"

Mary nodded quietly, suddenly feeling a stillness inside her. "Are you going to take that with you?" she asked pointing to her banjo.

Joe looked at his hand still clutching the instrument. They both burst out laughing as Joe handed it back to her.

"But when Irish eyes are smiling…" he began to sing, as he bowed out of the door, "Sure they steal your heart away…"

She watched till Joe disappeared round the corner of the close before going back inside.

The fire was burning low now as she sat down with her banjo again. She played 'The Mountains of Mourne' and the 'Londonderry Aire', two of her father's favourites. She'd play them for Joe Cassiday the next time he called, she decided. He'd like that.

Chapter 9

Annie's pregnancy progressed through the long winter months, despite Alex's moods, which seemed to swing between high elation and deep blackness, depending it seemed, on Annie's behaviour. No matter how she tried, she always seemed to do something to trigger his anger. She'd stopped seeing Mary, except when her sister secretly visited her, and seldom went out alone, except to go for the messages.

Alex's duty rota at the jail meant he ate and slept at different times and Annie had to rearrange her days to comply with his, which meant she would sometimes be asleep during the day and awake all night.

It was during one such wakeful night that Constable MacPherson called at the house. At first, she'd been reluctant to open the door, but had been assured by the Constable that Alex was on duty at the station and it was important that he speak with her.

Euan MacPherson had been a policeman for over twelve years and for the last seven of them, Alex had been his Sergeant.

"I'm concerned," he began, once he had taken off his helmet and sat down by the fire, "About your welfare."

Annie felt uncomfortable. Was this a trick by Alex to catch her with another man? "Are you sure Sergeant Melville's at the station," she asked anxiously.

Euan MacPherson nodded. "Please, Mrs Melville, I wouldn't be bothering you unless I was sure. If the Sergeant knew I was here... well!"

Annie remained on the edge of her chair.

"Is everything... alright?" he asked Annie. "I mean, are *you* alright?"

Annie's eyes narrowed, she never answered direct questions any more. "Why do you ask?"

Constable MacPherson's complexion deepened to brick red. "I know it's probably none of my business but I feel it's my duty to speak to you about my concerns and..."

"Please, Constable MacPherson," interrupted Annie. "What is it you want to say?"

Euan MacPherson coughed nervously and ran his finger round the collar of his tunic. "Has your husband..." he began. "I mean, Sergeant Melville, been behaving strangely recently?"

Annie tensed. "Strangely?"

The constable sucked his teeth. "What I mean is... well... I'll come right to the point, Mrs Melville. Has your husband ever behaved in a violent manner towards you?"

Annie froze. "Why do you ask that?" she said, a thousand thoughts racing through her mind.

Euan MacPherson stared at his polished toecaps. "Mr McKay, the butcher in Dura Street's my sister's husband and he's been concerned about your appearance of late..." Euan's voice tailed off.

"My appearance?"

The constable looked at Annie. "He thinks, maybe, Mr Melville's accidentally hit..."

Annie jumped up. "Well, he's *wrong*," she rounded, tears springing to her eyes. "I keep fainting and falling down," she lied. "It's the baby I'm expecting."

Constable MacPherson sprang to his feet. "Of course," he agreed anxiously. "I knew it was something like that. I'm sorry to have bothered you Mrs Melville, but I felt I had to ask..."

Annie tried to calm down. "Please tell Mr McKay, I'm fine," she asked trying to control the quiver in her voice. "And don't ever call here again." Annie walked towards the door. "I'll see you out Constable MacPherson."

The policeman followed, replacing his helmet and tightening the chinstrap. "I'm sorry to have bothered you, Mrs Melville," he said. "Goodnight."

Annie closed the door and leant against its firmness to steady herself.

People were noticing, speaking about her. It felt as if her whole world was closing in on her. She had not only ruined her own reputation but now, she was ruining her husband's.

Constable MacPherson emerged from the close into the night. His brother-in-law was right, he concluded angrily. Annie Melville was being beaten and by her husband.

On 17 April 1914, Annie gave birth to her daughter. It had been a difficult labour, lasting thirty-six hours and at the end of it, Annie had been too exhausted to even look at her child. The Doctor had insisted she was hospitalised to rest and arranged for her and the baby to be admitted to Maryfield Hospital in Mains Loan.

"Of course," Alex had agreed. "Anything for my lovely wife."

The spring sunshine was filtering through the maternity ward window as Annie nursed her babe, surrounded by other mothers with theirs. Everything was so different here and for the first time in a long time, Annie felt unafraid. She gazed at the tiny features of her daughter.

"Jessie," she whispered. "You're to be called Jessie, after my best friend in the whole world."

"Your husband's here to visit you, Mrs Melville," announced the Sister briskly, descending on Annie down the centre of the ward. "And to see his beautiful new daughter."

Alex was the picture of happiness. He kissed Annie on the forehead and presented her with a large bouquet of spring flowers.

"Thank you dearest," he whispered. "For my lovely daughter, Alexandra."

"Alexandra?" exclaimed Annie. "But," she stammered. "We haven't decided on a name yet, and I rather liked… Jessie."

Alex's eyes darkened. "Jessie?" he queried. "After your *good* friend?"

Annie flinched, the fear returning.

"*My* daughter will be called *Alexandra*, after *me*."

Annie swallowed. 'Is there to be no end to Alex's anger?' she thought.

"Yes, Alex," she agreed meekly. Of course."

"I suppose you'll be wanting your sister to know about Alexandra?"

Annie silently nodded.

"I'll send Constable MacPherson round to tell her when he comes on duty at three o'clock."

"Thank you Alex."

He bent over and kissed first his daughter and then Annie on the forehead. "Which reminds me, time I was on my way. Duty calls."

Annie watched his broad frame disappear down the ward and her thoughts went back to their first encounter. He had seemed so kind then, concerned for his sister, Isabella, and compassionate towards Mary and Isabella's husband, John, in their adultery. But most of all, he'd shown understanding and tenderness to Annie. She held Alexandra close and gently stroked the blonde wisp of hair on her crown.

"Lexie," she said softly. "I'll call you Lexie."

Constable MacPherson was instructed to deliver the news of Alexandra's birth to Mary.

"And spare no time with the woman once she's been told," Alex had insisted. "There's no need to encourage her to visit."

Euan MacPherson tightened his lips for fear of speaking out at his Sergeant, but saluted before turning on his heel and leaving the Charge Room. Since his visit to Annie, he'd watched Alex Melville from afar, trying to sense his moods but, as usual, Alex was cool and unemotional at all times.

He knocked officially on the door of Mary's single-end.

At first Mary had thought he was the bearer of bad news and her eyes filled with fear at the sight of him. "What is it?" she asked, immediately worried for Annie. "What's wrong?"

Euan MacPherson held up his hand. "Calm down, Mrs Dawson," he intoned in his steady voice. "Nothing's wrong. In fact, if you'll let me in for a minute, I'm the bearer of good news."

Mary stepped aside. "Come in then," she ordered, brightening.

Euan looked round the small room. 'Hardly room to swing a cat,' he observed. 'But neat and tidy nevertheless.'

"And who's this?" he smiled, spying a little girl playing in the corner with a peg doll.

"I'm Nancy."

"It's my daughter," Mary explained. "But hurry up Constable, tell me your news. Is it Annie, has the baby come?"

Constable MacPherson beamed. "It has indeed," he told her. "Or should I say, *she* has indeed."

"It's a girl!" Mary exclaimed, clapping her hands. "Do you hear that Nancy, your Auntie Annie's had a little girl, just like you." She crossed the room and hugged her daughter. "And is she alright… Annie, I mean," asked Mary, conscious of her sister's life with Alex.

Euan MacPherson nodded. "Mother and baby is both fine," he assured her. Mary breathed a sigh of relief.

"Is she at home? Can I go and see her?"

Constable MacPherson held up his hand again. "Snakes alive, Mrs Dawson, slow down. I've to tell you she's in hospital."

"Hospital!" Mary shrieked. "I thought you said she was alright!"

"She is, she *is*," Euan reassured her, becoming exasperated. "She's gone in for a few days for the rest."

Mary seemed to calm down.

"Now, I suppose if you want to go to see your sister, there's no one can stop you. She's in the Maternity Ward at Maryfield."

Mary's eyes clouded. "Did *he* say I wasn't to go?"

"Who?" asked the Constable.

"Never mind," she replied, not waiting for an answer. "I'd go anyway, whether he liked it or not."

"And why would Sergeant Melville want to stop his wife's sister visiting her in hospital?"

Mary's expression hardened. "Never mind," she murmured. "Least said…"

Euan replaced his helmet on his head, pulling the chinstrap under his chin, now surer than ever of Annie's situation.

"Say hello to your sister from me," he told Mary. "Tell her congratulations."

Mary smiled. "I will, Constable and thanks for bringing me the news."

After he'd gone, Mary hurriedly donned her coat and ordered Nancy to do the same.

"We're going to visit your Auntie Annie," she told the child. "While we've the chance."

The Ward Sister barred Mary's entry.

"Visiting's over for the day, I'm afraid," she informed her in her crisp starched voice.

"But you don't understand," replied Mary, wondering why she was whispering. "I'm going through to Edinburgh tomorrow for a fortnight and this is the only chance I'll have to see my sister. Pleeeeaaassse."

The Sister eyed her sternly. "Is that the truth?" she asked.

Mary nodded quickly, willing the nurse to believe her.

"Hhhhmmmmppphh!" she exclaimed, weighing up the possibility of disruption to her mother if she allowed Mary *and* Nancy into the ward.

"Very well," she conceded. "Follow me."

"Thank you Sister," Mary gushed.

"Ssssshhhhh," the starched one instructed. "There are babies trying to sleep."

Mary grabbed Nancy's hand and tiptoed after her.

Annie's bed was at the far end of the ward.

"You've visitors, Mrs Melville," the Sister whispered. "Would you like to see them?"

Annie propped herself up on her elbows and squinted into the low light of the ward. "It's my sister, Mary," she told the nurse, her eyes lighting up. "And Nancy."

The Sister seemed satisfied that Annie's visitors were welcome. "They can't stay long, you understand," she whispered to Annie, "But seeing as she's off to Edinburgh tomorrow, I've made an exception this time."

"Edinburgh!" Annie exclaimed.

"Sssshhhh," hushed Mary. "It was the only way I could get in to see you outside visiting hours."

The sisters giggled.

"I'm so glad you've come Mary."

"Are you alright?"

Annie nodded. "I'm fine," she whispered. "And the baby's fine too."

They both knew what Mary meant, but neither sister laboured the point.

"Are you calling her Jessie, then?" asked Mary.

Annie bit her lip. "Not exactly," she replied. "You see Alex wants to call her Alexandra, after him… so, that's her name. But I'm going to call her Lexie," she added defiantly. "How does that sound?"

"Lexie," Mary repeated to Nancy. "Now isn't that a nice name for your wee cousin. Lexie Melville."

Nancy beamed. "Lexie and Nancy," she breathed. "She can play with my dolly if she likes."

Annie ruffled her hair. "Thanks Nancy," she whispered. "You're a good girl."

"Are things any better?" Mary asked. "Between you and Alex I mean?"

Annie took a deep breath. "No," she replied, flatly. "I don't think they'll ever be right again, Mary. It doesn't matter what I do or don't do, there always seems something I do wrong to rile him."

Mary squeezed her sister's hand. "Perhaps when you and the baby are home, things will be different," she told her hopefully.

Annie smiled ruefully, "Perhaps. Anyway, enough of me, how are you and Nancy doing?"

Mary paused. "You'll never guess who's been visiting me."

Annie shook her head. "Don't know."

"Joe," replied Mary.

Annie hesitated. "Joe?" she repeated. "You mean, Joe Cassiday?"

"The very same."

Annie wasn't sure how to react to the news. "And what on earth was he wantin'?"

Mary pulled her shoulders back. "Well, originally, he called to see you. Thought you were still living at the single end… but now…"

"Now?"

Mary felt herself colour. "Well now, it would seem he calls to see me."

Annie didn't know whether to laugh or cry. "You… and Joe!"

Mary nodded enthusiastically. "There's nothing serious yet," Mary continued. "But… I'm hopeful."

Annie lay back on her pillows. Joe had been the one who'd replaced Billy in her affections, until he found out she wasn't the virgin bride he'd been looking for, then, he'd deserted her and joined the Black Watch. And now, he was courting Mary, whose past was even more colourful than Annie's.

"Does he know about… you and Billy?"

Mary nodded.

"And he doesn't mind?"

Mary shrugged. "No."

"Well, he's changed the colour of his coat since he joined up," Annie exclaimed. "And does he know about… Mrs Cook?"

Mary shook her head. "No," she whispered. "Not about Mrs Cook."

Annie raised an eyebrow. "And will you tell him?"

"No," Mary hissed. "And don't you either… pleeeeease."

Annie shook her head. "Remember he's a ladies' man Mary, with a God-fearing Catholic for a brother."

"I know, I know. But he's not like his brother. Honest he isn't."

"If you say so," replied Annie. "Anyway, enough of Joe Cassiday, when did Alex tell you about the baby?"

Mary looked perplexed. "Alex never told me. It was his Constable."

"Constable MacPherson?"

Mary nodded. "I think so. He came to the door. Said to tell you 'congratulations' by the way. He seems a nice man."

Annie tensed at the mention of the Constable's name. "What else did he say?" she asked.

Mary shrugged. "Nothing really, just told me you were in Maryfield Hospital and to go and see you."

"Why?"

"Nothing."

The rustle of a starched apron sounded behind Mary.

"That's long enough," said the Sister. "Mum needs her rest."

Mary nodded and rose from the chair, scraping it across the linoleum floor as she did so.

"Sorry," she whispered loudly.

The Sister frowned. "Get some rest now, Mrs Melville, it'll soon be feeding time for baby."

Mary leant over and hugged her sister. "I'll see you at home." she smiled. "When I get back from Edinburgh!"

Annie shook her head at her sister's cheek.

"Good night," she mouthed to Nancy as mother and daughter turned to go.

"Good night Auntie Annie," called Nancy before being ushered out by the Sister.

Annie closed her eyes. 'Joe Cassiday and Mary,' she pondered. 'Now there *is* a turn-up for the books.'

Chapter 10

"Do you really think there'll be a war Billy?" Josephine MacIntyre was gazing intently at her lodger over the rim of her teacup.

"Depends."

"What on?"

"Whether King George's looking for a good fight."

Josephine stood up and began to clear the table. "But we won't really be expected to join in… will we?"

Billy smiled. "If it means defending our country against 'them foreigners' then the answer's yes, Josie."

Josephine coloured. She liked when Billy called her Josie, in fact, she was beginning to like Billy a lot. He'd taken full advantage of her suggestion that he visit the little study with its book-lined shelves whenever he wanted and as his appetite for reading and literature had deepened, a common bond had formed between them.

"I hope you're wrong," she frowned. "Enough lives were lost in the African Campaign."

Billy saw a frown form on her forehead.

"Now then," he sought to reassure her. "Don't you be worrying your head about such things. Even if there is a war, it'll be something and nothing and over before the shouting starts." His hands were gripping her shoulders and his eyes were locked on to hers.

Josephine nodded. "I'm sorry," she said. "It's just that I've lost someone I loved already and I wouldn't want to lose anyone else…"

Billy's fingers held her shoulders tighter. "You're not going to lose anyone else," he told her. "Not if I have anything to do with it."

Josephine's breathing was barely perceptible as Billy released his grip. "What're you reading tonight?" she asked, her voice trembling slightly with the nearness of the encounter.

Billy gathered up the rest of the crockery and followed Josephine through to the small scullery. "Politics," he replied.

Josephine raised an eyebrow. "Which party?" she asked. Her late husband had been a Liberal all of his life and had been considering entering local politics when he'd taken ill with the disease which eventually killed him.

Billy folded his arms across his chest. "Labour Party, of course," he replied, his eyes developing a gleam in them. "Ramsay McDonald," he continued. "Now, there's a man of the people."

"Mr MacIntyre was very political," Josephine told him. "You'd have liked him."

Billy smiled at her kindly, "I'm sure I would," he replied. "But how about yourself? Which political persuasion are you?"

Josie grinned wickedly. "I'm a suffragette, of course."

Billy joined in the banter. "I hope you're not going to throw yourself in front of any horses, are you?"

"Ni," she responded, grinning. "But if you're not careful, I'll throw this dishcloth at you and insist you wash up."

Billy bowed deeply and draped the towel over his arm in mock servitude. "Your wish is my command, my lady," he intoned. "Chain me to the sink!"

Josephine MacIntyre giggled like a schoolgirl, as Billy plunged his arms into the hot water. The intimacy of the situation imperceptibly seeped into Billy's soul as the pile of dishes were washed and dried. "And how else can this simple working man repay such kindness as you've shown me these last six months?" he asked, drying his hands as he watched Josie stack the plates on their shelf.

"A day at the seaside would be nice," she laughed over her shoulder, jokingly.

"Done."

Josephine turned to face him. "What?"

"Done," repeated Billy, smiling gently.

A wave of acute vulnerability washed over her. "I didn't mean…" she began to explain. "That I would expect you to take me…"

Billy held up a finger to silence her. "I would be honoured," he said. "If you'd accompany me this Sunday to Broughty Ferry."

For the first time since the death of her husband, Josephine felt desire. "We could take a picnic," she half-suggested… perhaps?"

"A picnic would be wonderful," Billy replied, resisting the urge to take her in his arms.

"Sunday it is then." She smiled.

Billy ran his fingers through his hair and cleared his throat. "Well… I'll get on with some reading then," he said gruffly. "…unless there's anything else?"

Josie fought back the temptation to reach out to him. "Nothing," she replied quickly. "Unless you want some sewing to do!"

They both grinned sheepishly at one another as Josephine picked up her sewing basket.

Billy disappeared to the study.

By the time Sunday came round, Josephine had worked herself up into a state of nerves about the impending outing to Broughty Ferry. 'What if we have a dreadful time,' she thought first of all, then, 'What if it rains and the picnic's ruined,' followed by 'What if Billy's changed his mind?'

The third thought was the most nerve-racking of all, for she wanted to be with Billy more than anything else now in her world. She was so absorbed in her fears that she didn't hear him come into the room and jumped at the sound of his voice.

"How's the picnic shaping up then?" he asked jovially. "Looks like the sun is going to shine on this fine June morning," he added, looking out of the window at the blue sky.

Josephine felt all her fears disappear. "I haven't begun yet," she laughed. "I thought we'd have breakfast first."

Billy rubbed his hands together. "Ahhhh!" he grinned, sniffing the air. "Sunday breakfast, best meal of the week."

She had never seen Billy so relaxed as they ate their morning meal. It had been a long time since she herself had felt this happy and there had been times, since the death of her husband, when she felt she'd never find any kind of personal happiness again. But, in the short time he'd been lodging with her, Billy had, unwittingly, changed all that.

"I'll make us some sandwiches," she called from the kitchen. "And there's the Ginger Beer I bought on Saturday," Josie bubbled. "We could take that too."

Billy was leaning against the doorframe, his hands in his pockets as he watched her move around the small kitchen. Her fair hair was held in place with tortoiseshell combs and the simple cotton dress which draped itself over her shoulders was held at the waist by a narrow length of ribbon, tied in a bow at the back.

"Anything you say," Billy told her softly. There was something in the tone of his voice which made Josephine stop what she was doing and turn to face him.

"You're very beautiful, Mrs MacIntyre." Billy smiled.

Josephine felt herself blush fiercely and quickly looked at her feet. "Well, thank you kind sir," she replied, not knowing how to handle the compliment.

"I hope you're not going to call me 'sir' for the rest of the day, are you?" he asked smiling at her loss of composure.

Josie turned back to the sandwich making, her hands trembling and her wits deserting her.

Suddenly, Billy was beside her, removing the butter knife from her hand.

"Here," he said. "Let me. You go and get your bonnet on and I'll get these packed in the basket."

Josie offered no objection, glad of the excuse to escape with the turmoil which was developing inside her.

Billy finished filling the sandwiches and packed them in the small wicker basket along with the Ginger Beer. He'd make the day special for Josie, she deserved that. He only wished he could have made life special for Annie when he'd had the chance, instead of having her hate him.

The tram rumbled along Broughty Ferry Road and past the Stannergate, where children were scrambling over the rocks picking whelks from their craggy homes and dropping them into buckets for boiling and eating when they got home. The water sparkled in the sunshine and

Josephine felt safe, a feeling which had been lost to her since becoming a widow.

"Can we build a sandcastle?" she asked Billy, excited now at the prospect of revisiting the beach of her childhood. "And paddle in the sea?"

"If you like," he told her grinning at her simple demands.

The tram bell clanged.

"Church Street," bellowed the conductor. "Alight here for West Ferry."

"Let's get off here and walk the rest," suggested Billy, taking Josephine's hand. "See the fisherfolk."

Josie nodded and allowed Billy to guide her to the front of the tram.

The conductor smiled at them as they jumped off the step into the sunshine. "Wish it wiz me," he grinned at them, wiping his brow and pretending exhaustion. "Make sure your man buys you some ice-cream," he added, nodding at Josie.

"I will," called back Billy.

Josie felt a surge of happiness as Billy held out his arm for her to link into.

"To the beach!" he said, pointing to the sea which could be glimpsed at the foot of Church Street.

"To the beach!" echoed Josie, as they set off towards their goal.

As they turned into Fisher Street, they could see washing flapping in the warm sea breeze as it hung between poles at the edge of the shingle to dry. Fishermen's wives sat mending nets as their husbands attended to the small boats which rested high on the shoreline. Their scallywag children ranged amongst them chasing one another and searching under barnacles for small crabs and old women puffed on clay pipes as they sat by the doors of their cottages, gossiping and chiding the youngsters when they got too rowdy.

"Lovely day," called Billy to a nearby local.

The man nodded and indicated the sunshine, puffing happily on his pipe.

"Look!" exclaimed Josie. "The castle. Isn't it magnificent."

Broughty Ferry Castle jutted out on the headland in front of them.

"We'll walk round that way," said Billy. "On our way to the sand. Let you have a closer look."

Josie nodded eagerly. "I'd like that."

The fisherfolk's cottages gave way to the magnificent houses of the Jute Barons overlooking the estuary, as Billy and Josie made their way towards the castle. A flock of swans sailed past on their way to feed and nannies strolled by, pushing their charges in black coach-built perambulators, as they took the air.

"There's a lot of activity at the castle," Billy observed as they neared the ancient portcullis entrance to the fortress. A Black Watch soldier stood guard at its entrance.

"What's going on?" asked Billy, his curiosity getting the better of him.

The soldier gazed in front of him as if Billy hadn't spoken.

"Must be a military secret," he whispered loudly to Josie. But the soldier still did not respond.

"C'mon," he told her. "Let's build our own castle… in the sand."

They ran down onto the soft, biscuit-coloured sand of Broughty Beach. Billy untied his shoes and took off his socks. "C'mon," he urged Josie. "If you want to paddle, you'll need to take these boots off."

Josie glanced round her at the clusters of families enjoying the sunshine and forgot her staid upbringing. She unbuttoned her boots and rolling down the cotton stockings, took them off and slipped them inside the boots. Leaving their basket and inhibitions behind them, Billy and Josie ran towards the estuary.

The water was freezing. "Aaaahhhhh," squealed Josie, as Billy pulled her further into the shallow waves.

"It's too cold," she shouted, but Billy would hear none of it. Ribbons of green seaweed swished round their ankles as slow waves rolled over it. Billy pointed to a lighthouse on the Fife shore.

"We'll take the train over the bridge next time," he told her. "And walk to that lighthouse in Tayport."

"Next time?" asked Josie, her skin glowing with fresh air and happiness.

Billy let go of her hand, realising what he'd said. "If you'd like there to be a next time, that is?" he asked, a sudden seriousness in his voice.

Josie extended her hand towards him. "I'd like," she said. "Very much."

Chapter 11

Before the summer of 1914 was over, Britain was at war with Germany. Annie held Lexie tightly to her as Alex read out the news from the Dundee Courier.

"What'll happen now?" she asked, maternal fear for her child uppermost in her mind.

Alex shrugged and folded the paper. "Whatever happens," he told her. "It won't affect me. Policemen are exempt from wars."

Annie's heart fell. Did Alex always have to put himself first? "I was more concerned about Alexandra," she murmured. "I couldn't bear anything to happen to her."

Alex raised an eyebrow. "So, you wouldn't care if your husband was killed in a war, so long as your daughter's alright?"

Annie had said the wrong thing again and a pang of anxiety gripped her insides. "No Alex," she whispered, her eyes staring at the banner headlines of the newspaper on the table. "I just meant…"

She waited for the slap to arrive.

"First of all, it was your friends and that sister of yours that came first," Alex said, his voice cold and emotionless. "And now it's Alexandra." He snatched up the newspaper and stood up. "I sometimes wish I'd never given you a child."

Annie's grip tightened on Lexie. "I'm sorry, Alex," she answered softly. "I didn't mean it like that."

The door banged loudly and he was gone.

Annie had thought the arrival of their child would have rekindled the love Alex had once had for her, but if anything, as the days and weeks had passed since Lexie's birth, his coldness towards her had increased. If the mood took him, he'd rock his daughter in her cradle, but this was seldom, and more than not, he'd ignore both of them.

It was late afternoon when Annie's visitor arrived. She'd spent all day about her housewifely duties and had just got Lexie down for her nap and was looking forward to some time to herself when the doorbell had jingled.

Reluctantly, she opened the door.

"Isabella!" she exclaimed in surprise at the sight of her sister-in-law. "Come in, come in."

Isabella Anderson, Alex's sister, hugged Annie and followed her through to the parlour.

"Is John not with you?" asked Annie.

Isabella smiled. "No," she replied. "But I've got some news for you."

Annie could see Isabella was bursting with excitement. "Well?" she asked, putting a cup of tea in front of her visitor.

"We're coming back to Dundee," Isabella gushed. "No more exile in Edinburgh."

Annie was more than taken aback by the news. John and Isabella had been forced to stay in Edinburgh since John's infidelity with Mary and it had been made clear that the Salvation Army would never allow them to return to Dundee again.

"But how?" Annie asked.

"John's been offered a job," she explained happily. "A teaching post at Morgan Academy. The Rector's a friend of John's and he's been looking for a History teacher for some time now."

"But, John's life is the Salvation Army," Annie queried. "Surely…"

"*Was* the Salvation Army," finished Isabella. She hung her head. "They've never forgiven him, Annie," she said. "Despite the fact that I, his wife, have."

Annie squeezed her hand. "I'm sure it'll be for the best," she assured her. "And it'll be wonderful to have you near."

Isabella blinked back a tear. "Thanks, Annie," she whispered. "I knew you'd be happy to see us back." She looked around the room. "You're a fine housekeeper," she told Annie admiringly. "And I'm sure a wonderful mother too."

Annie smiled. "She's sleeping just now, but when she wakes, you can hold her if you like. After all, you are her God Mother."

Isabella had been so full of her news, she'd failed to notice the change in Annie and, when she had, she'd at first put it down to the strains of being a new mother.

"Are you coping alright?" she asked kindly. "You seem a bit drawn, Annie."

Annie drew a deep breath. She knew Isabella loved her brother dearly and wouldn't believe a word said against him.

"I'm fine, Isabella," she assured her pushing her hair back from her forehead and inadvertently revealing a large bruise on her arm as her sleeve fell back.

"What on earth's that on your arm?"

Annie quickly pulled the sleeve back. "Nothing," she responded quickly, "Nothing at all."

Isabella's eyes filled with concern. "But, Annie!" she exclaimed. "You're black and blue."

Annie had steeled herself over the past year to deal with anger, temper and pain, but she'd forgotten how to respond to kindness and couldn't deal with Isabella's concern except by dissolving into tears.

"Why Annie," asked Isabella. "Whatever's wrong?"

Annie fell into her sister-in-law's arms and sobbed for a long time. Isabella didn't try to speak again, till the tide of sorrow had ebbed.

"What is it, Annie?" she asked gently. "You must tell me."

The sobbing had rendered Annie emotionless. "He's beating me Isabella," she said woodenly. "No matter what I do to try to please him, it's never enough." She sighed deeply. "I thought once Alexandra was born, he'd stop, but…"

Annie waited for Isabella to defend her brother.

"Just like father," she heard her whisper. "God help him, he's turned out just like father."

Annie looked up.

Isabella's eyes were shining with painful memories. "Our father was the same," she told Annie faintly. "Mother had a terrible life with him. But, I thought… after what Alex had seen, he'd never treat *his* wife that way." She took Annie's hands in hers. "It would seem it's come through in the blood."

Annie didn't know whether to laugh or cry. "So, it's not me?" she asked.

Isabella shook her head. "Just like it wasn't mother."

"Oh, Isabella," Annie whispered. "What am I to do?"

Isabella smiled gently. "What are *we* to do," she told her. "John and me move back to Dundee at the end of this month, and quite near to you too, Janefield Place. I'll be able to visit you more often and Alex will have to stop his nonsense then."

Annie felt a glimmer of hope. "Do you really think so, Isabella?"

Isabella squeezed her hand. "I'm sure of it," she said. "Now, go wash you face and let me see that new niece of mine."

Lexie blinked at the light as she was brought through to be cuddled by her Auntie Isabella.

"Oh, Annie," she murmured. "She's beautiful." Gently, Isabella drew a finger over the tiny features. "May I take her for walks in her pram, sometimes," she asked softly.

"She'd like that," smiled Annie.

The sound of the front door closing alerted the two women to Alex's return.

Fear immediately gripped Annie's heart again. "Please," she hissed to Isabella. "Don't say anything."

Isabella nodded and squeezed Annie's arm, as she handed Lexie back. "It's alright," she whispered. "Trust me."

Alex's eyes widened in surprise when he saw his sister. "Isabella," he smiled, holding out his arms to embrace her. "What a lovely surprise." He turned to Annie. "You didn't tell me Isabella was coming."

Annie flinched.

"She didn't know," Isabella cut in. "No one did."

Alex turned back to his sister and reinstated his smile.

"And where's John?" he asked intently, steering Isabella back to a chair.

"Preparing for our move back to Dundee," announced Isabella for the second time that day.

"*Back to Dundee*!" exclaimed Alex. "Well, how wonderful." He turned to Annie. "Isn't that wonderful my dear?"

Annie smiled weakly. "Yes," she agreed. "Wonderful."

"You'll stay to tea, of course," Alex went on. "But I suppose Annie's already invited you."

"No, I haven't," Annie stuttered. "But, of course, Isabella, you must stay…"

Annie felt the weight of Alex's displeasure descend on her again.

"I'd love to stay," Isabella interjected brightly. "But I've a train to catch, but next time, Annie," she added, hugging her sister-in-law warmly. "I'll stay as long as you like."

Alex saw his sister to the door and returned to the waiting Annie.

"That wasn't very friendly of you now, was it," Alex began, knowing exactly where it was leading.

Annie ignored the remark. "I'll just put Lexie in her crib and get your tea."

"I said," repeated Alex loudly. "That wasn't very friendly."

Annie tucked the covers round her child and turned to face the wrath of her husband. "Whatever you say, Alex."

Alex crossed the room towards her, his eyes black as coal. "That's right, my *dear*," he spat. "Whatever I *say*."

For a moment, their eyes locked and neither spoke.

"You're a bully," Annie slowly whispered into the silence. "A coward and a bully."

Alex's eyes darkened further. "What did you say," he growled, his grip tightening on her already bruised arm.

"If I was a man," she continued, her knees trembling. "You wouldn't dare touch me."

His jaw was clenched with anger as he pushed her from him. "Baaahhh," he shouted. "You're not worth bothering with… *whore*." He slammed out of the room, rattling the pictures on the wall with the force of his departure.

Annie's heart was pounding. She knew he'd be back, but she'd stood up to him. And for the moment, she'd won.

Chapter 12

"Lance-Corporal Joseph Cassiday," barked the Sergeant.

"Sir."

"There's a bunch of volunteers due next week for basic training." He shuffled a mound of paperwork on his desk. "Report to the barracks at Forfar on the seventeenth and take this." He handed Joe a three-day leave pass. "Make the most of it," he instructed Joe. "Now there's a war on laddie, it'll be the last you get for a while."

Joe saluted. "Sir."

The sergeant waved his hand in dismissal.

The onset of the war with Germany had resulted in a quick promotion for Joe and he was determined to live up to it. Training volunteers, however, hadn't been his idea of heroics. He wanted to be at the front line, trouncing the Hun, but if this was what the Black Watch wanted of him, then so be it.

He picked up his rail warrant from the orderly on duty and returned to his barracks.

"Hey Joe," called Tam Gow. "Whut's happenin'?" Tam was scrawny and always looked in need of a good meal. His legs dangled over the edge of his bunk, more bone than brawn.

Joe grinned. "A bit of home-leave," he said. "Then off to the wilds of Forfar to train the volunteers."

Tam jumped from his bunk and landed with a thump on the floor. "*Forfar*," Tam echoed, in mock admiration. "Is that where you Irish lads are bein' sent? I'm off tae France," he announced proudly, pulling back his shoulders and attempting to expand his meatless chest.

"France, eh," smiled Joe. "Lucky you."

"Well," continued Tam proudly, strutting up the middle of the barrack room. "They ken where to send the *real* men."

Joe grinned. "Make sure you kill a few Germans for me, Tam." He swung his kitbag over his shoulder. "I'll have a pint ready for you at the Thrums when you get back."

Tam laughed, the gap in his front teeth showing black amongst the yellow. "Make it twa an' a wee nip besides an' you've got a deal."

Joe slapped him on the back and headed out of the barracks towards home. He wished he could swap places with Tam Gow.

"How are you going to spend your leave this time," asked Charlie, after Joe had dumped his kitbag in the corner and drained a mug of tea.

"Drinking," replied his brother.

Charlie raised a quizzical eyebrow. "No womanising?"

Joe grinned and gazed at the tea leaves in his mug. "Maybe."

Charlie took the mug from his hands. "You'll not find Mary Dawson in there," he added. "If that's who you're looking for."

Joe glanced at his brother. Charlie knew him better than anyone. "What made you say that?" he asked.

Charlie shrugged his shoulders. "Tell me I'm wrong."

Joe stood up. "I'll see you in the Thrums," he said. "If that's alright with you!"

"I've told you before, Joe, that woman's trouble, just like her sister, Annie."

Joe lit a cigarette. "I'll be the judge of that," Joe replied. "I'm a big boy now."

The elder brother shook his head. "See you in the Thrums."

But Joe's feet somehow ended up at Mary's door instead.

Her heart leapt at the sight of him. He was by far the handsomest man she'd ever seen and his Black Watch uniform only served to show off his physique.

"What's that?" Mary asked, pointing to the white stripe on the sleeve of Joe's uniform.

Joe gasped in pretend amazement. "Now, where did that come from?"

Mary giggled.

"Can Lance-Corporal Joseph Cassiday come in?" he asked bowing.

"*Lance-Corporal!*" squealed Mary.

"They've only promoted me so I could win the war single-handed," Joe grinned.

Mary's eyes widened. "They're not sending you to..."

"Forfar," Joe interrupted. "Training volunteers."

Mary breathed a sigh of relief.

"I don't think there's many Germans in Forfar," he added. "Now, can I come in?"

Mary pulled him inside the single-end.

"Where's Nancy?" he asked, noticing the absence of Mary's daughter.

"Mrs Ogilvie's keeping an eye on her. I'm not long back from the cleaning at Baxters, I'll be picking her up in about an hour."

Joe relaxed into the chair by the fire.

"I've a three-day pass," he told Mary. "Before I go to Forfar."

"That's nice," she replied, cutting some bread and trying to keep her desire for Joe under control.

"And, I was wondering..."

Mary stopped cutting the bread. "Wondering?"

Joe cleared his throat. "Wondering if you'd like to spend some of it with me."

Mary pushed a slice of bread onto the toasting fork and handed it to Joe, managing, with remarkable reserve, to stop herself from rushing into his arms. She was still married to Billy, she reminded herself, although in name only, and was only too aware of Joe's past.

"And what did you have in mind?" she asked demurely, as the toast burned.

Joe blew out the flames and handed the burnt offering to Mary. "Sorry," he said. "Nearly got my fingers burned."

Mary's eyes flashed as he held his hand up to show her.

"Maybe I should kiss them better," she whispered, all caution now deserting her in her desire for him.

His hand brushed her cheek. "My lips got burned too," he murmured into her hair.

The roughness of his khaki jacket pressed itself against her.

"Mary, Mary," Joe repeated, wrapping her in his arms. "Let me hold you."

For a long time, Joe and Mary stood transfixed by the power of their desire for one another and the wonder of the moment, till a sharp tap on the window made them both jump.

"Mrs Dawson," a voice called.

"It's Mrs Ogilvie," hissed Mary. "With Nancy. Coming, Mrs Ogilvie," called Mary, smoothing her hair and pushing Joe back into the chair.

"You took you time cumin' ti' the door," intoned Mrs Ogilvie, squinting past Mary to see inside.

"Sorry, Mrs Ogilvie," Mary lied. "I was just having a wee lie down and must have fallen asleep."

Mrs Ogilvie sniffed. "Here's your lassie, then."

Nancy ran past Mary into the room and stopped at the sight of Joe sitting beside the fire.

"It's a kiltie," she shouted to Mrs Ogilvie. "There's a kiltie in here."

Mary quickly shut the door on the startled face of Mrs Ogilvie. "Be *quiet*, Nancy," she urged her daughter. "It's only Joe Cassiday, come to say goodbye. He's off to the war."

Nancy's eyes widened in amazement. "Are you going to fight people?" she asked. "They said at school, the King wants us all to do our best and not be scared."

Joe pulled her towards him. "Now, don't you be getting scared about anything," he told her gently. "Your Uncle Joe's going to make sure nobody hurts you or your mammy. How's that then?"

Nancy smiled broadly and nodded, satisfied for the moment.

"I'd best be going," Joe said, standing up and taking Mary's hand in his. "Maybe… tomorrow?"

Mary nodded, still resonating from the passion she had felt when in his arms. "I'll ask Mrs Ogilvie to look after Nancy and we'll have a day out," she told him.

Joe felt a thrill of pride burn inside him. "I'll call about one o'clock," he said. "We could go for a walk together. It's a lovely view from the top of the Law. What do you think?"

"Anywhere would be a lovely view with you Joe," Mary replied.

They both nodded and burst out laughing at their delight in one another. "See you tomorrow then," Joe whispered. "Bye Nancy," he called.

"Bye Uncle Joe."

Mary stroked her hand down his back as he went through the door. "Till tomorrow," she smiled.

Joe felt he could fight the entire German army single-handed. "Till tomorrow."

Sleep eluded Mary that night. Thoughts of Joe and her, together, rushed through her head, one after the other. By morning though, instead of feeling exhausted, Mary felt utterly alive.

"C'mon Nancy," she urged her daughter. "Wakey wakey. We need to see Mrs Ogilvie about minding you this afternoon, your mum has a message to go."

Nancy rubbed her sleepy eyes. "Are you going the messages with Uncle Joe?" she asked, her childlike innocence too near the mark for Mary's liking.

"What made you say that?" she queried.

Nancy yawned and kicked her legs free from the bed covers. "Don't know."

Mary sat down beside her daughter. "Now don't you go saying that to anyone, will you? Especially not Mrs Ogilvie." The last thing Mary wanted was Billy finding out. She knew he saw Mrs Ogilvie regularly to pay for Nancy being minded and she well remembered his temper and hatred of Joe.

Nancy nodded. "Can I have some toast please?" she asked, her hunger more important than her mother's worried instruction.

"Only if you promise me you won't say a word about Uncle Joe to Mrs Ogilvie."

"Promise," Nancy nodded, becoming irritated at her mother's pressure. "Now, can I have my toast?"

Reluctantly, Mary relented. "Alright," she agreed. "You wash your face and hands and I'll make you some." A twinge of anxiety replaced the delicious thoughts Mary had been experiencing, but she pushed it from her head and forced her happy mood to return. No matter what, she was going to have her day with Joe Cassiday.

Mrs Ogilvie was in suspicious mood when Mary knocked at her door at midday.

"Oh, it's you, is it," she huffed, eyeing her young neighbour. "Suppose you want that lassie o' yours minded again?"

Mary forced a smile. "If that's alright," she said. "I've a few things to do this afternoon and Nancy would just be a hindrance."

Mrs Ogilvie's eyes narrowed. "Wouldn't be anythin' to do wi' that 'kiltie' would it?"

Mary felt herself colour and tightened her grip on her daughter's hand.

"Ouch," squeaked Nancy. "You're hurting me."

Mary released her grip. "No, Mrs Ogilvie," she replied, trying to gather her wits. "It's nothing to do with any kiltie. Now, can you mind Nancy or not?"

Mrs Ogilvie sniffed, sensing she had rattled Mary. "I can mind 'er alright, but it'll be a shillin' more, seein' as it's sic short notice."

Mary clenched her teeth. She knew if she wanted to see Joe, she'd have to agree. "Fine," she said in a clipped voice. "I'll call back for her around seven."

"Around *six*," retorted Mrs Ogilvie.

"Six it is."

Nancy was passed over to the child-minder. "Now be a good girl for your mammy," she told her, kissing the top of her head. I'll be back about teatime."

Mrs Ogilvie closed the door with a knowing look and Mary drew a deep breath. Joe would be here soon and she wanted to look her best.

Mary ran back along the close to the single-end. She had just over half an hour to get ready. She filled a small basin with water from the kettle and placed in in the sink. The red carbolic soap was rubbed into a lather on her skin and splashed off with the warm water and her hair was brushed till it shone. The choice of clothes was simple, as Mary's wardrobe was limited to the clothes she wore for her cleaning job and one dress. She slipped it on and looked at herself in the mirror. Small lines were evident around her eyes and lips but the sparkle of her optimistic spirit glowed in her smile. She pinned a small cream silk rose in her hair, which she'd been given by Annie from her wedding veil, just as Joe knocked at her door.

A rush of colour flew to Mary's cheeks at the sound, enhancing her appearance even further.

"Just coming," she called out.

The now familiar wave of desire swept over her at the sight of Joe Cassiday. "I'm ready," she announced breathlessly, her eyes locking onto his.

Joe smiled at the memory of their last encounter. "Me too," he said, taking her hand as she pulled the door closed behind her.

"Let's go up the Law Hill," he suggested. "I want to show you the world."

As one, they climbed the steps of William Lane into Victoria Road. Mary prayed they wouldn't meet anyone she knew, especially not Billy, but no one glanced their way as they turned into the steepness of the Hilltown, which led to the slopes of the Law.

"It's a fair climb," Joe said. "Are you sure you can manage it?"

Mary's skin was glowing with happiness and exertion. She nodded. "I can manage," she assured him.

Joe's arm swept round her waist. "I'll just give you a little help," he grinned, almost lifting her off her feet. His powerful grip never lessened till they reached the Hilltown clock.

"Not far now," Joe told her, pointing at the green mound in the distance. "Look, there it is."

Mary squinted into the sunshine.

"The first thing I saw when I came to Dundee across the Tay was the Law Hill," Joe told her. "It's a memory I'll never forget."

"C'mon," he urged, taking her hand again. "Wait till you see the view."

It seemed like another world to Mary as they scrambled over tussocks of grass and gorse bushes up the slopes of the Law. The air was clear and fresh and the noise and smell of the jute mills faded into the distance as they climbed.

"Almost there," called Joe over his shoulder. "Only a few steps more."

He hauled Mary up the last yard and caught her round the waist. "Now, turn around," he instructed her. "With your eyes closed."

Giggling, Mary did as she was told.

"Now," whispered Joe in her ear. "Open them."

Mary drew in her breath at the sight. The whole of the town lay before them, smoking and solid. Whalers with their sails furled were berthed at the docks and the River Tay shimmered in the sunlight.

"Look at the bridge, Mary," urged Joe, pointing to the metal wonder spanning the river. "And there," he enthused. "That's the university." His eyes misted. "Real learning, Mary," he whispered. "All the knowledge in the world is in there." His hands tightened round her waist as he stood behind her. "Look at it all," he murmured into her ear. "That's our world Mary, yours and mine." He turned her to face him. "Will you remember this day always, Mary?" he asked, a sudden urgency in his voice.

Mary felt tears tighten her throat. "I will, Joe," she replied softly.

"And will you wait for me," he asked. "Till this silly war's over?"

Tears of emotion touched Mary's eyes and a fear at Joe's going crept over her. "I'd wait for you forever," she told him, her heart taking over.

His kiss, when it came, teemed with the pent-up emotion he had built up since Annie's going and swept Mary into a place more passionate than she'd ever experienced before. The warm breeze that had accompanied them in their climb suddenly freshened as clouds blew in from the west and blotted out the sunshine, but neither of them noticed.

High on the hill, in this world of their own, Joe and Mary sealed their love for one another in a haze of overpowering passion. The raindrops landed softly on their faces as they both lay amongst the tussocks guarded by the flaming yellow gorse, wakening them from their world of love.

Mary turned her face towards him. "It isn't just the war, is it?" she whispered, reality forcing itself back into her heart.

Joe pulled her close to him. "No," he replied simply. "It's you, Mary Dawson and that Irish smile of yours."

Reassured, Mary snuggled closer. "I think it's raining," she giggled.

Joe stuck his bonnet on her head. "I think you may be right," he grinned. "Does that mean we've to go back now?"

Mary sat up, tilting Joe's Black Watch bonnet to one side and nodded. "Back to reality," she said, a sadness suddenly replacing the laughter.

"You do know I love you," whispered Joe. "Even in reality."

Mary's eyes swam with emotion. "Do you mean that, Joe?" she asked, hardly daring to believe him.

"I mean it," he replied, kissing her again. "If you'll have me."

Chapter 13

Billy had fallen into a silence since the day at Broughty Ferry and after a week of tension, Josephine MacIntyre could stand it no longer.

"Please tell me what's wrong," she asked bluntly one evening after they'd eaten another uncomfortable meal. Her mind had gone through every possible scenario over the past few days and she felt she could now handle anything he might say in reply.

Billy gazed at her, searching for a way to tell her. "Nothing," he'd replied, failing to find one.

Josephine pushed her chair back and began to clear the table. "Fine," she said, her courage deserting her. "Fine."

She scraped the remains of the food into the sink and ran the tap. Her face felt hot with embarrassment and she was glad of the spray of cold water reflecting from the porcelain.

"I'm sorry," Billy's voice reached her ears from the door. "There is something I have to tell you," he continued. "It's just that I don't know how."

Josie stopped what she was doing and turned to face him. What seemed like a thousand thoughts, good and bad, flashed into her head. "If you want to tell me you regret our day at Broughty Ferry," Josie began, tackling her biggest fear head-on, "Then go ahead."

Billy's eyes clouded. "Do you regret it?" he asked tightly.

Josie stuck her chin out and clasped her hands in front of her. "No."

Billy visibly relaxed. "Thank God for that," he murmured.

Josie folded her arms in front of her defensively. "Then I don't understand," she continued, nervously, "What is it?"

Billy dug his hands into his pockets and shrugged. "I've decided to…volunteer."

For a moment, Josie had thought he was going to say he'd decided to leave.

"Voluneteer?" she echoed. "Volunteer for what?"

"The Black Watch," Billy replied quietly. "I've given it a lot of thought, Josie, and I've decided to join the Black Watch."

Of all the things Josephine MacIntyre had imaged Billy would say, she'd never thought of this one. Her hands flew to her face.

"But, they'll send you to France… and the fighting…"Josie felt a terrible fear grip her.

Billy moved towards her. "Now, now," he began. "Nobody's going to send me anywhere. By the time they've taught me to shoot straight, the war'll be over."

Josie's eyes were wide with imagined horrors. "But *why*?" she asked, her voice noticeably shaking now.

"Because it's what I have to do, Josie," he replied steadily. "What kind of a man would I be if I didn't fight for my country."

"But, you're needed here, surely," she argued, searching for a reason for him not to go ahead. "They'll need skilled workers like yourself to run the mills, look after things at home…" Her voice tailed off as he pulled her towards him.

"Sssshhhh, now," he calmed her. "There's plenty women and old men who can do that. I can't not do my duty Josie."

She could feel his heart beating through the muscles in his chest as he held her.

"But what if…" she began in a muffled voice.

"Now, now," Billy smoothed her. "Let's have none of that. Nothing bad's going to happen, trust me."

For a few moments as he held her, Billy was back at the stream in Ireland holding Annie and telling her he was going to Scotland without her. He pulled Josie closer as his memories intensified.

"Everything will be alright," he murmured. "Come to me when you can."

"I'm here, now," Josie whispered, her voice bringing Billy back to the present.

He released his hold on her and the memory faded. "I'm sorry, Josie," he said hoarsely realising what she'd said, "I didn't mean to upset you." He ran his fingers through his hair and turned away from her. "I'll sign up tomorrow then," he told her. "I'm sorry."

Josie stood for a long time staring at the door which had closed behind him and tried to understand the confusion which was inside her. He had held her so tenderly, so warmly, but then…

As she prepared for bed that night, she heard him pacing the floor of his room. She wanted to go through to him, tell him how she felt, but something prevented her. Instead, she lay in the dark, listening to his footfalls till they stopped.

The next day, Billy seemed back to his usual self.

"No second thoughts, then?" she asked hoping that he had.

"None," he told her, rising to go. "I have to do this," he told her. "Please understand."

Josie nodded. "I understand," she told him, but she didn't. She didn't understand at all.

Billy joined the queue of men snaking into the Murraygate from the Town House, where the 4th Battalion of the Black Watch had set up their recruitment table. Everyone was in high spirits and Billy picked up on their mood instantly. One of the men behind him tapped him on the shoulder.

"Are you the gaffer from Baxters?" he asked candidly.

Billy nodded.

"Do you no' mind o'me?"

Billy looked closely at the small man, his flat cap pulled at a jaunty angle over one eye. "I'm afraid I don't," Billy answered honestly.

"It's Peem," he responded. "Peem Innes. I wiz a Tenter at Baxters wi' Joe Cassiday."

Billy vaguely remembered him. But his full attention at that time had been concentrated on Joe. Again, the painful memories of Annie, which he thought he'd buried, reared up.

"Peem Innes!" he repeated, unconvincingly. "Of course, I remember you. How's Mrs Innes doing?"

Peem shrugged. "Doin' what she's telt as uzual."

Billy smiled and nodded. "Nice to see you again, Peem," he said turning back to the moving queue and thoughts of Annie. He hadn't seen her since her wedding to Alex Melville and a wave of sadness washed over him as he remembered the hurt of that day.

"Next," called out a military voice.

Billy moved forward.

"Name?"

"Dawson," replied Billy.

"First name?"

"William."

The Recruiting Sergeant eyed Billy, measuring him up in an instant as fit. "Sign here."

Billy took the pen and signed his name.

"Over there."

The Sergeant indicated another queue, where the volunteers were in line awaiting further instructions.

"Next," intoned the Sergeant again.

Billy moved on.

"Report to the Black Watch Barracks at Forfar for basic training," he was instructed when his turn came. "Here's your rail warrant."

Billy looked at the piece of paper. He'd done it. He was in the Black Watch.

A surge of pride filled his soul as he turned to make his way back to Morgan Street. People smiled at him and nodded as he left the Town House.

"Well done," they called. "Guid man."

Billy acknowledged their praise. He hadn't felt proud of himself for a long time. But now, now he had the chance to prove to himself and to everyone else, he was a man again.

Josie was waiting for him on his return. She'd prepared a special meal for him and even baked a cake with his name on it.

"It's my way of saying sorry," she said. "And to tell you I'm very proud of you."

Billy acknowledged the compliment and ate appreciatively of Josie's cooking.

"You're a fine woman, Josie," he told her. "Far too good for the likes of me."

Josie flinched. "Don't say that Billy. We're different, that's all."

Billy nodded. "You're probably right," he agreed. How he wished he could feel the love for Josie that she plainly wanted.

"I'll be off to my room now," he said, feeling a tension building between them again, "I've a few things to sort out before I join the ranks, so to speak." He'd tried to keep the mood light but, seeing the look in Josie's eyes, realised he'd failed miserably.

"Good night then," she murmured, picking up her sewing basket.

In the silence of his room, Billy wrote a letter to Annie.

Dearest Annie, it began,

I know things haven't always been right between us, but I want you to know I've joined the Black Watch and will be going to war soon. Who knows if I'll return. But I want you to know Annie, I've always loved you and I always will.

I hope you're very happy with your new baby. Think of me sometimes.

I love you. Billy.

He addressed it to the single-end. Mary would pass it to Annie, he was sure.

His last thoughts as he turned out his light were of Annie. The next day and for many days after that, they would be of war.

Mary examined the small envelope addressed to Annie. Everyone knew she'd moved away when she married Alex and her curiosity to find out the identity of the writer was overwhelming. She held it up to the light at the window but this revealed nothing.

"Maybe, if I just hold it near the kettle," she mused. "The steam just might… accidentally…'

"What you doin' mammy?" asked Nancy, startling Mary in her endeavours.

"Nothing!" exclaimed her mother, stuffing the envelope in her skirt pocket.

Nancy's eyes followed the envelope as it disappeared into the folds of Mary's skirt.

"Can I have a penny for sweeties?"

Mary felt flushed with guilt. "Here," she said abruptly, handing her daughter a coin. "Now go and buy yourself some and make sure Mr MacIntosh fills your poke."

Nancy nodded sagely and disappeared out of the door.

Mary sat down and pulled out the envelope again. It was no use, she'd have to find out who sent it. It was her duty, she convinced herself, to protect her sister. Slowly, the steam from the kettle softened the glue of the envelope and curled the paper open.

Gingerly, Mary removed the sheet of paper.

She felt a strange mixture of anger and relief as she read it. She'd always felt total responsibility for the breakup of her marriage to Billy, but now... Billy had never loved her, ever. Even in the beginning. Annie must have known this all along, she reasoned, from the very first day she'd arrived from Ireland.

Mary felt betrayed by both of them.

The sound of the paper tearing as she ripped the letter in half filled her head.

"Go to war, Billy Dawson," she murmured to herself. "And damn you for what you put me through." The flames devoured the paper and the black ash disappeared up the chimney. "And as for you, my precious sister, you're getting the pain you deserve." A great wave of bitterness swept over Mary as she sat remembering all the times when she'd tried to get close to Billy and each time he'd rejected her. Now she knew why.

Her daughter's return brought her back to the present. "Does mammy want a sweetie?" she asked offering Mary her pokie.

Mary ruffled her blonde curls. "No thanks, darlin'," she whispered, looking into the innocent blue eyes. "You have them all.

Chapter 14

Isabella Anderson's return to Dundee was, for Annie, like coming across an oasis in the desert. Nearly every day, she stopped in to see Annie and Lexie, making sure Alex knew of her presence and, as she had predicted, the beatings stopped. Under the protection of her sister-in-law, Annie's confidence gradually returned and with it a renewed determination that she'd never let Alex hit her again.

"We're knitting socks for soldiers," Isabella announced one day over a cup of tea. "Why don't you come along and join us?"

"What?" queried Annie.

"Socks for soldiers," she grinned. "We women have to do our bit for the boys out in France," she said. "So once a week, we meet and knit and some of us write little notes of encouragement and fold them in with the socks before they're sent to the front."

Annie's interest was caught. "We?"

"The WVS, of course - we women can be volunteers too you know."

Annie felt a wave of excitement. "I'd like that, Isabella. Do you think Alex would mind?" she added, suddenly hesitating.

"Not if I tell him," she laughed. She liked Annie, a lot, and had grown closer to both her and Lexie as the weeks had passed. "I'll tell him next time I see him," she said, cradling Lexie in her arms. "Now that's decided, how about one of your lovely pancakes?"

Isabella was a good as her word and coerced Alex into agreeing to Annie's joining the WVS.

"As long as she's here for my dinner," he'd concluded grudgingly…

"I will be, Alex," Annie interrupted. "And it's only once a week."

Isabella winked at Annie as she took her to the door. "See you on Friday then, about one o'clock."

Annie squeezed Isabella's hand. "Thanks," she said softly.

"What for?"

"For being here," she said. "For being you."

Isabella nodded. "See you Friday."

Annie hummed a little tune to herself as she returned to the parlour and Alex.

"You won't manage to go, of course."

Annie stopped humming. Alex's voice held the old familiar menace.

"Why not?"

"Because I say so," came the cold reply. "You may have fooled my sister, but you don't fool me."

Annie sat down across from him. This was the battle she had to win. "I don't understand Alex," she began, trying to keep all emotion out of her voice. "It's voluntary work to help the war effort."

"Huh!" Alex retorted, his anger bubbling under the surface. "An excuse to meet soldiers more like."

Annie flinched. "You're wrong Alex," she replied standing up. "I will be going with Isabella. It's my duty to help."

Alex's anger burst through. "And what about your duty to your *husband*?" he shouted, moving closer to her. "Just because I can't be a bloody *hero*." His face was close to hers now and she could feel the heat from his breath as he raged at her.

"I'm going," she told him, her voice steady and her knees shaking.

His fist flew past her and crashed into the door behind her, splitting the wooden panel with its force. "Bitch!" he cursed, pushing her out of the way. "Go to your bloody meeting then," he growled. "But don't blame me for the consequences." The threat hung in the air as the door slammed behind him and his feet thudded upstairs to their bedroom.

Annie flopped down into a chair and waited for her breathing to steady. Before Isabella's return, the argument would have surely resulted in a beating and Annie thanked God for her sister-in-law's return. Now she knew for certain Alex daren't mark her for fear of losing the respect of his sister, but she also knew he would get back at her, somehow.

She waited till midnight before softly climbing the stairs to bed. Alex was sure to be asleep by then.

"I've been waiting for you," he said as she entered the bedroom.

Annie's heart sank as she closed the door. "I was seeing to Alexandra," she told him, a shimmer of panic forming in her stomach. "I thought you'd be sleeping by now."

"You mean, you hoped I'd be sleeping," he replied sarcastically.

Annie pulled on her nightdress, praying he would leave her alone.

"No need for that," Alex told her slowly. "Duty calls."

Reluctantly, Annie did as she was told. So this was what he'd meant by 'consequences', she realised. Anger always seemed to heighten his desire for her and tonight was to be no exception. It was the first time since the birth of Lexie and Annie was fearful.

"Please be careful Alex," she whispered, but he chose not to hear.

Isabella noticed immediately that Annie wasn't herself when she called in on the Friday.

"Is anything wrong?" she asked, worry in her voice. "Alex hasn't been beat…"

"No, no," Annie quickly reassured her. "I'm still not over the birth yet, that's all. Maybe… maybe, I'll not go this week. Perhaps next week."

Isabella's eyes narrowed.

"What is it, Annie?" she asked quietly. "You know you want to come to the meeting."

Annie hung her head. "Please, Isabella, I can't."

"I don't know what's wrong, Annie," she said. "But I do know if you don't come with me today, you'll never come, and Alex will have you right back where he wants you."

Annie's eyes searched Isabella's for the courage she lacked.

"C'mon, Annie," she urged. "Trust me."

Shakily, Annie nodded. "Alright," she said. "I'll get my coat."

"And I'll get Lexie," added Isabella, picking up the child from her crib before Annie could change her mind.

Once out in the fresh air, Annie began to feel better and in the company of Isabella, her fear slowly diminished.

"You'll meet the Dow sisters and Miss Watson and the Reverend Wilson," enthused Isabella, as they made their way to the Ogilvie Church Hall at the top of Albert Street. "And they'll be so pleased to meet you and baby Alexandra."

The Hall was abuzz with activity. Women, young and old, were laughing and talking as their knitting needles clacked and cups and saucers clinked and rattled as tea and biscuits were organised under the watchful eye of Miss Watson.

"Isabella," she called, nodding to one of the Dow sisters to take over supervision of the refreshments. "How lovely to see you again, come away in." She ushered the little party into the middle of the activity.

Holding up her hand for silence, she introduced Annie.

"Ladies," she began. "Isabella's brought another volunteer along to join us today. Mrs Annie Melville." Annie blushed as all eyes turned to look at her. "And not forgetting her new baby, Alexandra."

There were smiles and nods all round. "Now, I want you all to make her welcome, and no spoiling the baby," she added, twinkling. "They will," she whispered in Annie's ear. "They always do."

The jollity was infectious as Annie joined the group and was handed a ball of wool and her knitting pins.

"They say the mud oot there's affy bad," informed one of her fellow knitters. "The sodgers socks fa' aff thir feet in no time," she added knowingly.

Annie began to cast on the woollen stitches.

"They need oor socks as fast as we can knit thum," she continued. "Are yi a fast knitter?"

Annie nodded. "Fairly," she replied.

"When yir finished a pair," she added. "Mind an' put a wee note in wi' them. Cheers the lads up alricht."

Annie smiled. "I'll remember," she said.

Isabella approached her bearing two cups of tea. "Over here," she called indicating a corner of the hall. Annie put down her knitting and joined her.

"I see Olive Dow's been looking after you."

Annie took her cup of tea. "She says I've to remember to enclose a note with the socks."

Isabella nodded. "Very important, that," she said. "Lets our fighting boys know we're thinking of them."

Annie finished her tea.

"Are you glad you came?" asked Isabella.

Annie knew what she meant. "Very glad," she replied, "And now I know our small effort matters, nothing will stop me coming back next week."

Isabella smiled widely. She knew how much courage it had taken Annie to be there. "Not even Alex?" she asked gently.

Annie shook her head and jutted out her chin. "Not even Alex."

The train pulled into Forfar Station with a relieved rush of steam. The Black Watch Sergeant who had been impatiently pacing the platform, now stood to attention as the doors of the carriages opened, disgorging their assortment of volunteers. He was accompanied by two Privates who began rounding up the men, sorting them into groups of twelve ready for their lorry drive to the training camp. There was much banter and humour amongst the men, but it was a cover for the nerves most of them felt and Billy was no exception.

News had broken just two days before about the massive losses of the Expeditionary Force at Mons and no one was under any illusions any more that this war was going to be a picnic. The casualty list was growing daily and the Black Watch had been in the thick of it. Billy climbed into the back of a lorry along with eleven others and held on to the edge of the wooden seat as the wheels bumped and rattled over the rough road to the camp.

"The things I do to get awa' frae the wife," announced one man, shaking his head in feigned dismay.

"I've heard them Madmozells over in France are daft aboot kilties," added another.

"They'd have to be mad right enough to fall for you in a kilt. No' wi' your legs," came the joshing reply.

Billy smiled. He was only twelve miles away from Dundee but already it seemed like another world. It had been a long time since he'd been in the company of men on anything other than a drinking level and then it hadn't mattered who they were. But this was different. His life could depend on any one of them in battle and their lives, on him. He pushed the thought from his head as the lorry pulled up at the gates of the camp. Coils of barbed wire ran the full length of the fence and two Sentry Boxes stood either side of the entrance.

The guard waved them through. His life as a soldier had begun.

The first day went by in a never-ending queue. Billy moved in shuffling steps from line to line as he was issued with kit, bedding and weaponry, he was examined, injected with needles and given a number. His bunk bed was one of forty-eight ranged along the walls of a wooden hut and he and his companions jostled for the top bunks as each sought to secure the most favourable resting places.

"The name's Thomson," announced the voice in the bunk below Billy. "Jock Thomson."

Billy leaned over the edge and acknowledged the introduction.

"Billy Dawson," he replied. "Private, Number 4426859."

Jock grinned amiably. "Never thoucht I'd end up a number either."

Billy swung his legs over the edge of his bunk and jumped down. "What made you volunteer then?" he asked his new companion, fishing out his tobacco tin and rolling a cigarette.

Jock shrugged. "The Mester sent wiz."

"Master?" asked Billy.

"Yon Laird at Achterhoose, Sir John Graves. Said it was our duty to serve the King."

Billy nodded.

"I waz one o' the Gamekeepers on the estate. He says if we could shoot deer we could shoot the Hun." Jock accepted a cigarette from Billy and drew the tobacco smoke deep into his lungs. "An' you?"

Billy pondered his reason for joining. At first, he'd thought he'd joined out of duty, but his real reason for joining was more to do with regaining his sense of pride in himself.

"Same as you, to serve King and country."

The barracks door swung open and a tall, kilted figure strode into their midst. He was fully kitted out in the Black Watch Uniform and had a single white stripe on the arm of his tunic.

"Stand by your beds," he barked. There was a rumble of feet as forty-eight men obeyed the instruction.

"Attenshun," came the next order. "Eyes front."

Shoulders were pulled back and eyes fixed onto nothing in particular.

"My name is Lance-Corporal Cassiday," announced the figure. "And it's my job to turn you into a fighting unit. Any questions?"

Billy glanced at the soldier as he strode past him. There was no doubt. It was Joe Cassiday alright and he was in charge.

Chapter 15

Despite Mary's bitterness at Billy's love for Annie, she was the first person she turned to when she discovered she was pregnant with Joe's child.

"I was just passing," she announced at Annie's doorstep one afternoon in late September.

"Mary!" exclaimed Annie. "Oh, I'm so glad to see you. Come in."

Mary hadn't seen her sister since her visit to the Maternity Ward in Maryfield Hospital.

"Where's Nancy?"

"School," Mary replied bluntly.

"Would you like to see Lexie, I'm just about to feed her."

"Suppose so," Mary replied, flouncing down into a chair.

Annie knew her sister well and sensed Mary was about to tell her something she didn't particularly want to hear. She disappeared upstairs and returned bearing her daughter in her arms.

"There," she said, handing her to Mary. "Hasn't she grown?"

Mary felt a lump in her throat as she looked at the toothless grin of her niece. "She's beautiful Annie," she said huskily. "Alex must be very proud."

"I'll make us some tea," Annie said. "It's a thirsty walk up here from William Lane."

Mary cooed a little Irish song to Lexie, who chuckled obligingly. "I'm sorry I haven't been to visit since the baby," she called through from the kitchen. "And I've so much to tell you."

Annie came through with a tray of tea things. "Help yourself," she told Mary, taking Lexie from her. "And I'll give this young lady her tea."

Lexie nuzzled into Annie and began to suck vigorously. "Here, here," Annie chided her. "Not so fast."

Mary poured out the tea and pushed a cup towards Annie.

"You'll never guess who's back in Dundee?" Annie began.

Mary lifted an eyebrow. "Who?"

"Isabella Anderson," Annie announced, watching for her sister's reaction before adding, "And John."

Mary shrugged. "That's nice."

Annie hadn't expected such disinterest. "She's been helping me out a lot, with Lexie," she continued. "And I've joined the WVS."

"The what?" Mary asked.

"Womens Voluntary Service," Annie told her. "We do things to help the war effort."

This news was met with the same disinterest as the previous snippet.

"Is there something wrong, Mary?" Annie finally asked. "You don't seem your usual self."

"Have you heard from Billy lately?"

"Billy!" exclaimed Annie shaking her head. "Why should I have heard from Billy?"

Mary shrugged her shoulders again. "No reason, I just wondered if you knew, that's all."

Annie's brow furrowed as she changed Lexie onto her other breast. "Knew what, Mary?" she asked, becoming irritated at her sister's procrastination. "And stop playing games."

"He's volunteered."

Annie let the news sink in. "You mean…"

"Yes, yes," Mary interrupted cheekily. "Gone to fight for his King and country."

Annie felt a twinge of anxiety for him. She hadn't heard anything about him since the fire and, apart from their brief meeting at the mill when she'd gone to tell Jessie about her pregnancy, hadn't seen him either.

She held Lexie closer to her. "I'll pray he comes back safely," she said. "The reports that are coming back from France don't bear thinking about."

"You don't still care for him, do you now, Annie?" Mary suddenly asked.

"No." Annie eyed her sister suspiciously. "That's a strange thing to say, after all this time."

Mary shrugged again. "No matter," she continued. "Anyway, I've something to tell you too."

Annie lifted Lexie upright and began gently patting her back and waited for Mary to speak.

"I'm pregnant," she announced vehemently. "And Joe Cassiday's the father."

Annie stared at her in disbelief. "Oh, Mary…" now she knew why her sister was so on edge. She hurriedly put Lexie down in her crib and returned to her sister. "Does Joe know?"

Mary shook her head.

"Does *Billy* know?"

"No."

"Oh, Mary," Annie whispered. "How are you going to manage?"

Mary sighed. "I was hoping my sister would help me."

Annie grasped her hands. "Of course I'll help," she exclaimed. "You know I will. It's just… Alex… you know what he's like…"

"Not really," Mary countered. "He never speaks to Irish trash like me."

Annie flinched. "That's not true, Mary," she countered. "He's just… busy, that's all." Annie was angry at herself for defending Alex and at Joe Cassiday for taking advantage of Mary's nature.

"Oh, Mary," she cried. "Why did you let him?"

Mary stood up. "Cause I love him Annie, and he loves me."

Annie wasn't sure if it was more of Mary's bravado or she was speaking the truth.

"If that's the case then, he'll want to know," she said.

"He's on embarkation leave next weekend before he goes to the front. I'll tell him then."

The two sisters stood facing one another each with their own thoughts.

"Why don't you come to the WVS on Friday," Annie ventured. "It'll get you out of the house and let us keep in touch."

"Maybe," replied Mary. "I hope you and the baby are happy," she added, quoting the line from Billy's letter as she headed for the door. "Maybe I'll get a little bit of happiness now too."

Mary patted her womb. "At least the man I love will know I'm carrying his child."

The obvious reference to Annie's son to Billy struck home.

"Goodbye Annie, dearest, give my love to Alex." If Mary had set out to hurt her, she'd succeeded and the encounter left Annie confused and upset but Mary smiled all the way home.

Joe Cassiday had done his job well. The bunch of raw volunteers had shaped up into a fighting unit and were to embark for France on 1 October and he was going with them. He'd requested active service and got it, along with another stripe. But now, he had some leave to take and he planned to spend it with Mary.

His brother welcomed him home.

"Tonight's for drinking," Joe told his brother. "But tomorrow…" He laid his hands on Charlie's shoulders. "Tomorrow's for Mary."

His brother shook his head in resignation. "Whatever you wish, Joe," he said. "Just be happy."

The Thrums Bar was overflowing with soldiers just like Joe. "Have one on me, Joe Cassiday," called the landlord. "You're a brave man."

Joe acknowledged the compliment.

"That's to pay for a whiskey and two pints for my friend Tam Gow," he called to the barman, tossing a half-crown towards him. He's due back from France soon, but not till I've gone and I promised him." The barman kissed the coin and placed it on a shelf. "Done, Joe."

The drink flowed like water and by closing time, Joe and Charlie were in fine form.

"I don't want to go to bed ever," announced Joe, as they tumbled out into the night air. "There's so much to see, so much to do." His eyes misted over as he looked at his brother.

"You've been like a father to me Charlie," he said, wrapping his arm around his brother's shoulder, "And I know you worry, but I wish you'd like Mary. She's not what you think."

"Is that right," Charlie countered. "Well, you know best Joe."

Joe sighed. "I'm going to marry her, you know."

Charlie's eyes levelled with his. "If that's what you want," he said quietly. "Then that's what you'll do. But I'll never take to her, Joe, never."

Joe nodded, suddenly weary. "So be it," he said. "But let's not argue about it, not before I go to France."

Charlie nodded. "You'll take care of yourself now, won't you Joe?"

"I will, brother. And you take care of yourself while I'm gone. I just wish…"

"I know," Charlie said. "That I was going too. Well, you know my views on war Joe and they're not going to change."

The two men agreed to differ and returned home to their room in Todburn Lane. The fire was almost out and the gas mantle was turned down low, giving the room a softness which it didn't have in daylight. Joe's eye took in every fuzzy detail, wishing to remember the room where he'd lived his life since being brought from Ireland as a child. His mother and father were gone now, but Charlie, solid reliable Charlie, will still be there, looking out for him. He felt tears prick the edges of his eyes. He loved his brother deeply, but now, he loved Mary too. He closed his eyes and tried to picture her through the alcohol that clouded his senses but fell asleep instead.

He was wakened by Charlie shaking him gently. "Wake up Joe," he said, a mug of tea steaming in his hand. "You've slept all night in the chair."

Joe shook himself to wakefulness and felt the dull ache of a hangover. His throat felt bone dry and he gulped down the hot tea.

"How's the time?"

Charlie looked at the mantelpiece clock. "Seven o'clock."

Joe slumped back into the chair and closed his eyes again to blot out the dizziness.

"Did you mean what you said last night?" asked Charlie.

"What was that then?" Joe muttered, his eyes still closed.

"About marrying… Mary Dawson."

Joe's eyes opened and focused on his brother. "Did I say that?"

"You did."

"Must have been the drink talking," replied Joe, not wishing to get into another discussion over Mary.

"Will you be seeing her today?"

Joe felt himself becoming irritated. His head ached and his stomach was now catching up.

"Questions, questions," he said. "Don't you ever stop asking questions?" He could see the remark had stung Charlie and cursed his hangover. "I need some fresh air," he said standing up. "I'll see you later." He turned at the door, his whole body aching. "Sorry," he said.

"Me too," acknowledged his brother. Charlie watched him go from the small window of their room. "God keep you safe, Joe," he said quietly to himself. "Though you'll be safer in France than you will in the hands of that woman."

Mary was drinking her tea in the silence of the early morning when she heard the noise at her door. She pulled aside the curtain to see Joe standing there and rushed to the door.

"I wasn't expecting you this early," she whispered. "But you're more than welcome." She noticed he was looking bleary-eyed but said nothing. "Tea's made," she said instead. "Can I get you a cup?"

"Later," he said, pulling her towards him.

Mary melted into his arms. "You haven't changed your mind then," she whispered.

"No," Joe murmured into her hair, holding her more fiercely, "I'll never change my mind."

Nancy stirred and turned over in bed and Joe slackened his hold on Mary.

"Sshhhh," he said, holding his finger to his lips. "I know, I forgot."

Mary suppressed a giggle and pushed Joe into the chair by the fire. "Tea!" she stated firmly, gazing fondly at his tousled, black hair. She settled in the chair opposite his and leant forward anxious not to speak too loudly in case Nancy should be awake enough to hear.

"I've something to tell you Joe," Mary began.

"That you love me," finished Joe.

Mary smiled. "Oh, I love you alright… but there's something else."

Joe put down his mug and reached out to take her hand. "Before you tell me anything," he said. "There's something I want to ask you."

Mary felt his grip tighten on her hand.

"When this war's over, Mary," he said, a seriousness in his voice Mary had never heard before. "Will you marry me?"

Mary felt a huge surge of happiness course through her. Her eyes glowed with love for the man in front of her. "I will Joe. There's nothing I want more."

Joe's whole face broke into a smile. "Then that's settled," he concluded. "Leave Billy to me and start putting your 'bottom drawer' together." He kissed her hand gently. "Now, what's your news?" he asked.

Mary drew a deep breath. "We're going to have a child."

Mary's heart was in her mouth as she watched for Joe's reaction.

"The day on the Law Hill?" he asked incredulously, his hungover mind trying to take in the news.

Mary nodded anxiously.

"First time lucky," he said grinning.

Mary let herself relax. "You're pleased?" she asked softly.

He pulled her towards him and sat her down on his knee. "Pleased?" he whispered. "I'm delighted, ecstatic, proud and so in love with you."

"What's happening?" asked a sleepy voice from the bed in the corner of the single-end.

In their excitement, Joe and Mary had forgotten about the slumbering Nancy.

"It's alright," Mary assured her, crossing the room and pulling the coverlet back over her shoulders. "It's just Uncle Joe."

Nancy glanced at Joe through half-shut eyes. "Uncle Joe…" she murmured, before her eyes closed again.

Joe returned Mary to his lap. "Everything will be alright now," he told her. "There's nothing but happiness ahead for us. And when this war's over, we'll be together forever."

The word 'war' brought Mary back to the present.

"Don't let anything happen to you in France, Joe," she whispered. "I couldn't bear it."

Joe held her tightly round the waist and smoothed the side of her cheek. "Nothing's going to happen to me," he soothed. "Not now that I've found you."

Mary kissed the palm of his hand and traced his life-line with her tongue. "Promise," she said.

"Promise."

Chapter 16

As Annie's confidence grew, Alex's ability to threaten her diminished. She knew it was mostly due to Isabella's influence but it was also partly due to her own courage in facing up to him. She looked at him reading his newspaper while she knitted and wondered how someone could change so much from the wonderful man she first fell in love with, to the one she lived with now.

"What's the news from the front?" she asked, her voice seeming to echo into the silence of the room.

"They've sunk three of our cruisers," he said solemnly. "Damned Hun." He folded the paper and lit his pipe, ending the conversation.

"How's Constable MacPherson?" Annie continued, trying to build some kind of bridge of words across to him.

Alex looked at her. "Why do you want to know?"

Annie felt herself become defensive. "I'm just making conversation, Alex," she replied. "We don't seem to talk much anymore."

Alex blew tobacco smoke into the room and lapsed back into silence.

"Isabella's looking well," she tried again. "She was telling me about when you were both little…"

Annie suddenly had Alex's full attention.

"And what was she telling you, exactly?"

Annie looked up from her knitting aware she had touched a nerve. "Just how happy you all were," she told him. "Your mother sounds lovely."

She returned to her knitting.

"She was lovely," Alex said, his voice soft at her memory. "She didn't deserve…" he began but stopped himself. The pipe smoke formed a smokescreen around him and the door to his heart slammed shut again.

"What didn't she deserve?" pursued Annie, but the moment had passed and Alex picked up his newspaper again and resumed reading in silence.

Isabella called for Annie the next day. "We're packing the sock boxes today," she announced proudly. "Twelve pairs to a box. I hope you've got your notes written."

Annie smiled and tucked Lexie into her pram. "I don't know what to write," she told Isabella as they made their way to Ogilvie Church Hall for the WVS meeting. Her sister-in-law tutted. "Just say who you are and wish them a safe return."

Annie wheeled the pram into the hall and was met with the now usual bright greetings from the other women.

"How's wee Lexie?" asked Miss Watson, gazing fondly into the pram. She had never married and had no children of her own, favouring instead to become a teacher of arithmetic at the Academy. "Getting a double-chin I see." She tickled Lexie who chortled with delight.

Annie made her way to the piles of socks and boxes ready for packing.

"I didn't realise we'd knitted so many!" she exclaimed to Olive Dow.

Olive beamed. "Aye, we've been busy," she said proudly. "And your contribution has been gratefully appreciated," she added.

Annie flushed with pride. "I'll just write my notes then," she said, picking up some small sheets of paper and a pencil.

Annie sat down at a small table. Now, what did Isabella say… 'Knitted by Annie Melville in Dundee. In my prayers till you return home. God bless you and keep you safe.' She tucked the note inside the sock and placed it with its partner in the box. Eleven more times she wrote the note, till her box was full.

"Here's mine," she announced to Olive Dow. "Do we know where they're going?"

Olive smiled wistfully. "To some brave boy in the Black Watch," she said. "My nephew's out there, with the forty-second Battalion," she said. "Dundee's own." She wiped a stray tear from her eye. "But whoever gets them, they'll know they're loved."

Annie nodded. "Let's hope so."

It was Isabella's smile disappearing off her face which alerted Annie to Mary's arrival at the hall. She quickly crossed the space between them and intercepted her.

"Mary!" she called. "You've come." She'd never seen Mary so happy. "And you've brought Nancy with you."

Annie bent down and cuddled her niece as Mary's eyes swept the room.

"So, this is where it all goes on," she said, her eyes widening in surprise at the bustle.

Annie nodded in agreement. "Isabella's here," she said. "Over there." She tipped her head in the direction of her sister-in-law.

"She looks well," Mary acknowledged. "Will she speak to me, do you think?"

"There's only one way to find out," Annie replied. "C'mon."

"Mary's here to help," Annie said to Isabella's back. "Can she join?"

If Isabella had any resentment towards Mary, she hid it well as she turned to face the woman who had taken her husband away from her.

"Of course you can, Mary," she said calmly. "Everyone's welcome here."

"That's decided then," Annie said, hurrying into the gulf between the two women.

"There's a lot of water passed under the bridge since the Salvation Army," Mary said quietly. "I hope you've forgiven me."

Annie held her breath.

"No," Isabella replied, equally quietly. "But I have chosen to forget."

Mary nodded. "I can ask for no more than that."

With a sigh of relief, Annie suggested some tea and pointed Mary in the direction of the cups and boiling water. "Thanks Isabella," she whispered. "I know how hard that was for you."

Isabella inclined her head and blinked back a tear. "There's a war on Annie," she replied softly. "That's far more important than any war I may have of my own."

Annie nodded and squeezed her hand in acknowledgement and gratitude. "Please don't let this spoil our friendship," she asked. Isabella brightened.

"Oh, Annie," she smiled. "Nothing could spoil that."

Mary was sipping her tea and munching on a piece of shortbread when Annie returned to her.

"I'm very pleased you've come," began Annie. "But what made you decide to join us?"

"You mean, apart from you being my sister?"

Annie grinned. This was more like the Mary she knew.

Mary patted her womb. "Well, what else can a girl in my condition do?"

"You could stay at home with your feet up," suggested her sister.

Mary's eyes became serious. "Joe's been sent to France," she said simply. "And I feel so useless..." Her voice tailed off. "I wish I could be a weaver, like you. Jessie says they're crying out for skilled women in the mill to help with the war effort."

Annie's ears pricked up. "What do you mean?"

"Well, with all the men away at the war, it's the women who're doing all the mill work now and Jessie says the government wants more and more jute sacking to make sandbags and linen to make tents for the boys at the front. Baxters Mill is working day and night."

Annie let the information sink in. "Is Mr Campbell still the Manager?" she asked.

Mary shrugged. "I suppose so, but Jessie would know."

Annie nodded.

"You're not thinking of..." Mary began.

Annie smiled. "That's exactly what I'm thinking."

Mary's eyes widened in disbelief. "Alex'll never let you!"

Annie pulled herself up to her full five foot four inches, her face taking on a new determination. "We'll see," she said, "We'll see."

Annie broached the subject with Isabella on their way home. "...so, I think I'd be more use to the war effort if I went back to the weaving," she concluded. "But there's Lexie to consider and well, I don't suppose Alex'll be too happy."

Isabella had listened intently to all Annie had said. "If it's what you want to do," Isabella began, "Then I'll do all I can to help."

Annie felt a surge of hope. She was realising how much she had changed since her marriage to Alex and also how much she had missed working at the mill. The friendship of Jessie, the banter of the Tenters. 'It's an ill wind…' she thought, 'that doesn't blow somebody some good.' This was her chance to feel needed again and she was determined to take it.

"Does that mean you'd mind Lexie for me?" Annie asked, praying silently that her sister-in-law would say yes.

Isabella's eyes lit up. "Oh, Annie," she smiled. "I'd love to."

The two women's eyes told each other that their mutual needs had been met.

"I'll pay you, of course," added Annie, but Isabella held up her hand.

"Please, Annie," she said. "Being able to have Lexie all to myself every day will be payment enough. She's beautiful and I love her dearly."

Annie nodded. "It's agreed then."

Alex noticed immediately the change in Annie's demeanour on his return from his shift at the Jail in Bell Street.

"You look pleased with yourself," he stated with a hint of suspicion in his voice.

Annie took a deep breath. "We packed the sock boxes today," she said brightly. "That's all. No more turning heels for a while." She put his plateful of food in front of him and sat down opposite him.

"Isabella's asked if she could look after Alexandra more often," she began.

Alex put down his knife and looked at her, his suspicions now fully aroused. "Why?" he asked.

Annie backed off. "Nothing," she replied. "Let me do more for the war effort, I suppose."

Alex returned to his food. "You do enough already for the war effort," he said morosely. "Bloody socks."

This wasn't going to be easy by any means but Annie persevered. "She was saying there's a lot of women needed in the mills now the men are off fighting…"

Alex slammed down the cutlery, bringing Annie's voice to a complete halt. "So," he glowered. "That's it."

Annie felt her heart begin to quicken.

"You want to go back to the bloody mill do you?"

Annie knew the signs and pushed her chair back, quickly standing and picking up her plate.

"I'll just clear these things away," she said turning to go to the kitchen.

"*Sit down,*" commanded Alex. Annie's heart sank.

"Yes Alex," she whispered, resuming her seat at the table.

His eyes had darkened as the demons in his soul reared up.

"Back to the weaving, is it?" he said. "Is that what's brought the colour to your cheeks?"

Annie hung her head, searching for the courage which had suddenly deserted her. "It's just something I thought I could do… for the war effort," she whispered faintly.

"LIAR!" shouted Alex. "This isn't about the *war*, is it Annie?" His anger was building now and Annie felt all the old fear returning with a vengeance.

"Stop shouting at me," Annie pleaded, her voice trembling as tears threatened to fall. "Why do you always have to shout at me?"

Alex's hands lifted her out of her seat. "Because you *don't bloody listen,*" he roared. "*That's why!*"

The last dregs of Annie's courage flowed from her as his hands wrapped themselves round her neck.

"Alex," she gasped, trying to force open his fingers. "Let go… please. You're hurting me…" She felt her head shaking wildly as he pushed and pulled her back and forwards before blackness engulfed her.

Annie didn't know how long she'd been unconscious, but as vague shapes began to form in front of her eyes, the memory of Alex's face once more filled her with dread. Her head was aching and dizzy as she tried to sit up. Thankfully, she was alone in the kitchen and the house was silent. Her neck felt as though it was on fire as she pulled herself to her feet. With shaking hands she ran some water from the tap and splashed it on her face, sipping a mouthful from her hand. Her whole body was trembling with cold and fear when she heard voices and one of them was Alex.

The front door burst open and he rushed in followed by John Anderson and Isabella, carrying Lexie.

Annie shrank back into the darkness of the kitchen as he led the way in.

"She must have fallen," he was saying, his voice laden with distress and concern. "And I didn't know what to do, Isabella, so I…" His eyes found Annie, leaning against the sink. "Annie," he called in exaggerated joy. "You're alright."

Alex ran towards her. "I thought you were dead," he exclaimed pulling her towards him. "Look Isabella," he shouted to his sister. "Annie's alright."

"Praise be to God," added John Anderson.

Isabella's face was white as she hurried towards her and Lexie began to whimper.

"Here," she said, handing the child to her father. "Take her into the parlour and leave me with Annie."

Suddenly meek, Alex did as he was told. John Anderson followed.

Isabella guided Annie to a chair. "It's alright, Annie," she murmured. "It's alright now." She reached over and stroked Annie's cheek. "What happened?" she asked, hoping it wasn't what she'd feared.

Annie tried to speak, but her voice was barely a whisper. Isabella leant forward to hear her better and, as she did so, she noticed the red marks on Annie's neck and her blood ran cold. Her hand gently tilted Annie's head upwards revealing the full extent of the abrasions.

"Alex?" she asked, the one word implying all the rest. Isabella swam before Annie's eyes as they filled with tears in answer.

"That's the end," she said. "You're coming with me and John. Lexie too."

Annie made to protest but was too shaken to argue.

Isabella smiled reassuringly. "Wait here." She returned moments later, bearing Lexie and followed by John Anderson.

"John will look after you both till I get back," she said, helping Annie to her feet. "Alex and me need to have words."

All thoughts of propriety deserted Isabella as she rounded on her brother.

"You could have killed her," she said icily. "And, if you'd succeeded, you'd be making the acquaintance of the hangman, police sergeant or not."

Alex hung his head. "I didn't mean to hurt her," he wept. "I love her."

Isabella felt a pang of pity for her brother but the memory of her mother's suffering at the hands of their father soon replaced it with reality.

"Then stay away from her," she retorted. "You're not to be trusted Alex."

"But, she's my wife," he protested. "And..."

Isabella's eyes flashed with anger. "And that doesn't give you the right to beat her," finished Isabella. "She stays with me and John till she's well enough to look after herself and Lexie," stated Isabella firmly. "And unless you want the world to know about what you've done tonight, you'll do as I ask and stay away from her."

Alex sat defeated, his head in his hands, as Isabella swept from the room. "I love her," he shouted into the emptiness, but no one answered. Alex was alone.

Chapter 17

1 October 1914 dawned cold and clear. The first chills of winter were already making themselves evident in the hoar frost which coated the roofs and smoke-blackened chimneys of the city. Corporal Joe Cassiday blew tobacco smoke into the air as he waited, with his Black Watch company, for the train that would take them to England and the South coast port of Dover. From there they would be shipped to the fighting in France. Joe thought of Mary and the child she carried - his child - and grew warm.

"Train's comin'," called a voice. The hubbub of conversation ceased as the soldiers strained their ears, listening for the rhythmic pulse of the steam which would herald the beginning of their journey to the battlefields of France.

"There she blaws," called another. All eyes were fixed now on the plume of smoke as it came nearer, until there was no doubt. The men, as one, began shouldering their kit bags and hugging their loved ones who'd came to see them off. Children began to whimper as they picked up on their mothers' distress and soldiers eyes glistened as the reality of their departure to war gripped them.

"Look oot for the bairns," instructed Jock Thomson to his burly wife. "An' dinna be greetin' nor nothin' like that, I'll only be away for a wee while."

Effie Thomson nodded and bit her lip. "Right Jock," she managed to mutter, before Jock kissed her briefly on the forehead and boarded the train.

"Take care of yourself, Billy," whispered Josie, who despite Billy's protestations, had insisted on seeing him off.

Billy smiled. "I will," he said. "And I'll write and let you know how things are going."

Josie nodded vigorously. "I'd like that," she said, forcing back a lump which had formed in her throat.

"All aboard," yelled the Station Master. Billy looked over his shoulder at the scrabble of men lurching themselves and their bulky kitbags through the carriage doors.

"I'd better go," he said. "I'll see you when I come back."

Josie could hold back the tears no longer.

"Oh, Billy," she burbled. "I love you."

Billy's jaw clenched. This was what he'd wanted to avoid.

"Goodbye Josie," he murmured grimly, in response. "I'll write soon."

Josie sniffed loudly and watched as Billy's back disappeared amongst the throng of khaki jackets and Black Watch bonnets.

"Goodbye," she called into the noise of the train as she tried to pick out Billy's face, but couldn't. A great rush of steam, accompanied by the shrill sound of the whistle blown by the Station Master, signalled the train's departure. Everyone was waving and cheering now, caught up in the emotion and atmosphere of the bravery of their men going to fight for the King and for their country. Jose waved her hankie till the train rounded the bend of the track and disappeared out of sight.

"I love you, Billy," she whispered to herself. "Even though you don't love me."

"Are you throwin' oot a h'uppny fir luck?" enquired a voice behind Billy, as the train puffed slowly over the Tay Bridge. It was Jock Thomson. "It's good luck if you can toss it intae the watter withoot hittin' the girders," he continued, fishing in his sporran for a coin.

Billy smiled. "We'll need all the luck we can get," he said, spinning a penny high into the air. Silently, it cleared the iron girders and disappeared over the edge of the bridge, followed by Jock's in similar fashion.

A wide grin split Jock's face. "There," he said. "We've nothin' to worry about now, that means we'll come back to Bonnie Dundee safe and sound."

The glint of another coin flashed past them and chinked off the metal before falling onto the wooden planking of the bridge.

Billy turned. Joe Cassiday was grinning behind him. "Some folk have all the luck," he said to Billy. "Just as well I've the luck of the Irish to protect me." Billy smiled and shook Joe's offered hand.

"You've trained us well, Joe," he acknowledged. "I mean Corporal."

Joe smiled broadly. "Just remember, keep your gun clean and your head covered. And make sure you come back to that bonnie lassie who was waving you goodbye," he added, winking knowingly at Billy.

"She's just my…" Billy began to explain, but decided not to bother. Instead he nodded. "I'll make sure," he said, turning away from the window and dumping his kitbag in the packed corridor of the train. "Do you know where we're bound?" he asked Joe, but was met with a shrug.

"Wherever it is, Billy," he replied. "It'll be muddy. You can be sure of that."

The journey to Dover was long and arduous, despite the men keeping their spirits up with songs and jokes, card games and banter and it was a relief to smell the sea air of the port as they tumbled and stumbled into the late night air.

"Sleep where you can," Joe ordered his men. "We sail on the early tide, then it's a long march at the other end."

Billy wrapped his army blanket around him and lay down on the hard ground overlooking the harbour and their troopship ablaze with lights preparing for their embarkation and thought of Annie. How he wished he could have seen her before he'd left for France. What if he were to be killed and never see her again? The thought shook him. If that happened, it was better she had not seen him go. Billy closed his eyes and, despite his troubled thoughts, fell into a restless sleep.

An army boot nudged him awake. Grey streaks of dawn light interspersed with black filled the sky. "We're on the move," hissed Jock, pointing to the cluster of men forming along the road to the dock.

Billy scrambled to his feet. "Right," he murmured back, picking up his kitbag and throwing his blanket over his shoulder. "Lead on." He followed Jock to the road and fell in with the rest of the Company.

Joe Cassiday was at their head and signalled them to move off. The ship's engines were rumbling in its bowels and the gang plank leading to the deck, creaked and groaned in the swell and the wind.

The Captain stood at its top as the men climbed, in single file, up the sloping slats of wood and filed past him. He nodded occasionally in the direction of a soldier, but apart from that offered no welcome. Billy was just glad of the warmth as he followed the others down into the galley where hot food was waiting. The sailors were more cheerful as they ladled out steaming porridge and huge mugs of tea and soon the atmosphere began to lighten.

"What's the weather like for the crossin'?" asked someone.

"Bloody rough, mate," replied the Cockney voice of the ship's cook. "It'll soon get rid'uv that there porridge you've just gobbled."

There was laughter all round, but as the ship cast off and edged its way out into the choppy waves of the English Channel, the cook's prediction came to pass as soldier after soldier made a hurried exit from the galley. None of the men could have imagined just how grim their next months would be, judging by the soft, rolling countryside of France, as they marched inland from the coast. French farmworkers greeted and hugged them as they passed through their villages and their daughters smiled coyly and giggled at the kilted soldiers.

Joe drew much admiring glances as he stepped out at the head of the column and even Jock Thomson had a spring in his step as he marched confidently along.

"This war's more fun than I first thoucht it wid be," he said to Billy, winking at a rounded frenchwoman who giggled and hid her face behind the edge of her headsquare.

Billy nodded. "We'd best enjoy it while we can," he replied. "The Corporal says we're heading for a place called Ypres."

Jock frowned. "Where's that?"

Billy shrugged. "Let's just say, it's somewhere in France and the lads there are having a hard time."

Jock huffed. "Dundee's own'll soon sort out the men from the laddies," he advised Billy proudly. "Then we'll be home afore yi ken it."

"I hope you're right, Jock," Billy replied, hoisting his pack higher on his shoulders. "I just hope you're right."

The weather broke as they reached Ypres and deluged them with soaking rain as they set up camp two miles from the front line. For days, their trench coats and tin helmets were a permanent part of their attire and, along with their rifles, were seldom parted from them. They could hear the shell bursts from the German guns by day and by night they lit up the sky with their luminous glow of death.

Everything was sodden, their food, their tents and their bedrolls and their only comfort was a cigarette and a helping hand from their fellow combatants.

"We move up to the front tomorrow, lads," Joe told his men one night after a particularly bad day of shelling. "The Lieutenant thinks one more push and we'll have them on the run."

The men muttered to one another. The battle was in its ninth day and the wounded and dead were being ferried through to the field hospital in droves, filling every heart with fear for their lives. "So get a good night's sleep and write any letters you want to write." Joe's grin was no longer evident. "And we'll give them a run for their money tomorrow."

Joe sat hunched over a wooden box with the glow of a storm lantern lighting the page in front of him.

Dearest Mary, he wrote,

We move up to the front-line tomorrow and it may be a while before I can write again. Remember I love you very much and am longing to see you again. How are you keeping, with the baby and all? I hope this letter reaches you and that you still love me too. France is a Hellish place, Mary, and I miss you so much. Pray that the war is over soon and I'll be home again. Your ever loving Joe.

Billy wrote to Josie, wishing it could have been Annie. He wondered how she'd felt when she got the letter he'd sent via Mary. He hung his head. Perhaps now he'd never know. A strong feeling of foreboding had been with him since he'd first set foot in France and was now accompanied by a steep mountain of fear.

Dear Josie,

I hope this letter finds you well. Dundee feels very far away and I sometimes wonder if I'll ever see it, or you, again. We move up to the front tomorrow and we've been told to write our letters home. I came here to fight and that's what I'll do to the best of my ability, but I fear this war won't be over as quickly as we first thought. Pray for me. Billy.

The full extent of the horror of Ypres was more than any of them could have imagined in their worst nightmares. Their lives were lived in a warren of dugouts and connecting trenches which were knee-deep in mud and water. Duckboards were swamped by the sea of brown sludge as quickly as they were laid and men slept where they fell. The guns roared their wages of death back and forward day and night, as medics with their stretchers and first-aid kits tried to stem the blood of the wounded long enough to get them back to the field hospital for treatment, which usually meant amputation of shattered limbs. Only death released them from their muddy Hell and for the lucky, that came quickly in the burst of a German shell.

Joe was given his orders. "We go over the top tomorrow," his Sergeant said quietly. "Gather your men and prepare them for the push."

Joe saluted. "Yes Sir."

"And Corporal," added the Sergeant. "We'll be heroes back home if we succeed."

Joe allowed himself a smile. "Yes Sir."

The air seemed still and expectant as Joe and his men lined up in their trench overlooking the emptiness of the waste ground between them and the German guns. Barbed wire coiled its vicious path before them and long-dead branches of trees stood stark against the eerie light of the dawn.

"There's a machine-gun dugout just over the ridge to our left flank and one to our right," the Sergeant told the men. "The big guns are directly in front." Billy peered into the gloom as the Sergeant continued his briefing. "Dawson," he ordered. "Take six men out to the left and knock out that machine gun. "Thomson, you do the same to the right." Jock and Billy nodded. "The rest of you, on the command 'CHARGE', follow me."

Billy suddenly grasped what the Sergeant was planning. To his horror, he realised he was going to draw the machine gun fire to himself and the remainder of the men, including Joe, giving cover while he and Jock went around the blind side of the machine guns.

For a moment, Billy's eyes met Joe's, but there was no time to speak or even offer up a prayer as the shout went up. "CHARGE!"

The bagpipes began their wailing as the men rose from their trench as one and marched forward. Billy took his unit and began to make their way towards the machine-gun when it began ack-ack-acking its terrible sound. The big guns opened up in support and everywhere Billy looked, men were falling wounded and dying, some in silence some screaming in agony.

"C'mon lads," he encouraged, all fear suddenly leaving him as they advanced towards their target. "Let's get the bastards."

The Germans and their machine gun never saw them coming, so intent were they on firing at the advancing Scotsmen. In a frenzy of killing and hatred for what they were doing, Billy and his men stabbed and stabbed at the bodies of the gunners with their bayonets.

The machine gun fell silent as Billy slumped beside the last of the dead Germans.

Almost simultaneously, the machine gun to the right ceased firing. Jock Thomson had done his job too.

"Let's get back," Billy ordered the men. "While we've the chance."

With shells exploding in their ears and the smell of cordite filling their nostrils, they crawled and stumbled back to their lines. The Lieutenant was waiting for them on their return.

"Well done, men," he intoned. "There'll be medals in this for you."

Billy could have wept. Medals! What need did he have of medals?

"Is the Corporal alright," he asked. "Corporal Cassiday?"

"Check with Sergeant MacIntosh," replied the Lieutenant. "He'll be able to tell you."

Billy barely saluted. "Thank you sir." He made his way back to his underground shelter, exhausted and trembling.

It was several hours later before Sergeant MacIntosh pushed aside the hessian sacking which served as a door and stepped into the sodden gloom of Billy's world.

"I'm afraid I have some bad news for you," he began, sitting down on a sandbag beside Billy.

"I know he was your Corporal, but I believe he was also your friend."

Billy pulled himself upright. "Joe Cassiday?" he asked shakily. "What's happened to him?"

Sergeant MacIntosh loosened the strap of his tin helmet. "I'm afraid he's been badly wounded. He caught some heavy shrapnel out there today and his leg's looking pretty bad."

Billy hung his head, the news seeping the last ounce of strength from his body. "God help him," he whispered.

The Sergeant cleared his throat, conscious of the tears now coursing down Billy's face.

"He's in the field hospital," he went on, his voice sounding unreal to Billy's shell-shocked ears. "But he'll need more than we can offer here if he's not to lose his leg."

Billy nodded. "Thanks," he said, from the emptiness where his heart used to be. He tried to imagine Joe Cassiday with one leg, but refusal to believe it clouded the picture. Billy shook his head. "Not Joe Cassiday," he prayed out loud to God. "Dear God, not Joe."

All that night Billy lay trembling till Jock Thomson found him the following morning.

"Billy," he enquired anxiously. "What is it man?"

Billy tried to stand, but couldn't. "I'm sorry, Jock," he said. "I've had it."

Jock wrapped another blanket around him, wincing at the patches of blood which had soaked through Billy's tunic. "C'mon," he said. "You're goin' to see the medics."

The field hospital was a terrible place. Men lay on cots, their bandages red with blood and their minds broken, as they waited for ambulances to take them back to the coast for shipment home.

"You'll be alricht now," comforted Jock, "Yi'll soon be home."

Billy stared blankly at him. "Home?" he repeated, his voice shaking uncontrollably.

"Aye, laddie," said Jock, kindly. "Home."

Billy closed his eyes and tried to blot out the horror of the last few weeks but failed.

At the hospital, doctors came and went and eyed Billy with suspicion.

"Coward," he heard one mutter. "He'd know all about if he'd really been wounded."

Billy felt an anger fill him. "I'm not a coward," he managed to shout. "They're giving me a medal!"

The Doctors shook their heads. "Send him home," one of them said.

"Shoot the bugger," responded another. Billy felt tears welling in his eyes, despite his endeavours to remain steady. "I'm *not a coward*," he screamed through his pain, both physical and mental.

"Home," was the eventual verdict. "He's no use to us, blubbering like a baby."

Billy's papers were stamped MEDICALLY UNFIT, but his heart was stamped COWARD.

"Lucky bugger," said a fellow inmate. "Wish it was me."

Billy gazed at him as his uniform, washed and patched up, was brought to him.

"There now," said the orderly. "All nice and smart for going home."

Billy looked at the Black Watch Uniform.

"New socks for you too," he continued, handing Billy a pair made of grey wool. "We'd to cut the last pair off your feet."

Billy gazed at the neat weave of tiny stitches and bent to pull them on. "Thank you," he said. Slowly, he pushed his hand inside and as he did so, he touched something smooth and thin and pulled out a piece of lined paper.

'Knitted by Annie Melville of Dundee,' he read. 'In my prayers till you return home. God bless and keep you safe.'

Billy gazed at the words. "Annie Melville, of Dundee." I seemed in the midst of all his suffering and misery, God had sent him Annie. With trembling fingers, Billy folded the note and pushed it into the breast pocket of his tunic. "Everything will be alright now," he told himself, a tiny flame of hope flickering inside him along with his tears. "Annie's found me."

Chapter 18

"I can't thank you enough, Isabella, for all you've done for me and Lexie," began Annie, a few weeks after Alex's last attack on her. "But I can't depend on your charity or kindness forever."

Isabella smiled. "Knowing you, Annie," she said kindly, "Dependency isn't a state which comes easily to you."

"Do you remember saying you'd be glad to mind Lexie if I went back to the weaving?"

Isabella nodded. "I was wondering when you'd remind me," she said. "You must be feeling stronger."

Annie touched the fading bruises on her neck and trembled at the memory of Alex's fingers tight around her throat, throttling the life out of her. "I am," she said, firmly. "And as soon as I can afford a place to stay, I'll move…"

Isabella held up her hand to stop the words. "No, Annie," she said anxiously. "You must stay for a while yet. Alex may be quiet just now, but I know him better than you. Believe me, it'll be safer for you and Lexie if you remain in this house."

Annie felt fearful. "I don't underestimate his capacity for violence Isabella," she said. "But I can't live with you and John forever."

Isabella held her shoulders. "I'm not saying forever, Annie," she said. "But just till I'm sure Alex is over this."

Reluctantly, Annie nodded in agreement. "But only if I pay my way," she added. "Neither me nor Lexie need charity."

Isabella's eyes misted. "You're a brave woman Annie and I respect your wishes. Alex must be a fool to have treated you so badly. I only hope God forgives him for what he's done."

"God will have to," replied Annie bitterly. "For I can't."

Mr Campbell, the Manager at Baxters Mill, welcomed Annie into his office. He seemed different. The war had brought out the best in him and his usual gruffness was replaced by a friendlier tone as he addressed Annie.

"Times have changed," he told her. "And not just with the men away fighting in France." He nodded sagely. "Women have proved more than their worth in the mills," he said. "And I'd be the first to admit it, our own Dundee weavers are the salt of the earth."

Annie acknowledged the compliment. "Then, when can I start?" she asked, anxious to ensure her return to the mill.

"Monday morning," Mr Campbell told her firmly. "Seven o'clock."

Annie stood up, a broad smile lighting her face. "Thank you, Mr Campbell. You don't know how much this means to me."

The Manager raised a quizzical eyebrow. "Report to Mrs Greig on Monday then, she'll set you on."

"Jessie!" Annie exclaimed.

Mr Campbell nodded. "Aye, Jessie, I've made her a Chargehand and, between you and me," he whispered out of the corner of his mouth. "She's not bad at all."

Annie practically skipped home. Things were looking up.

Mary was waiting for her at the end of Janefield Place on her return to Isabella's. Even from a distance, Annie could tell by her agitation, something was badly wrong. She hurried towards her sister, all thoughts of her recent excitement gone.

"Mary," she called out, close enough now to see the distress in her face. "What is it?"

"It's Joe," Mary wept. "He's been badly wounded... he may even die."

Annie folded her into her arms. "No, Mary, no," she comforted her sister. "Come away now, it'll be alright."

Mary was sobbing uncontrollably. She thrust a letter into Annie's hand.

Mrs Dawson, it read,

I've had word that Joe's been wounded in action. I know he'd want you to know, so hence this note. I think it's pretty bad but I'll let you know when I hear anything further. Yours truly, Charles Cassiday.

Annie held Mary tighter. "When did you get this?" she asked.

Mary blew her nose and pushed the note back into her apron pocket. "It was there when I got back from the cleaning this morning and I don't know what to do. Oh, Annie…" Fresh tears began to flow.

"Have you spoken to Joe's brother?"

Mary shook her head.

"Then perhaps that's where we should start," Annie reasoned. "As Joe's next of kin, he'll be the one to get any more news."

"But what if…"

"Now, now," Annie interrupted gently. "Let's go and see Charlie first, find out exactly what he knows."

Mary blew her nose again. "Alright," she agreed. "As long as you stay with me."

Annie hugged her sister. "Of course, I'll stay with you."

The two sisters walked back down Dura Street and into Victoria Road, finally turning into the steepness of Dens Brae and Todburn Lane at its foot.

Charlie Cassiday eyed Annie and Mary with mistrust. "You got the note then," he said gruffly. "Joe would've wanted me to tell you."

"May we come in for a minute Mr Cassiday?" Annie asked.

Charlie turned and walked back into the small room leaving the door open to indicate his agreement.

Annie ushered Mary inside and closed the door.

"We're sorry to bother you, Mr Cassiday," she began. "But as you can see, my sister's quite upset and…"

"I know, I know," Charlie interrupted, "And you want to know if there's any more news, well the answer's *no*." For a moment there was silence. "And if I could go out there and bring him home, that's what I'd do," Charlie continued. "But I too, must just wait." His voice was heavy with resignation and Annie realised how much he loved his younger brother.

"I understand," Annie said softly. "And I'm sorry we've bothered you at this time, but Mary's concerned too."

At the mention of her name, Mary raised her eyes to meet those of Charlie Cassiday. "I'm pregnant, Mr Cassiday," she said flatly, "With Joe's child."

For a long moment Charlie gazed at her. "So, that's it," he said slowly, as if the last piece of some giant jigsaw had suddenly fallen into place. "That's another good man you've caught out Mistress Dawson, is it, my gullible brother's fallen for your ungodly charms too has he?"

Annie felt her back stiffen at the hurtful remark. "Your brother's a fine man, Mr Cassiday," she said. "But he's no angel."

"It's alright, Annie," added Mary, finding her fighting spirit again. "Mr Cassiday's made no secret of not liking me and that's his choice, but the fact remains, me and Joe are going to have a babe and we're going to be married." She stood up and swiftly moved to the door followed by Annie. "If you hear anything further, Mr Cassiday," Mary said. "I'd be much obliged if you'd let me know. But I'm sure I'll hear from Joe myself soon. Thank you for seeing us."

Out in the lane, Mary breathed in the late Autumn air. "Will you come back with me to the single-end," she asked Annie. "Just for a while?"

Annie put her arm around her shoulder. "Of course," she whispered. "C'mon."

A small brown envelope awaited them at the single-end and it was addressed to Mary. It had a crown on it and was postmarked Edinburgh. Mary felt her blood run cold.

"You open it, Annie," she said, trembling. "It's word about Joe, I just know it is."

Annie sat her down and opened the envelope.

Dear Mrs Dawson,

I have to inform you that Private William Dawson has been discharged from duty with the 4th Batallion Black Watch as medically unfit, but regrettably, it is my firm opinion that he was discharged due to cowardice in the face of the enemy at the Battle of Ypres, France, November 1915.

Colonel John W McKay.

Annie felt a rush of shock wash over her.

"Tell me, Annie," Mary gasped. "Tell me what it says."

Annie handed her the letter. "It's not about Joe," she said her voice faint with disbelief. "It's about Billy."

Mary quickly read the words. "Cowardice," she gasped. "*Billy, a coward?*"

Both Annie and Mary had known Billy at his best and at his worst and knew he'd never run from a fight. "Why, he volunteered," ventured Mary. "How can they say he's a coward?"

Annie's mind tried to picture Billy, tall and handsome as she remembered him on the day she first set eyes on him at the farm in Ireland and a softness formed inside her.

"There's a lot of water passed under the bridge since Ireland," she said to Mary. "And God knows, Billy Dawson has a lot to answer for, but…" Annie felt a longing inside for the safe feeling Billy had given her along with his love. She brushed a tiny tear from her eye as the memories crowded into her heart. "But, he's a strong man," she finished. "And no coward."

Mary watched her sister. "Annie," she whispered, "I've something to tell you."

"Not more bad news," she said sadly. "I don't think I can bear it."

Mary hung her head. "There's another letter," she began, her voice barely audible. "Or there was."

"Mary," Annie said. "You're not making sense…"

"Please, let me finish." Mary took a deep breath. "There was a letter for you, sent here, from Billy."

Annie felt a knot of confusion forming on her forehead. "When?" she asked.

"Before he was sent to France."

Annie waited.

"He still loves you Annie," Mary told her. "He always has."

"And where is this letter?" Annie asked disbelievingly.

Mary's lips tightened. "I burnt it," she said. The silence was tangible. "I was jealous," she muttered, "So I burnt it."

Annie let the statement sink into her subconscious. "Thanks for telling me," she said finally. "I know how much you must have hurt."

Mary shrugged with relief that Annie wasn't angry at her. "I've got Joe now, anyway," she added briskly, before suddenly remembering that, if the fates were unkind, she wouldn't have.

Annie nodded and stood up. "And I've got a daughter to see to," she said. "And she'll be wanting her tea."

"Do you forgive me then?" Mary asked.

"There's nothing to forgive," replied Annie. "Billy's in the past now and I'm more concerned with the future, for me and for Lexie."

Alone with her thoughts, Annie walked past the Mill and up Princes Street. Workers were scurrying home for their tea and children were playing in the street trying to cram as much fun into their lives as the winter light would allow. The Leerie passed Annie on his round, lighting the street lamps and whistling as he went. Annie's mind drifted, at random, into the past and back to the present. Thoughts of Billy and Alex Melville mingled with Mary and Isabella. She had come far since leaving the Poor House in Ireland and she wondered where she would end up. One thing was sure, she decided. She would never depend on a man again for her happiness. Not Alex, not anyone.

Chapter 19

The clatter of the looms greeted Annie on her first day back at the Mill. She breathed in the familiar smell of the jute and smiled at the small boys delivering their barrow-loads of bobbins to the weavers. Jessie was at the far end of the weaving flat, her arms waving wildly at one of the Tenters as he tried to oil life back into a silent pair of looms.

Annie nodded to the remembered faces of the other weavers as she approached Jessie and tapped her on the shoulder.

Jessie's eyes lit up with delight on seeing Annie standing there. "Good God," she cried above the din. "Where have you sprung from?"

Annie grinned. "I'm back to work," she shouted, pointing to the row of looms. "Which pair?"

Jessie hugged her tightly and took her hand. "Follow me," she mouthed. She took Annie past where the Tenter was finishing his work. "This do you?" she laughed.

Annie patted the Tenter on the shoulder as she went by and winked at Jessie.

"This'll do me just fine," she said, "Gaffer."

Jessie threw back her head and hooted. "See you at half-twelve," Jessie signed above the din.

Annie nodded. It was good to be back.

"You're the last person I thought I'd see back here!" exclaimed Jessie as they settled down on a pile of jute sacks to eat their mid-day dinner. "Not that I'm no glad to see you, mind," she added quickly.

Annie smiled. "Thanks Jessie. I'm glad to see you too. And promoted to Chargehand."

Jessie beamed. "Mister Campbell says it's just till the war's over, but wha kens what's afore you."

Annie began to eat her bread and cheese, the mention of war bringing back to her mind again the letter about Billy's cowardice.

"But what aboot yoursel' Annie, what's been happenin' to you and that wee bairn o' yours?" Jessie's voice brought her back to the present.

Annie'e eyes darkened. "It's not been good Jessie," she sighed. "Lexie's fine, but Alex and me are living apart."

"Oh, Annie," sympathised her friend. "What happened?"

Annie hesitated, reluctant to remember the pain of the beatings, let alone speak of it. "Let's just say, we didn't get along."

Jessie instinctively knew not to quiz Annie further and, instead, squeezed her arm. "Least said," she murmured, "Soonest mended."

The 'bummer' sounded shrill in their ears signalling it was time to return to work.

"Will you bring Lexie to visit one Sunday, Annie?" Jessie asked as they walked back down the weaving flat. "The laddies would love to see her."

"That'd be lovely, Jessie," Annie replied. "Once I get myself sorted with a place to live and such, I'd like nothing better."

Jessie nodded and squeezed her arm again. "When you're ready, lassie," she smiled kindly. "When you're ready."

The weeks flew by, with Annie falling back into the pattern of early rising and late finishing as if she'd never been away. Lexie seemed happy too, being looked after by Isabella, and there were even times when she almost forgot she was still married to Alex. But, late one Friday afternoon, he was waiting for her at the mill gate and all the feelings of fear and pain returned to Annie's soul with a vengeance.

Bracing herself for an onslaught of verbal abuse, Annie cautiously approached him.

His face was gaunt and his eyes bleak and empty. "Will you speak with me," he asked quietly, "Please?"

Annie's ears strained to detect any anger in his voice, but there was none. "What do you want with me Alex?" she asked, her eyes avoiding his.

"Just to speak with you Annie," he answered. "And to say how sorry I am for the way I've treated you."

Annie raised her eyes to meet his. Sorry!"

It was Alex's turn to look away. "Yes, Annie. Sorry."

"You look ill," she said, her anxiety easing and a compassion for his plight replacing it.

His eyes glistened with tears as he looked at her.

"I don't deserve your concern," he told her. "But thank you anyway."

Annie nodded and shifted uncomfortably closer to him as a group of workers pushed past them.

Alex caught her arm. "Can we go somewhere," he begged. "Anywhere, so I can talk to you alone." Annie pulled her arm away and Alex released his grip instantly. "I'm sorry," he rushed, "I didn't mean to… to touch you."

Annie looked around her at the darkening evening sky and nodded.

"You can walk me back to Isabella's if you like, but that's all."

Alex's eyes flickered with hope. "Anything you say, Annie." He fell in step alongside her. "I've missed you," he said simply. "More than I ever thought possible."

Annie's lips tightened. "I'm fine," she replied. "And so's Lexie."

Alex kicked a stone onto the road. "Havn't you missed me?"

"No," she replied. "You don't miss pain."

Alex clenched his fists and thrust his hands into his pockets. "You know I didn't mean any of that," he said, his head bowed. "You know I love you and I always will."

Annie felt her eyebrows frown with disbelief. "Love?" she echoed, "You tried to kill me Alex!"

Alex pulled his shoulders up to his ears in an effort to parry the verbal blow. "No, Annie," he insisted. "I never meant to hurt you, I was just jealous, that's all, jealous with love for you." His shoulders dropped with his voice. "Maybe I love you too much."

Annie fell silent, his words conflicting with her common sense and setting up a confusion in her heart.

"How's Alexandra?" he asked, changing the subject and confusing her further. "Does *she* miss me?"

Annie breathed deeply, her steps slowing as they made their way up the steepness of Albert Street where it joined the Arbroath Road. "I told you, she's fine. We're both fine."

"Come home, Annie," he murmured. "Come back to me."

Annie froze at the words and turned to face him. Tears began to stream down his face and his tall frame appeared hunched and broken. Annie felt a wave of compassion flow through her.

"I didn't mean it," he cried. "I didn't mean any of it." His voice was trembling with emotion. "Just come back."

Annie stared intently at his eyes, looking for any indication of deceit but found none. "If I come back," she began slowly…

"Anything, Annie," Alex cut in, hope suddenly bursting through the tears. "I'll do anything you want… just, come back."

"Do you mean that, Alex?" she asked steadily. "No more hurt?"

Alex grasped her hands in his. "No more hurt, Annie. Just come home." His eyes sought hers for their answer and got it.

Annie nodded.

Alex threw his arms around her to the amusement of passersby. "You won't regret it," he cried, hugging her to him. "I'll make up for everything."

Annie felt all the anxiety of the last months flow away. This was the man she'd fallen in love with. "I'm sorry for doing anything to upset you," she began, tears of relief beginning to fill her eyes. "For causing any of this."

Alex pulled her towards him. "I forgive you," he murmured. "Now, let's get Alexandra and go home."

Arm in arm they returned to Isabella's, who greeted their news with a mixture of disbelief and happiness.

"I'm going to miss this little lady," she smiled, cuddling Lexie close to her before handing her back to Annie.

"I'll bring her round tomorrow to be minded as usual," Annie said firmly. "I'll still be working at the mill."

The two women's eyes met briefly as Annie turned to go. "Are you sure?" was all Isabella said.

Annie nodded. "I'm sure."

It was strange returning to her home, part of her felt she'd never been away but another part felt as though she didn't belong there anymore.

Alex's arms circled her on her return from Lexie's room, where she'd laid her child to sleep.

"Kiss me?" he asked more than demanded.

Annie leant towards him and kissed him gently on the cheek. "Not like that," he whispered, his voice low and pleading. "Like you used to."

Annie felt a strange discomfort settle on her shoulders as she looked into her husband's eyes. "How did I used to kiss you?" she asked, trying to sound light-hearted.

Alex's arms tightened around her. "Like you loved me," he replied.

Annie's lips touched his, softly at first, then more intensely, as he responded fully to her nearness.

"Do you love me still?" he asked, searching for her breasts with his hands. "Tell me you love me."

Memories of Alex's violence suddenly filled her head as he pulled her to the floor and lay on top of her. Annie's arms flopped by her sides and she offered no resistance to his urgency.

"Tell me," he insisted again. "Tell me Annie."

"I love you Alex," she said, but her heart felt like ice and her voice was devoid of emotion. Whatever love she had once felt for Alex had gone for good and her spirit dimmed within her.

"What have I done?" she asked herself later, as she gazed sadly at her reflection in the mirror of their bedroom where Alec now lay sleeping. "What have I done?" But there was no one to answer and Annie wept quietly for a long time before going to bed.

Next day, she rose early and prepared Lexie and herself for the day ahead, but the tone of Alex's voice filled her ears with dread as he came into the small kitchen and realised Annie's intentions.

"You're not really going to continue this stupid working are you?"

Annie turned to face him. "Anything, you said," Annie told him. "Do anything you want, you said."

Alex suddenly smiled and put his arms around her. "Yes, yes, I know," he said, "But I didn't think you'd want to…"

"Well, I do," interrupted Annie, "I want to work." She pushed him away and gathered Lexie quickly up into her arms. "I'll be home about half past six." Before he could say another word, Annie was out the door and down the stairs into the close.

"Annie, *wait*," Alex called after her, his voice echoing off the stone walls of the stairwell. But Annie was gone and life would never be the same again for either of them.

Chapter 20

Dundee West Station was cold and empty as Billy emerged from the milk train from Glasgow into the vastness of the platform. His army greatcoat served to keep out the blast of the East wind as it whistled around him but he still shivered violently within. The smell of the station brought back memories of the excitement he had felt going to war. He remembered the cheerful waves of his comrades as they said goodbye to their loved ones and then the journey through France with its smiling peasants.

Joe Cassiday's face flashed before him, marching at the head of their column, his kilt swinging and his head held high. Billy felt tears prick the corners of his eyes and wiped them quickly away with a trembling hand. 'Brave Joe,' he thought. 'Now wounded and lying somewhere in France, with God knows what fate awaiting him.'

"Billy!" He heard a voice call his name, somewhere in the distance.

"Billy, over here!"

He looked in the direction of the sound and saw Josie MacIntyre came running towards him.

"Billy!" she cried, closing in on him. "Welcome home."

He felt Josie's arms fold around him and her face, cold and rosy with the wind, press against his cheek.

Josie's voice babbled on in his ears. "It's so good to see you again, Billy," she said. "You look fine, just fine." Billy tried to fix his attention on her voice and form a coherent reply, but failed. Instead, he just nodded.

Josie linked her arm in his. "You're home now, Billy," she said, softer this time, as she became aware of Billy's lack of response. "Everything's alright now."

His eyes turned towards her and for the first time, Josie saw the terrible sadness and confusion they held and her heart hesitated inside her. The letter she had received from Jock Thomson had been brief, telling her of Billy's discharge and to make sure she met him on his return home. She hadn't known what to expect but the man in front of her wasn't the Billy she had waved goodbye to and who she had fallen in love with.

She held his arm tighter and led him slowly from the station platform out into the cold morning air. The city was already bustling with activity. Dock workers were assembling in grumbling bunches to be allocated their work for the day, shopkeepers were laying out their wares to meet the needs of the mill workers and leeries doused the streetlights at the end of another night. Horses clopped past, their breath gushing in clouds from their nostrils as they pulled carts piled with jute or coal to feed the mills.

"Can you walk alright, Billy?" Josie's voice was concerned now.

Billy nodded.

"We'll soon be home," she added quietly. "There's some hot porridge waiting for you and your favourite jam. You'll like that."

Josie became aware she was speaking to Billy like she would to one of her pupils who needed encouragement and fell into silence till they reached Morgan Street.

"Your room's waiting for you," she told him. "For as long as you want it."

"A room for a coward to hide in," Billy said shakily, speaking for the first time.

Josie stopped walking. "Why did you say that, Billy?" she asked gently. "Jock said you'd been sent home for your health and I can see he was right. You're not well, Billy, but a coward…?"

But Billy's mind had closed again and he didn't speak again till he was in the study in Josie's house surrounded by the shelves of books he had grown to love. He fingered them individually before removing one from its resting place on the shelf.

"*Pilgrim's Progress* by John Bunyan," he whispered to himself. "The slough of despair."

Josie laid a hand on his arm. "Is there anything I can do, Billy?" she asked sadly, realising she was unable to penetrate the wall of pain that was around him.

His eyes looked at her without seeing her need of him and he shook his head.

"I'll make us some tea," said Josie softly, "If you'd like?"

Billy nodded once.

"Right then," Josie smiled nervously. "It'll be ready in five minutes." She left him sitting in his shell of impenetrable blackness and made her way back to the kitchen powerless to help him and yet resenting his need for her support. She had nursed her husband through the slow death of tuberculosis and had never wanted to live with that burden again.

Billy gazed at the pages of John Bunyan's book, till the print blurred in front of him. The shrapnel wounds were healing and his body was recovering from the horror of the trenches but his mind was still lost somewhere in the death and blast of war. He closed his eyes and leant his head back against the leather of the button-backed chair, immediately reliving again the fear and pain of battle.

Joe Cassiday's face reared up before him as it rushed over the top of the trench and into the fire of the German guns. "CHARGE" he heard Joe roar. "CHARGE."

Sweating and trembling, Billy jerked back into reality. "*No Joe*," he heard himself shout as the vision faded and the book-lined walls of the study replaced the blackness of Ypres.

The door of the room burst open and Josie ran towards him, her face white with concern.

"Billy, Billy, what is it?" She gathered his trembling hands in hers, holding them tightly to let him know she was there. "What is it?"

Uncontrolled tears of fear washed Billy's face and the trembling grew worse.

"Please, Billy," pleaded Josie. "Tell me what's happening to you."

But Billy couldn't and Josie grew afraid.

Nothing had prepared her for this. She had prayed and prayed for Billy's safe return and hoped, somehow, he would fall in love with her as she had done with him, but now…

Eventually, his grip loosened and the trembling eased as Billy fell into an exhausted sleep. Josie slowly removed her hand from his and stood up, her mind trying to understand and her heart heavy with fear. Billy's face looked colourless and haggard in the dim light of winter, not the handsome face she'd waved off to France at all. She pulled up the step-stool and sat down on it watching him sleep his uneasy slumber. A ripple of disquiet formed in her heart and slowly developed into a tidal wave of anxiety as memories of her husband's last months resurrected themselves into her consciousness.

She couldn't go through that again, she told herself as she felt again the strain of caring, of watching the man she loved suffer and waste away. Calling out to her to help him in the darkness of night as the sweats and his gasping tuberculor lungs had created their panic and fear of death. Josie clamped her hands over her mouth to suppress the involuntary sob which was forcing its way to the surface and ran from the room.

'How cruel God is,' she told herself. 'To do this to me again.' She steadied herself at the kitchen sink and ran some cold water from the well into a cup. She gulped it down and inhaled deeply to try to dispel the memories. "Please God," she whispered aloud. "Don't ask this of me again."

"He doesn't hear you."

Josie swung round at the sound of Billy's voice and met his empty eyes.

"There is no God."

Josie felt herself shrink back against the hardness of the sink. "I'm sorry, Billy," she heard herself say bleakly. "I'm not strong enough."

Billy's eyes gazed at her devoid of everything but pain. "Nor am I," he whispered. "Nor am I."

Josie watched him turn away from her and heard him close the front door behind him. "*Billy*!" she cried, tears of guilt filling her voice. "*I'm sorry*!"

But there was only silence in answer.

The sound of knocking at Charlie Cassiday's door was barely audible. He squinted at the clock above the fireplace. It had gone midnight but the worry for Joe meant he was still awake.

"Who's there?" he called brusquely, pulling a woollen blanket round his shoulders. But there was no answer. "Who is it at this time of night," he repeated, opening the door and allowing the faint glow of the firelight to illuminate the figure in front of him.

"Can I come in?" an Irish accent asked.

Charlie squinted into the gloom. "Who is it?"

A white face with sunken eyes raised itself to be seen. "It's Billy Dawson."

For a moment, Charlie failed to recognise the gaunt features of the man before him, but immediately recognised the desperation in his eyes.

"You'd better," he said calmly. "You look as though you're done in."

Billy entered the tiny room.

"Sit down," Charlie said, indicating a wooden chair by the dying fire.

Without asking, Charlie took a bottle of Irish Whisky from the kitchen press and poured a measure into a nip glass.

"Here," he said, offering the tiny tumbler to Billy. "You look as though you need it."

Billy's fingers wrapped themselves round the cool smoothness of the glass as he drank its contents down. He felt the burn of the alcohol sweep over his larynx and into his gullet.

Charlie watched him carefully. "Another?" he asked. Billy nodded.

The second drink followed the first.

"Better?" asked Charlie. Billy nodded and handed back the glass.

Joe's brother took up a position opposite Billy and waited.

"I'm sorry," began Billy. "But I'd nowhere else to go."

Charlie nodded. "I understand," he said. "You did the right thing."

"How's Joe?"

Charlie's head dipped. "He's wounded, Billy," he said. "Somewhere in that God-forsaken country across the sea." He fought back anger for his brother's plight. "But, he'll be home soon, God willing."

"I was there," Billy said quietly. "When Joe was in the thick of it."

Charlie leant forward. "Did you see him, Billy," he queried anxiously. "How bad is it?"

Billy shook his head. "I don't know, Charlie," he whispered, the memory of the fighting overwhelming him again. "I think it was his legs that took the blast."

Charlie sank back into his chair. "Christ!"

The muscles of Billy's face trembled as he fought to control his anguish. "Help me?" he muttered, his whole body shaking uncontrollably again.

Charlie grasped his shoulders. "Hold fast, man," he told him urgently. "You're safe now."

"I'm going mad," Billy whimpered. "I can't hold on any longer."

Charlie pulled him to his feet and wrapped his arms around him. "It's alright, Billy," he said firmly. "I've got you now. You're not mad, Billy boy, you've just had more than you can bear." Charlie held on to him while great waves of sobbing wracked his body and mind. "Let it all go," Charlie murmured, as the painful memories overwhelmed Billy again and again. "You're safe now."

Eventually, the sobbing eased and Charlie lowered him back into the chair.

"You're safe now," he told him again. "Safe with me."

Billy's empty eyes acknowledged the compassion of the man in front of him.

"Stay here," Charlied added. "Till Joe comes home."

But it would be a long time before Joe returned to Todburn Lane and Mary's concern for him deepened as the weeks passed and her pregnancy advanced.

"Do you want me to go round to Charlie's?" asked Annie, one day in late Spring when Mary was into her fourth month.

Mary shrugged. "What's the point?" she replied. "He said if there was any news he'd tell us."

Annie nodded in agreement. "I just thought it would help."

"Nothing helps," responded Mary sadly. "I just wish he was back."

"I know," said Annie. "Let's go on a picnic, tomorrow. We'll take Nancy and Lexie out to Linlathen and get some fresh air into our lungs. All this work and worry's making us blue."

Mary brightened. "Oh, I'd like that," she said, then remembering Annie's husband, she hesitated, "But… what about Alex?"

Annie took a deep breath. "I don't think he'll want to come," she said simply.

"I didn't mean that," replied Mary. "I mean, won't he mind?"

Annie grimaced. "I went back on the understanding I did what I wanted to do and I want to go on a picnic with my sister. Anyway, Alex on duty this Sunday, so he won't even notice."

Mary relaxed. "We'll come up around ten o'clock then," she said. "After Mass."

Annie looked at her sister and felt a wave of empathy for her plight. "After Mass it is," she said. "And don't forget to say a Hail Mary for your sister."

Annie didn't tell Alex about the proposed picnic till the Sunday morning over breakfast.

"And what else have you arranged behind my back?" he asked from behind his newspaper.

Annie drew a deep breath. "I haven't arranged anything behind your back Alex," she said evenly. "I just didn't think you'd be all that interested, that's all."

The newspaper slapped down on the table beside him and a remembered fear suddenly reacted in Annie's heart. "Not interested!" Alex exclaimed. "Not interested in what my wife's up to behind my back?"

Annie could feel the words being twisted against her as she turned to face him.

"Isn't it enough I let you go back to that damned weaving job of yours that you love so much?" Alex shouted angrily. "Without you flouting it in my face."

She'd seen it before, the unreasoning anger, the blindness to common sense and her heart stood still. 'Surely, not again,' she told herself. 'He said no more hurt, if only I'd return to him.' But Alex was beyond reason as his hand struck her across the face, drawing blood from her nose and lips.

Annie knew it was useless to try to fight back and curled up in a ball on the floor, pulling her arms and hands around her face and head. His boot found her back and kicked her aside like a rag doll.

"Hussey," he screamed. "Whore."

Annie lay motionless, fighting to control her breathing and waiting for the next blow, but the doorbell shrilled in her ears before it landed. She heard Alex curse as his footsteps thudded over the floor and out into the hall.

"Enjoy your *picnic*," she heard him shout, before his footsteps echoed down the stairwell and into the distance.

Mary's hands gently turned her over onto her back. She heard the involuntary intake of breath as her sister saw the damage Alex had inflicted on her face.

"Oh, Annie," Mary repeated again and again, as she attempted to staunch the flow of blood from her sister's nose and lip. Annie forced herself to sit up and pressed the cloth to her face as Mary helped her onto a chair.

"See if Lexie's alright?" Annie whispered through the hurt.

"Nancy," Mary called urgently to her daughter. "Bring Lexie down from her cot."

Nancy nodded and hurried from the room. Life had matured her beyond her seven years and she needed no second bidding from her mother.

"You can't stay here," Mary begged. "Please Annie, he's going to be the death of you."

Annie felt the fear overwhelm her again. "Where can I go?" she said. "Where can't he get me?"

"Come to the single-end with me," urged Mary. "We'll manage."

"He'll find me there," replied Annie. "I know now nothing will stop him."

Mary sighed in desperation. "It'll do for now," she said. "I'm not leaving you here."

Nancy brought Lexie into the room, still bleary with sleep.

"Give her here," instructed Mary, taking control. "And fetch down her clothes… *all* of them."

Nancy disappeared upstairs.

"Pile them all onto a sheet," shouted Mary. "And bring the whole bundle down."

Mary fed Lexie while Annie gathered her wits back together and managed to stop the bleeding. She looked at her face in the small mirror on the kitchen window ledge and recoiled in shock. Her nose was swollen to twice its normal size and her top lip was split and purple. Mary was right, she couldn't stay here.

Nancy dragged the bundle of clothes into the kitchen. "Is there anything else you want me to do mammy?" she asked. "Is Auntie Annie alright?"

Annie forced a smile. "I'm fine Nancy," she murmured. "And me and Lexie's coming to stay with you for a while, if that's alright?"

Nancy's face broke into a wide grin in answer.

"I'll just be a few minutes," Annie told Mary. "I need one or two things of my own before we go."

Mary nodded, "But be quick," she said. "Nancy and me'll manage Lexie and her things."

Both women froze in their tracks as they simultaneously heard heavy footsteps coming up the stair.

"Is it Alex?" Mary asked, her voice wavering with fear.

Annie held her finger to her lips. "Sssshhhh," she said as the footsteps stopped outside the door.

"Mrs Melville!" called a deep voice. "Are you alright?"

Mary looked at Annie. "Who is it?" she hissed.

"I don't know," Annie mouthed back.

"Mrs Melville, open the door… please."

The voice sounded familiar but Annie couldn't put a name to it.

"It's not Alex," she whispered to Mary, moving closer to the door. "Who'se there?" Annie called out.

"Mrs Melville," came the relieved voice. "It's Constable MacPherson. Can you open the door?"

Annie signalled to Mary to open the door.

Constable MacPherson's black police uniform filled the entrance to Annie's house. He removed his helmet. "Can I come in?" he asked quietly.

Annie covered the lower part of her face with her hands. "If Alex's sent you," she began bravely. "You're not welcome."

The Constable moved further into the kitchen. "No Mrs Melville," he replied. "I'm here because I want to help you."

Annie glanced at Mary. "My sister's doing that," she said. "I don't need any more help."

"Please, Mrs Melville," he continued, gently lowering her hands from her face. Constable MacPherson winced at the sight. "I knew it," he said, anger blazing into his eyes. "He's been up to his old tricks again I see."

Annie turned away unable to meet his gaze.

"Mrs Melville," the Constable continued. "You know I've been aware for a long time that Sergeant Melville's been doing this to you and I just want you to know that I'll be looking out for you and if there's anything I can do, you only have to ask."

Annie felt her chin tremble. "Thank you," she said simply. "Now please… we have to go."

The Constable replaced his helmet and nodded.

"Constable MacPherson," Mary said. "There is something you can do."

Euan MacPherson inclined his head towards her expectantly.

"Annie's coming to live with me for a while in William Lane. Maybe, when you're on your beat and it takes you near there, you could just check that Alex isn't anywhere about."

Euan touched the edge of his helmet. "Enough said," he replied. "As I said," he turned to Annie. "I'll be keeping an eye on things."

Annie felt a wave of gratitude to the policeman. It couldn't have been easy for him, Alex being his Sergeant at the station.

"Come on then," Mary urged. "We'd best be out of here in case Alex comes back."

The little procession made its way through Stobswell and down Dura Street, hurrying as fast as their bundles and small children's legs would allow. The church bells were chiming out their message of Christianity and the April sunshine shone brightly down on the God-fearing folks of Dundee as they gravitated towards the church doors. But no one noticed Annie's plight or glanced at her battered face as she hurried by, her daughter clasped tightly in her arms and her sister and niece struggling with their bulky burdens.

'There is no God,' she thought sadly. 'Not for the likes of me anyway.'

Chapter 21

Annie pulled her shawl over her head and held it tightly beneath her chin as she entered through the gates of Baxters Mill the following day. It was essential now that she worked and the luxury of staying indoors till her face healed was not an option. The other weavers were wrapped up in their own Monday morning depression and, if they did notice the bruising, didn't comment on it, but Jessie did.

"Annie!" she exclaimed, her expression shocked and concerned. "What in God's name's happened?"

"Alex," she said in reply, again, the one word being explanation enough.

Jessie steered her to the corner of the weaving flat. "Oh, Annie, are you alright to work?"

Annie nodded. "I'm fine Jessie, just a bit sore, that's all."

"Ye ken if there's anythin' I can do, you've only to ask."

"I know, Jessie," Annie replied, appreciating once again the loyalty of her friend. "Me and Lexie's living with Mary in William Lane. We'll be fine there just now. I'd just ask if you see Alex hanging about outside the mill, would you tell me?"

Jessie grasped Annie's hands. "I'll set Mister Greig an' the laddies on 'im if I see 'im," she replied loyally. Annie smiled and winced as the movement pulled at the split in her lip.

She nodded and shook Jessie's bony hand. "Just let it be, Jessie," she added softly. "Least said… remember."

Jessie nodded in agreement. "C'mon," she said. "Let's get you to your looms."

Jessie linked her arm into Annie's. "By the by," she added. "You'll never guess who's hame frae the war already?"

"Who?" Annie asked, not really caring.

"Only Mister Da'son."

Annie stopped in her tracks. "Billy Dawson!" she exclaimed. "But how do you know this?"

"Mister Campbell got word he was back. He says I've to make way for 'im when he's ready to come back to work. Seems he's no' very well."

"Did he say what was wrong with him?" Annie asked, hoping that she wouldn't know.

Jessie shrugged. "Just that he's no' well. An' you'll never guess where he's livin'?"

Annie's heart involuntarily leapt in her chest. "Where?"

"With Charlie Cassiday," announced Jessie loudly. "That's where."

Annie's eyes widened in disbelief. "Are you sure, Jessie?" she asked.

Jessie nodded sagely, "I'm sure," she replied. "Take my word for it."

Annie knocked on at her looms, her mind whirling. Why was Billy staying with Joe's brother, of all people, and where was Joe!

Annie hurried home to the single-end as soon as the bummer sounded signalling the end of her shift.

"Mary, Mary," she called as soon as she was in the door. "I've something to tell you."

Mary stopped feeding Lexie and stood up in alarm. "Alex's not been at the mill, has he?" she asked anxiously.

"No, no, nothing like that. Billy's back," she said. "And he's living at Charlie Cassiday's."

Mary took the news with the same look of incredulity as Annie and flopped back down into a chair.

"Charlie's!" exclaimed Mary. "But how?"

Annie threw down her shawl and pulled up a chair. "Jessie told me," she began. "And Mr Campbell says he's coming back to work at Baxters when he's well again."

Mary frowned. "Does Mr Campbell know the real reason Billy's back?"

Annie shook her head. "I don't know, Mary," she replied. "I only know what Jessie's been told, that he's been ill."

"And Joe?" Mary continued slowly. "Where's Joe in all this?"

Annie shook her head. "I don't know, Mary," she said. "I don't know."

Mary's eyes clouded over. "You don't think he's back and doesn't want to see me anymore, do you Annie?"

Annie knelt down beside her younger sister. "No, Mary," she replied quickly. "Not Joe. He'll come to you as soon as he's back from the war."

"I'm five months pregnant with his child Annie," Mary said shakily. "And never a word in three months."

"It's the war Mary," Annie tried to reassure her. "These things are difficult in war time."

Mary's lips formed a thin line as she tried to control her fears. "What if he never comes back, Annie," she whispered, "What will I do then?"

"He *will* be back," Annie replied, willing a confidence into her voice she didn't feel.

"Will you go to Charlie's and find out where Joe is… please?"

A thousand questions filled Annie's head, none of which had an answer. "I don't know if I can face…"

"*Please*, Annie," urged Mary. "I have to know what's happened to him."

Annie nodded, slowly. "I'll try Mary," she said softly, her heart full of misgivings and doubts. "For your sake and Nancy's."

"When?"

Annie sighed. "When I find the courage Mary," she replied. "That's when."

Mary urged and pleaded with Annie for a full week before she finally relented and agreed to visiting Charlie Cassiday's.

"Don't expect too much," she told Mary. "You know what Charlie's like and how he feels about both me and you."

Mary nodded. "I have to know what's happened Annie," she said quietly. "I miss him so much."

Annie's feet dragged as she made her way along Todburn Lane the following Sunday morning. Her heart was a mixture of fear at what she may find out about Joe and misgivings at meeting Billy again, but she plodded on.

Tentatively, she tapped on the green painted door of Charlie and Joe's house in the Lane.

"It's you, is it," murmured Charlie, opening the door to reveal the still bruised face of Annie. "You look as though you've been in the war yourself."

Annie pulled her shawl closer round her face. "Can I come in Mr Cassiday?" she asked, her skin colouring under his piteous gaze.

But, instead of opening the door wider to allow her to enter, Charlie pulled it closed behind him and indicated she should sit on the steps outside.

"How's that sister of yours," he asked, sitting himself down beside her.

Annie leant her elbows on her knees and gazed ahead of her avoiding Charlie's eyes. "She's pregnant, Mr Cassiday," she answered. "And there's still no word from Joe. How do you think she is?"

Charlie nodded. "He's back home," he said simply.

Annie's bruised face turned sharply towards him. "*Home*," she echoed. "*When*?"

Charlie ran his fingers through the hair on his bowed head. "He's been home some two months now."

"*Two months*!"

"But…" Charlie silenced her with a look. "He doesn't want to see her," he said. "Doesn't know what he saw in her in the first place."

Annie felt the heat of anger surging in her veins. "Doesn't want to see her?" she shouted, all thoughts of pity for Joe flying out of the window.

Charlie placed a finger to his lips. "Sssshhhhhh!" he ordered. "you'll have the whole land up with your wailing."

Annie's lips tightened. "And the babe," she added. "What about that?"

Charlie sighed. "Yes," he said, thoughtfully. "There is that."

"Has your brother no shame?" Annie interrupted, not waiting for an answer, her voice shaking with temper.

"Calm down," Charlie told her. "Things have changed. I'll make sure there's money comes to her and the babe."

"MONEY!" shouted Annie. "My sister doesn't want your money." Annie felt tears begin to spring to her eyes. "This'll break her heart," she cried. "Can't you see that?"

The voice of Joe Cassiday sounded behind her from the space which had opened up between the door and the lintel.

"It's alright, Charlie," he said. "I'll speak to Annie."

Charlie stood up and moved towards the door. "You'd better come in," he said, his voice heavy with resignation.

Annie entered the dimness of the small room.

Joe Cassiday was sitting in his chair by the fire, the wooden armrests of a pair of crutches leaning against its back. Annie's heart was pounding as she drew closer and her eyes accustomed themselves to the low light.

"It's Annie, Joe," she said. "Mary's sent me."

"I suppose it had to happen, sooner or later," he said quietly, his eyes never meeting hers.

"Is it true," Annie asked. "You don't want to see Mary again?"

Joe's head dropped further. "Aye," he said. "It's true."

Annie flinched at the confirmation. "And the babe?" she added. "Don't you want to know your own child?"

Joe shook his head. "No."

Annie looked to Charlie for some explanation, but was met with a shrug, as he too avoided her eyes.

Annie felt the strain of exasperation overwhelm her. "But, *why*, Joe?" she asked tearfully. "She loves you so."

"And how long do you think she'd love this?" Joe shouted, pulling aside the blanket that had covered his legs.

Annie looked at the emptiness where Joe's left leg should have been and clasped her hands over her mouth to stifle the gasp of shock which rushed to her vocal chords.

Joe's eyes were blazing with anguish and self-hatred. "Answer me that then, Annie Melville," he cried. "How long?"

Charlie moved with a swiftness which belied his size. "Joe," he said quickly. "Hold fast." He replaced the blanket over Joe's leg and turned to Annie, shielding his brother from any further questions. "I think you should go now," he told Annie. "There's nothing more to be said."

Annie felt sick with shock and concern for her sister and for Joe Cassiday. He'd been so proud of himself in his Black Watch uniform, marching off to war and now, this was what he had to show for his bravery.

"I'm sorry, Mr Cassiday," she whispered. "I'm sorry Joe."

The green door closed softly behind her and the image of Joe burned into her brain as she made her way back to William Lane. Great tears of sympathy and injustice fell from her eyes as she wondered frantically how she would tell Mary.

Her sister was waiting for her, her eyes wide with apprehension.

"Well?" she asked as soon as Annie was near enough to hear her. "Have you found out what's happened?"

Annie nodded solemnly. "You'd better sit down," she said gently. "I've bad news."

Mary turned pale in front of her eyes. "He's not… dead. Please, Annie, tell me he's not dead."

Annie knelt down beside her and took her hand in hers. "No, Mary," he's not dead.

Mary visibly relaxed. "Thank God," she whispered. "Then what is it?" she asked. "Where is he?"

"He's home, Mary," Annie replied. "He's back with Charlie at Todburn Lane."

Mary let out a whoop of joy. "I knew it," she squealed, "I knew he'd come back safely. Is he well, Annie?" she burbled on. "When is he coming to see me? When did he get back…?" Mary's flow of questions ceased as she realised that Annie wasn't smiling. "Annie!" she exclaimed, anxiety suddenly returning to her voice. "He *is* coming to see me?"

"Oh, Mary," Annie began. "He's been badly wounded. He's… not the Joe you knew."

Mary's eyebrows frowned in confusion. "I know he's been wounded," she said. "But he's home now. He'll get better. I'll look after him…"

Annie felt her throat tighten with tears as the picture of Joe filled her mind. "He doesn't want to see you Mary, because…" Mary waited while Annie drew a deep breath. "Because, he's come back with only one leg." Annie let the words settle into Mary's heart before continuing speaking to her brain. "He's always been a proud man, Mary, handsome and proud and to be a cripple is more than he can bear. Especially in your eyes."

Mary sat still and tearless for what seemed like an eternity while Annie silently continued to hold her hand. "Does he really believe I'd stop loving him because of this?"

Annie nodded. "He's stopped loving himself, Mary, so how can he expect anyone else to love him?"

Mary released her hand from Annie's. "Will you keep an eye on Nancy for a while?"

Annie nodded.

"I must see him." Mary continued, a new determination replacing the fear that had been there earlier. "Whether he wants me or not."

"Are you sure, Mary?" asked Annie, already knowing the answer.

"I'm sure."

Charlie Cassiday knew, even before opening the door, who'd be standing on the doorstep.

"Come in," he said to Mary. "I've been expecting you."

"Is Joe here?" she asked. "Like Annie said?"

Charlie stepped aside to let her pass. "See for yourself."

Mary entered the gloom of the small kitchen, made darker by the drawn curtains. "Joe," she whispered to the hunched figure by the fireside. "It's Mary. Will you speak to me?"

"Go away, Mary," said Joe hoarsely, never looking up at her. "Just leave me be."

Mary stepped further into the room. "And where shall I go to, without you?" she answered softly.

Joe's shoulders shook with the effort to control the tidal wave of emotion which was threatening to drown him.

"I'm no use to you Mary," he managed to stammer. "I'm no use to anyone anymore!" A great rush of self-pity swept over him, forcing him to bury his face in his hands. "Please," he begged her. "Go away and leave me be."

In an instant Mary was on her knees at his side, carefully unfolding his fingers and taking his strong hand in hers.

"I love you, Joe Cassiday," she whispered. "Do you hear me? I love you, just as you are."

"No you don't," answered Joe. "I'm not the man you fell in love with." He pulled away the blanket from his lap. "Look at me Mary," he cried with an anguish of the hopeless. "Half a man. What good is half a man?"

"You'll never be half a man to me, Joe," Mary whispered. "You'll always be my Joe, no matter what."

"I wish I could believe you," Joe answered through his pain.

"Believe me," said Mary. "Please, Joe, believe me."

Joe's trembling fingers reached out and touched Mary's cheek and, for the first time, his eyes met hers.

"You… you wouldn't lie to me," he murmured, barely audible through his pain. "Not about this, Mary, I couldn't bear it."

Mary pressed her face to his hand and kissed the tip of each finger. "No Joe," she told him. "I wouldn't lie to you, not now, nor ever."

Joe's breathing became easier. "How's our baby doing?" he asked shakily.

"Our baby's doing fine," said Mary. "He'll be with us come the Summer."

"Oh, Mary," Joe breathed, wrapping her in his arms. "Thank you for loving me."

"Thank you for letting me," Mary replied. "Now, when are you really coming home?"

"Soon now," Joe replied. "Now I know I've got you to come home to."

Charlie Cassiday watched in silence as Mary's love for his brother formed around him, lifting him from his despair and restoring him to wholeness.

"Will you come and see me, tomorrow?" she asked gently. "Nancy's always asking about you."

Joe nodded and sniffed. "Tomorrow," he said. "Tomorrow it is."

"I owe you an apology," said Charlie as he took Mary out of the door into Todburn Lane.

"No need," said Mary. "Everything you said about me was true. We all make mistakes but Joe saw past them and loved me still. Now it's my turn to show him how much I love him too."

Charlie nodded. "You're a strong woman, Mary," he said. "And Joe's going to need you to stay strong."

"I know, Charlie," said Mary. "I'll do my best and, maybe with your help, I'll succeed."

The two of them acknowledged their dependence on one another in that instant and Charlie extended his hand. Mary took it.

Chapter 22

Constable MacPherson was sitting in Mary's kitchen on her return, with Annie, sobbing quietly in the chair opposite him.

"What is it?" she cried immediately. "Annie, tell me what's wrong?"

Constable MacPherson stood to attention. "I'm sorry, Mrs Dawson, to be the bearer of bad news, but…"

Mary tightened her arm around Annie's shoulders. "Not more bad news," she whispered. "Haven't we had enough to bear?"

"It's been my duty to inform Mrs Melville that her husband was found last night, hanging by his belt in one of the cells at Bell Street Police Station…"

Mary's eyes filled with disbelief. "Hanging?" she asked, her voice barely audible. "You mean…"

"I'm afraid so," Euan MacPherson confirmed. "Mr Melville is dead." Constable MacPherson's eyes misted with concern as he uttered the final word. "Suicide."

"Oh! Annie," whispered Mary, unable to think of words to comfort her. "Hold on to me."

"He punished me in life," Annie muttered. "And now, he's punishing me in death."

"No, Annie," said Mary. "Don't think like that."

Your sister's right, Mrs Melville," interrupted Euan MacPherson. "He couldn't live with his guilt it seems to me. I wouldn't wish to speak ill of the dead but don't forget his harshness to you."

Annie felt numb and detached from the sounds of the world around her. Everything she'd ever tried to do to build some happiness for herself had somehow always crumbled around her, but she hadn't counted on this.

"I don't know what to do?" she told Mary after Constable MacPherson had gone. "Tell me what to do."

"Hush, now," said Mary soothingly. "He's with God now."

"I hope so, Mary," said Annie. "For his sister's sake."

"You've got Lexie," Mary reminded Annie. "She needs you more than ever now."

Annie smiled faintly at the sound of her daughter's name. "Alexandra," she said. "Named after her father." Annie felt herself shudder with emotion. "Where did it all go so wrong?" she asked, almost to herself.

"Who knows, Annie," replied Mary. "Who understands any of it."

"I must go back to Maryfield tomorrow," Annie said. "Make arrangements for the funeral."

Mary acknowledged her sister's practical way of coping. "Shall I come with you?" Mary asked.

Annie shook her head. "Isabella will be there. She must be distraught. Alex was her only brother and, despite everything, she loved him dearly."

Annie called Lexie to her. "We're going home tomorrow," she told the child.

Lexie giggled and returned to her innocent play.

"One day," said Annie. "I'll have to tell her about her father."

"I know," replied Mary. "But not today." She sat down opposite Annie and placed some more coal on the fire, bringing it back to life. Both sisters retreated into their thoughts as their two daughters played quietly together in the corner of the room, Mary wondering about her future with Joe and Annie trying to understand Alex's suicide.

Alex's funeral was a public acknowledgement of his life in the police force. His coffin was carried by six uniformed constables and the cemetery was a sea of black serge. To Annie's surprise, several town councillors and local business men, who nodded solemnly at Annie as they passed, were also present.

"If there's anything I can do, Mrs Melville," whispered one of them respectfully. "You've only to ask." He handed Annie a small printed card. 'Councillor Matthew Reagan', it read.

Annie glanced up at his earnest eyes. "Mr Melville and I were friends," he added. "And fellow-brothers."

Brothers?" she asked. "I didn't know Alex had a brother."

The Councillor smiled. "There are other kinds of brothers," he said, closing her fingers round the card with his. "Let's just say we look after our own." He moved on, leaving Annie puzzled.

"Is everything alright, Mrs Melville?" asked Constable MacPherson. "This can't be easy for you."

Annie frowned and smiled at the same time. "Thanks for your concern Constable…?"

"MacPherson," Euan added. "Euan MacPherson."

Annie nodded. "Sorry, I'm not thinking properly…"

"Very understandable, Mrs Melville," he continued. "No need to apologise. Just remember, I'm here if you need anything." Euan melted back into the weave of black tunics. Annie Melville was in his thoughts a lot nowadays. At first, it had been as a concerned onlooker, but the more he came to know about her life the more he admired her courage and dignity.

Mary stood by Annie's side the whole time, with Nancy holding one hand and Lexie the other. It was almost the turning of a year and it was year Annie would rather not have lived through. But she was alive, despite Alex's efforts to throttle her and he was dead. She knelt by the freshly-dug earth and thought of the last time she'd knelt at a graveside.

Her mother's burial, in a pauper's grave in Belfast, had happened without ceremony or assembled dignitaries, yet she'd never hurt a fly during her life and had always toiled to ensure the lives of those around her had been enriched.

Annie touched the petals of the assembled wreaths which lay, side by side, the length of Alex's grave. "These should have been for you, mammy," she whispered sadly, breaking a flower free from the others and placing it inside the bible she was carrying.

"In memory o' your man?" asked the gravedigger kindly. Annie remembered the gravedigger in Ireland who'd been the only other witness to her mother's burial and smiled gently.

"Something like that," she said, standing up and looking around the leafless trees and grey headstones. Annie watched, as the final mourners disappeared from the scene, back to their own lives and realities.

"Are we going home now Auntie Annie?" Nancy's frozen little hand slipped into hers.

Annie turned to the pinched face of her niece and bent down beside her. "You've been a good girl," she said, pushing back a stray curl from her forehead. "And your Auntie Annie's going to make sure you and Lexie have a better life then me and your mammy have had."

Nancy nodded solemnly, trying to stop her teeth from chattering. "Can we go home now?" she asked again.

Annie straightened up and squeezed her hand. "Yes Nancy," she said softly. "Let's go home."

"Are you alright?" asked Mary as they walked together back to Mary's single-end in William Lane.

Annie nodded. "It's all so false," she said. "All these people singing their praises to a wife-beater, and there was mammy, buried without…" Annie felt her chin quiver at the memory.

Mary squeezed her hand. "She understands," she said gently. "You were always her rock. Not like me, who caused her nothing but worry."

Annie smiled. "She loved you very much," Annie told her. "Just like I do."

The sisters walked past the gaol in Bell Street and up Meadowside into Victoria Road in quiet reflection.

"Do you think mammy ever forgave me for leaving when I did?" asked Mary.

"Of course, she did," Annie reassured her. "She knew you had to go."

"I hope so, Annie," Mary said. "I hope so."

It had felt strange returning alone to her home in Maryfield. Annie had anticipated all sorts of unhappy feelings as she remembered the pain of her time there, but on entering the door, she felt only peace. The parlour was cold with lack of use, but she soon had a fire burning brightly in the grate and it's glow lit up the sheen of the mahogany table and the soft drape of the velvet-covered armchairs at either side. Lexie played happily around Annie's feet as she prepared their meal. If she noticed Alex was no longer there, she didn't show it and Annie prayed that she was too young to understand. One day, she would tell her about her father, but only the good times.

Annie watched her daughter as she spooned soup into her mouth. She was as fair as Mary's child was dark. Her deep-brown eyes and golden hair was from Alex but her easy personality was Annie's. This was her child now, hers alone, and she would love her like she'd not been able to love her firstborn son, John. Her thoughts turned to Bella and her last letter, which Alex had burned. She must write to Bella, even go back to Ireland and see her. Anything was possible now. The thought filled Annie with excitement. To see Bella again would be wonderful, but even more wonderful, would be the chance of seeing her son, for the first time since his birth.

Annie cradled the thought to her heart. She would write to Bella that night, once Lexie was in bed. The doorbell interrupted her thoughts.

"Who is it?" Annie called, hesitating to open the door to a stranger. A hesitant female voice answered.

"My name's Mrs MacIntyre. You don't know me Mrs Melville, but I must speak with you… please?"

Annie frowned and unlocked the door.

"I'm sorry to bother you," Josie began. "But I think it's important that we speak."

"What about?" asked Annie, barring Josie's entrance. "I've just buried my husband and I'm not really ready for visitors, let alone people I don't know."

"Please, Mrs Melville," the woman repeated. "I wouldn't bother you unless I thought you should know. It's about Mr Dawson, Billy Dawson."

Annie stepped back and allowed Josie MacIntyre to pass into her home.

Josie carried herself well and had a refinement which made Annie immediately feel self-conscious. She glanced at herself in the hall mirror and frowned.

"Well?" Annie said, closing the parlour door behind her.

Josie lowered her eyes to avert Annie's penetrating gaze. "May I sit down?" she asked quietly.

Annie indicated a chair by the fire. "What about Billy Dawson?" Annie asked. "And what makes you think I need to know?"

Josie took a deep breath. "He's in a bad way, Mrs Melville," she began. "And I think you're the only one who can help him."

Annie's eyes narrowed. "How do you know of me?" she asked.

"Billy told me," she replied. "Before he disappeared, and John Anderson confirmed it."

"John Anderson!" Annie exclaimed. "How do you know him?"

"We're both teachers," she said. "At the Academy... Morgan Academy."

"I wasn't aware I was interesting enough to be the subject of conversation for teachers at the Academy," Annie said. "But go on." A hostility had crept into her voice which made Josie flinch.

"Please, Mrs Melville, let me finish."

Annie softened and sat down opposite her. She was pale and pretty, about Annie's age, but somehow seemed almost childlike in her mannerisms.

Josie cleared her throat. "Mr Dawson... Billy... lodged with me in Morgan Street for a while, before he went off to the war. I had hoped we would..." her face coloured and she pulled a handkerchief out of her pocket and blew her nose to conceal the pinkness.

"Go on," Annie said gently, aware of Josie's discomfort.

"Well," she sniffed. "I had hoped we would marry... I'm a widow," she added hastily, seeking Annie's approval, but Annie remained impassive.

"Well," Josie continued. "When he came home from the front, he was... different."

"Different?" Annie queried.

Josie lowered her eyes again. "He's... he's..." her chin began to quiver. "I don't know how to explain it," she said, her voice rushing ahead of her tears. "It's was as if he's died inside," she ended in exasperation. She blew her nose again, this time in real sadness. "I don't know what the war did to him Mrs Melville, but he trembled all the time and would wake up screaming in terrible night sweats..." Josie's voice tailed off and her small shoulders shook in despair.

Annie felt every nerve in her body scream as her mind conjured up pictures of Billy. She stood up quickly. "Please go, Mrs MacIntyre," she said. "I don't know what you expected of me, but I'm sorry, there's nothing I can do for him. Do you understand... *nothing*."

Josie's face paled further, but she remained seated. "He kept talking about Annie's socks," she said, the words making no sense.

"Socks!" echoed Annie. "What socks?"

"It seems that just before they sent him home," Josie continued steadily. "He'd been given new socks... knitted by Annie Melville of Dundee."

Annie dropped back into her chair. "They reached *Billy*?" Annie whispered incredulously.

Josie nodded. "They saved his life," she said. "He felt as if somehow, you'd found him again."

Annie felt her heart pound in her chest and her eyes searched Josie's for more understanding. "Where is he now?" she asked, memories flooding through her head.

Josie's sniffed loudly and shook her head, "I don't know," she said. "But John Anderson says he's living the life of a beggar around the West Port and…" Josie's twisted her handkerchief round her fingers and they both fell silent as Annie tried to piece together the meaning of Josie's words and her reaction to them.

"Thanks for telling me," Annie said eventually into the silence. "And tell John Anderson to look out for him when he's doing his good work for the destitute, but there's nothing I can do to help him." Annie stood up and walked to the door of the room. "I think you should go now," she told Josie tiredly. "And I'm sorry things didn't work out for you and Billy." She looked at the genteel figure of her visitor. "He must be blind not to notice you," she said. "And foolish not to see your love for him."

Josie sighed and extended her gloved hand to Annie. "He's blind alright," she said. "Blinded by love for you."

Annie felt her throat tighten.

"And it's perhaps it's you who is the foolish one," she added. "To deny it."

Annie leant against the closed door and listened to Josie MacIntyre's light footfalls fade into the descending stairwell.

"You've no right to do this to me Billy Dawson," she called into the emptiness, tears threatening to overwhelm her anger. "No right at all."

Chapter 23

Joe Cassiday combed his black hair and gazed at his reflection in the mirror above the fireplace of the single-end in William Lane.

"Do you think I'll do?" he asked Nancy. "I mean, do you think your new baby brother'll like me?" Nancy placed her small hands on her hips and cocked her head to one side, mimicking her mother to perfection.

"You'll do nicely," she giggled. "And I want to hold him first."

Joe threw his head back and laughed loudly at his step-daughter's comic stance.

"Of course you can be the first to hold him," he said adjusting the wooden crutch under his right arm. "And if you're a really good girl, you can have a pokey of sweeties on the way home."

Since he had come to live with Mary in February, Joe had not only become Nancy's unofficial step-father but now he was the natural father of his own brand-new son. The June sunshine spread its warmth into his bones and even the loss of his leg seemed almost forgotten as he and Nancy made their way up the steepness of Infirmary Brae leading to the hospital where Mary had been delivered of their son.

"We've come to see Mrs Cassiday," he told the starched Sister who'd met them at the door of the Ward.

"Wait," she intoned, in a voice that brooked no argument.

Nancy's eyes widened and her grip tightened on Joe's hand. "Is mammy alright?" she whispered.

Joe squeezed her hand reassuringly. "She's fine," he whispered back.

The starched one indicated they could enter. "She's in the end bed," she nodded. "I'll bring baby in myself for you to look at but, you mustn't touch," she instructed, eyeing Joe and Nancy from top to bottom.

Joe pulled his bonnet obediently from his head. "Right," he said. "Right you are."

Nancy suppressed a nervous giggle which was forcing itself up the back of her throat.

"You've visitors Mrs Cassiday," she told Mary, tucking in the covers of the hospital bed and straightening the pillow under Mary's head. "I'll just fetch baby," she added, turning to Joe. "She's very tired, so don't stay too long."

Joe nodded and pulled a chair over to the bedside and helped Nancy on to it.

Mary smiled weakly.

"How are you, my love?" Joe asked, his eyes taking in every inch of Mary's pale face.

Her hand reached out to him and he grasped it's tininess in his. "I'm fine Joe," she whispered. "Just tired, that's all."

"Of course you're tired," Joe said softly. "But you'll be home soon and I'll look after you till you're strong again, just like you've looked after me."

"I'll help," piped up Nancy.

Mary stroked her soft curls, "You're a good girl, Nancy," she whispered. "And your mammy's very proud of you."

The Sister rustled to the end of the bed carrying a white bundle.

"Here's your new man," she said to Mary. "Isn't he just like his daddy?"

Mary indicated to Joe to have a look.

Gingerly, he pulled back the soft whiteness of the blanket around his son. A shock of black hair spiked from his head and long, dark lashes edged his closed eyes. Joe gazed at the tiny features and his heart wept with joy.

"Hello wee Joe," he whispered. "I'm your daddy, don't you know." The bundle moved and began to wail.

"He's saying hello back," called out Nancy in delight. "Say hello from me."

Joe pulled her towards him. "Say hello yourself," he told her gently. "And maybe, if you're good, the nurse'll let you hold him."

Nancy's eyes were round with wonder.

"Oh, just for a minute," sniffed the nurse, her starchiness fading under the influence of the magic of a newborn child.

Nancy cupped her arms and, for a moment, held the sweet-scented bundle. "He's got hair," she breathed in child-like awe. "Just like me!"

"And me," added Joe, helping her to return her baby brother to the nurse.

"Now then," continued the sister, remembering her position of authority. "Just a few minutes with mum, then you'll have to go."

Joe nodded and turned his eyes back to his beautiful wife. "I love you Mary Cassiday," he whispered. "And I love you for making me a man again."

Mary smiled and nodded. "And I love you for making me a woman again," she said.

"And I love *everybody*," squealed Nancy, making them all laugh.

"Hurry home, Mary."

"Soon," replied Mary, feigning a strength she didn't feel. "Very soon."

"Auntie Annie," called out Nancy, running towards the figure at the door of the ward. "It's Auntie Annie."

Joe fixed his eyes on Mary. "You'll be wanting to be alone with your sister for a while," he said. "I'll take Nancy for a walk and we'll come back tomorrow, if that's alright?" His eyes were full of an earnest desire to be understood. "It's not that I want to go," he said hurriedly as Annie approached Mary's bed, dragged by the grinning Nancy. "But maybe it's best." He leaned heavily on the crutch as he bent over to kiss Mary, glad of an excuse not to meet Annie's eyes. The man in him was unable to have Annie look at him with pity but there was no quick escape.

"I was just going," he stammered, pulling his bonnet low over one eye and moving nervously aside to let Annie pass.

"Please Joe," Annie said. "Not on my account."

Their eyes met and Annie could see the pain of loss etched in Joe's face, as he could in hers. For a moment neither spoke and it was Nancy who broke through the curtain of discomfort which hung between them.

"He's got *hair*, Auntie Annie," she squealed. "Little Joe's got hair just like me."

Annie smiled. "I'm sure he's as handsome as his daddy too."

Joe relaxed and a wide grin spread over his face. "Thanks for that Annie," he said. "And thanks for looking after Mary while I was away."

Annie nodded in acknowledgement of their mutual love for Mary and turned her attention to her sister as Joe and Nancy bade their goodbyes.

"How was it?" Annie asked, knowing Mary's concern about the birth.

Mary nodded. "It was fine, Annie," she said. "I was so afraid the abortion would somehow have damaged the babe but everything's fine. I'm just very tired."

Annie squeezed her hand. "Of course you are my pet," she said softly. "But at least, this time, you're with the man you love and Joe's very proud and happy."

Mary agreed. "I just wish we were able to be married," she said. "It doesn't sit well bringing little Joe into the world a basta…"

"Hush now Mary," Annie interrupted. "You mustn't speak like that. You know Joe would marry you in a minute were it possible."

"I know that," murmured Mary. "But I just wish… that's all."

Annie frowned. "Perhaps if you asked Billy…"

Mary sighed, "I don't even know where he is Annie," she said. "He only stayed with Charlie for a few days, then disappeared into the night and no one's seen him since."

"Someone's seen him," Annie told her quietly.

Mary's eyes widened. "Who?"

"John Anderson."

Mary flinched at the mention of his name.

Annie nodded. "He saw him up the West Port… he was begging in the street, Mary."

Mary gasped involuntarily and her eyes filled with tears of pity. "Oh, Annie, *no*."

Annie too felt her heart lurch at the thought. "Seems the war's left him badly damaged," continued Annie. "In fact, someone's been to see me about him."

Mary tried to sit upright, her whole attention now focussed on Annie's words. "Tell me, Annie," she asked urgently, "I must know."

Annie took a deep breath. "Her name's Josephine MacIntyre. Billy lodged with her after the fire."

"Where?"

Annie folded her arms around herself and looked at the point of her shoe protruding from beneath her skirt. "Morgan Street."

"Morgan Street," Mary repeated in amazement. "But, that's near where you and…"

Annie held up a hand. "I know," she said. "Just round the corner from me and Alex. God knows how we never met."

Mary steadied herself, and slid back down her pillow, the exertion of balancing on her elbows exhausting her. "Maybe that's the way he wanted it, Annie," she said. "Maybe he just wanted to be near."

Annie felt a wave of frustration wash over her. "Don't say things like that Mary, it's bad enough Josie MacIntyre going on at me, don't you start too…" There was a silence while Annie composed herself again and Mary allowed Annie's reaction to seep into her mind.

"I'm sorry," she said, "But I think we both know…"

Annie jumped up and clamped her hands over her ears. "No," she said loudly. "We don't know anything."

The ward sister hurried towards them drawn by the noise. "Please, please," she urged. "Remember the babies."

Annie sat down abruptly and straightened her back. "I'm sorry, sister," she said. "It won't happen again."

The sister sniffed and nodded. "It had better not," she said sternly. "Or you'll have to leave."

Annie hung her head. "I'm sorry Mary," she whispered. "I don't know what I'm doing anymore, what with Alex killing…" She forced her lips to tighten, closing up the door to her emotions.

"I know," Mary whispered. "It's not been easy for either of us this last while." Mary closed her eyes, the tiredness of the exchange overwhelming her. Annie watched her sister's breathing deepen into sleep before slipping away.

'You'll get your divorce from Billy,' she vowed silently. 'And you'll be free to marry Joe.'

Annie knocked at John and Isabella Anderson's door.

"It's only me," she said as Isabella opened it to let her in. "How's Lexie? Has she been a good girl?"

"She's been lovely, as usual," smiled Isabella. "And Mary," she continued. "How's Mary and the new babe?"

Annie slipped off her coat and picked up Lexie who had crawled into the hall at the sound of her voice. "She's fine Isabella, a bit tired, but quite well."

"And the babe?"

"Do you know, I never saw him." Isabella's eyes widened in disbelief. "I got distracted, I think, and the sister had whisked him away before I got the chance to do anything about it."

"Well, I'm sure there'll be plenty times to see him once she's home," Isabella assured her. "And you don't have to rush away do you, I've hardly seen you this last while since Alex…?"

Annie pressed her arm, as Isabella stumbled for words.

"I'm sorry," Isabella murmured. "It all just seems such a waste."

"I know," Annie agreed. "I'm just sorry things ended the way they did."

"Oh, you've nothing to be sorry for," Isabella said sadly. "No one could have done more."

"Is John in?" Annie asked, hoping the change of subject would distract Isabella from the train of thought she was now on.

"Yes, yes," she replied. "He's in his study. Why?"

"Oh, nothing much," replied Annie. "Just something I wanted to ask him."

"I'll see if he's busy, shall I?" Isabella offered.

"And I'll put the kettle on." Isabella nodded and disappeared upstairs to John's study.

Lexie was gurgling in Annie's arms as she waited for the water to boil. Imagined pictures of Billy, begging in the street, crowded into her mind, despite every effort to dispel them and it was only a deep voice behind her that brought her back to reality with a jolt.

"You wanted to see me Annie?" John Anderson stood just inside the door of the kitchen. Calm eyes, black as coal, perceived her, unblinking and steady. He had lost the thinness which had made his angular face look pinched and since his reinstatement back into the Salvation Army, his stance was once more upright and confident. Returning to Isabella had been the right thing for him to do, but Annie could see why Mary had fallen for him and why she had given up so much to be with him.

Annie forced a nervous smile. "I believe we've a mutual acquaintance," she said.

John lifted the steaming kettle from the black range and poured its contents into the teapot Annie had prepared.

"And who might that be?"

"Mrs MacIntyre," Annie replied. "Josie MacIntyre."

John set three cups in their saucers and placed a sugar bowl and milk jug on the table before responding.

"I think you might mean it's Billy Dawson who's the mutual acquaintance," he said pouring the tea into the cups. "Am I right?"

Annie took the proffered cup of tea. "She says you've seen him."

"I've seen him, Annie," John confirmed. "And to say he's got all he deserved is, perhaps, unfair."

Annie felt herself bristle. "No one deserves to be begging in the streets," she said defensively. "Especially after fighting for his country."

"We all serve in different ways," John Anderson replied, unflinchingly. "And I would have thought you'd be the last person to defend him."

"I'm not defending him," Annie retorted, angry at herself for reacting emotionally and at John Anderson for touching a raw nerve. She drew a deep breath to try to calm herself down. "I need to speak to him," she said as evenly as she could. "That's all."

"And you want me to take you to him," finished John. "Is that it?"

Annie felt herself becoming more and more irritated at John Anderson's self-control. "I suppose that is it," she replied curtly. "If that's possible."

John shrugged his shoulders and picked up the third teacup. "I'll just take this through to Isabella. She'll be wondering where we are."

"Will you then?" Annie asked again, anxiety now evident in her voice. "Take me to him?"

John Anderson stopped at the door and turned. "The Salvation Army runs a soup kitchen in Artillery Lane. I'll be there on Saturday night… and so will Billy Dawson."

"Thank you," Annie said, her heart pounding in her head. She gathered Lexie up into her arms again and followed John Anderson into the parlour where Isabella sat wooden-faced. She forced a smile as John and Annie entered the room.

"Ah, my tea at last," she said, taking the cup from her husband's hand. "And did you get whatever it was sorted, Annie?" she asked quietly.

"We did," John replied, before Annie had a chance to answer. "And it's nothing for you to worry about."

The reply signalled that the subject was closed and Annie quickly prepared to depart amidst an air of tension which now seemed to fill the room.

"Thanks for looking after Lexie again, Isabella," she said, moving towards the door. "I'll see you again soon." Annie hurried along the street back to her home and was conscious of a deep confusion which had been building since Josie MacIntyre's visit. But, one way or another, for Mary's sake, she was going to have to see Billy again, whether she liked it or not.

Chapter 24

Annie slept badly on the Friday night. Old memories kept flashing through her sub-conscious, mixed with recent ones. It seemed in her fitfulness that one minute she was back in the poorhouse in Ireland giving birth to her son, the next she was walking through Baxters Park arm in arm with Joe Cassiday and then Alex's face would suddenly appear from nowhere calling her name over and over. She was glad when the early dawn light pierced the darkness and brought calm to her heart and mind. She would be glad too when the meeting with Billy was over.

She could hear Lexie squealing from her cot, demanding to be fed and quickly rose.

"C'mon little one," she whispered into the silky hair of her daughter's warm head. "Time for breakfast." Annie looked at the kitchen clock pointing to five thirty and pulled back the curtain that covered the window. Strands of light and warmth fell onto her face and she closed her eyes for a moment, savouring the stillness and hope of the June morning.

"Everything will be fine," she told herself. "God willing."

She had to work at the mill that morning, but was glad of it, as her need to seek Jessie Greig's help, yet again, was now paramount. Annie deposited Lexie at Isabella's as usual and if she had wondered about the reason behind Annie's wish to speak with John Anderson, she didn't pursue it.

"I'll pick her up round about two o'clock," said Annie. "If that's alright."

"Of course it is Annie," replied Isabella. "You know I love having her."

Annie bade her goodbye and hurried down into Princes Street and through the gates of the mill. On entering the weaving flat she made a beeline for Jessie.

"Jessie," she called breathlessly. "Can I speak with you before knocking on time."

Jessie eyed her quizzically. "Aye, Annie," she said, trying to understand the obvious urgency. "What is it?"

"It's a long story Jessie," Annie rushed. "But I have to go out late tonight and I need Lexie looked after."

"Is that all?" Jessie responded warmly. "Then bring 'er round an' me an' the laddies'll see to her."

Annie relaxed. "Thanks Jessie," she said gratefully. "Did I ever tell you you're the most wonderful friend in the world?"

Jessie beamed. "He must be affy speciall," she nodded, winking dramatically. "You can pick the bairn up on Sunday morning if you like…"

"No, *No*, Jessie," Annie interrupted, blushing wildly. "It's nothing like that, it's… well, it's just that I've to meet Billy Dawson… to ask him…"

Jessie's eyes widened in disbelief. "*Mister Da'son*," she echoed. "After all he's done!"

Annie shook her head and held up her hand to stop Jessie's train of thought. "It's not like that, Jessie, it's about Mary…" Annie began to feel something akin to panic as she tried to give Jessie enough information without actually telling her anything. "Please, Jessie, don't ask any more questions, just trust me!"

The older woman shook her head, "I trust you, Annie," she said. "It's Billy Dawson I dinna trust."

Annie clasped her hands in exasperation. "It's nearly knocking-on time," she said. "I'll bring Lexie over around seven o'clock." Thankfully, the clatter of looms beginning their noisy day put an end to any further questioning and Annie fell to work with a sigh of relief.

Time and time again throughout the day, Annie talked herself out of meeting Billy, then remembered her silent vow to Mary and scolded herself for being so cowardly. Mary and Joe needed to be married. With two children to look after now, it was unthinkable that they would have to go through life with the stigma of their parents living in sin, but first of all, Billy had to agree to a divorce. The thought strengthened Annie's resolve and by the time she'd dropped Lexie off at Jessie's she was fired with the indignation of the righteous.

The Masonic Hall in Artillery Lane had been converted into a large canteen. At one end huge pots of soup bubbled away while the men and women of the Salvation Army sliced bread and brewed tea. The smell of food and the unwashed bodies of the ragged men assembled for their daily hand-out, only added to the discomfort Annie already felt in her stomach and she pulled her shawl over her mouth and nose as she entered the hall.

John Anderson was directing operations at the far end of the room and again, Annie understood Mary's attraction to him. He had a naturally commanding air about him which demanded respect and obedience and Annie felt, to her surprise and discomfort, a desire that he should like her.

"John," she said, close enough now to be heard. "It's Annie."

John Anderson immediately turned his attention to her and for a moment seemed to look right through her. Annie felt herself blush under his gaze.

"You said…"

"Yes," he interrupted. "I know what I said. He usually turns up around eleven o'clock, so you may have to wait a bit."

Annie nodded. "Perhaps… perhaps I could help while I'm waiting…?"

John pursed his lips. "I don't see why not. Here." He handed Annie a large ladle. "Stir the soup," he said abruptly. "Then maybe you could give me a help with the songsheets."

Annie took the ladle and plunged it into the bubbling broth. The steam hissed up at her and Annie felt it blast over her face.

"Gently does it," said a voice next to her. The smiling face of Euan MacPherson looked down at her.

Annie blinked through the steam. "Constable MacPherson?" she gasped in amazement. "What on earth…"

"Oh, I've been a Salvatonist for years now," he said amiably. "And it's Sergeant MacPherson, by the way."

"Well… congratulations, Euan," Annie stammered. "I'm… very pleased for you."

Euan's mouth dropped. "Oh, I'm sorry, Mrs Melville," he said hurriedly. "It's, of course, only down to Mr Melville no longer being with us that they promoted me." He cleared his throat in embarrassment at causing Annie any distress.

Annie resumed the soup stirring. "It's alright," she said. "We all know there was no love lost at Alex's passing."

"Can I ask why you're here?" Euan enquired.

"I'm actually here to meet someone," Annie said. "It's important that I see my sister's husband and I believe he comes here."

Euan surveyed the throng of thieves and beggars queuing for their sustenance. "You don't mean…"

Annie nodded. "Yes, Euan," she said sadly. "Billy Dawson. He's one of them now."

"If you're finished gossiping, perhaps you could hand these hymn sheets out." John Anderson's voice was cool and emotionless. "They have to sing for their supper," he added.

Annie nodded and handed the ladle to Euan. "Here," she said. "I'd best do as I'm told." She followed John Anderson into the midst of the gathering and tried to keep her eyes lowered and her breathing shallow, as she handed out the songsheets.

An organ began to play 'What a Friend We Have in Jesus', just as she had handed out the last songsheet and a rumble of voices began singing the words. John Anderson moved to the front of the hall and Annie followed.

His sermon was short and to the point. God loved everyone, including them.

"And now, if you'll all join me in a prayer of thanks for the food we are about to receive." There was a mumble of words before John Anderson nodded to the men that they could now eat.

"Is he here yet?" Annie asked anxiously. "Perhaps he's not coming."

"He'll be here. Hunger will drive him in."

Annie flinched at his lack of concern and sat down on a chair at the side of the hall near a boiling urn of tea. Her shoulders slumped and she closed her eyes to blot out the mass of human wreckage in front of her, shuffling and grumbling over their soup bowls. How could it have all come to this, she wondered sadly, wishing she had never came to this awful place.

John Anderson's dark-brown voice sounded in her ear. "Here's what you've been waiting for," he said almost mockingly.

Annie opened her eyes. "Where?" she asked, peering into the smoke and foetid air which now seemed to fill the hall.

John pointed to a figure hunched over a bowl of soup. Annie tensed.

"Are you sure?" she asked, suddenly nervous and unsure.

"Allow me to introduce you." John Anderson took her hand and propelled her between chairs and bodies towards the figure sitting alone at the end of one of the trestle tables.

"Someone to see you Billy," he said evenly. For a fleeting minute Annie sensed John Anderson was enjoying Billy's despair.

Annie sat down opposite the figure and nodded her thanks to John Anderson.

"I'll leave you to it then," he said, irritated that he would not be remaining to witness Billy's pain.

Annie stared at the hands wrapped around the soup bowl. Nails bitten to the quick and skin encrusted with dirt and scars. They protruded from the sleeves of an army greatcoat stained and blackened with constant used as a blanket in some close or courtyard to protect its owner from the elements.

"Billy?" Annie said softly. "It's Annie."

She watched as the knuckles of the trembling fingers showed white against the grime.

"How are you, Billy?"

Two dark-brown eyes rose to meet hers and Annie gasped at the pain they held within their bloodshot rims.

"Oh, Billy," she cried, tears of pity surging from her soul.

The black hair, which had once framed his handsome face, hung in grey-streaked strands over his ears. Lines were carved deep into his forehead and around his eyes, curving to his mouth and pulling his lips down in a permanent scowl. Involuntarily, she reached out to touch him but he drew back.

"Annie Pepper," he whispered, his voice almost inaudible and his eyes staring madly. "My Annie, come for me at last."

Annie clutched the shawl around her shoulders, suddenly shivering despite the heat of the soup kitchen. "I-I… I need to s-s-speak to you, Billy," Annie stammered, all at once realising the depth to which Billy had been reduced.

"Socks," Billy replied, slowly and childlike. "Thank you for the socks."

Annie felt a huge lump in her throat and found it difficult to speak. "No need for thanks," she said. "They were knitted for you."

For a second Annie saw the flicker of a smile play at the corner of his mouth, then it was gone.

"What's happened to you?" she whispered. "What has this war done to you?"

Billy's lifeless eyes looked at her. "Annie Pepper," he said again. "My Annie."

Annie looked round in helpless confusion. She could no more ask Billy to agree to a divorce from Mary than she could have asked him to dance the Can-can.

"Had enough?" John Anderson was suddenly alongside of her.

Annie looked at him in despair, her eyes filling with tears and confusion. "Help him!" she said. "Please."

John sat down beside her. "Billy," he said, as if addressing a child. "Annie doesn't want you any more, nor does Mary."

Annie felt herself draw back in horror. "What are you saying?" she screamed, "Stop, please stop."

But John Anderson would not be stopped. "There's no woman wants you Billy Dawson," he continued, louder and louder. "You're all washed up."

Annie leapt to her feet as the words hit Billy like sledgehammer blows.

"*Stop it,*" she shouted. "He's sick!"

John Anderson pushed the chair away from him and stood up, pulling Annie behind him. "He's sick alright, but not as sick as everyone is of him."

Billy sat staring at his aggressor, his eyes never leaving his face. Annie felt she would faint and made a bolt for the door.

"See how they run away from you Billy, they all hate you, and *especially Annie.*"

The cold air rushed into Annie's hair and she gulped in its chill. She thought she was going to vomit and clutched her stomach as she prayed for the waves of nausea to cease.

"Annie, Annie, are you alright?" Euan MacPherson was holding her arm and guiding her down the cobblestoned lane into the gloom of the West Port.

"Take me home," she whispered, her voice barely audible.

"It's alright," Euan murmured. "I'll take you home."

Annie clung on to the policeman in shocked silence during the long trek back to Maryfield.

The image of John Anderson venting his anger at Billy was burned into her brain. How could he have been so cruel? Tears ebbed and flowed into Annie's heart as she realised he was wreaking his revenge for Mary and that his love for her was still there, despite having returned to Isabella.

"Thanks Euan," whispered Annie as they reach the door of her home in Maryfield.

"Where's Lexie?" he asked.

"Jessie Greig's minding her," replied Annie. "I'll collect her tomorrow."

"Good idea," said Euan. "Would you like me to make you some tea? It'll settle you down."

Annie nodded wearily. "Please," she said. "If you don't mind."

Euan guided her through to the kitchen and sat her at the table. "Show me where the teapot is," he said. "And I'll have a brew going in a jiffy."

The tea was hot and sweet and Annie drained the cup as though it were lifeblood itself.

"Another?" asked Euan.

Annie nodded and began to allow herself to relax.

"Do you want to talk about it?"

Annie looked at the concerned eyes of Sergeant MacPherson and forced a smile. "I wanted to see Billy to ask him to agree a divorce from Mary," she began. "Joe Cassiday and her want to marry and Mary's just given birth to Joe's son and…"

Euan stopped her flow of words. "Slow down," he said. "I hear what you're saying, but why is it you need to see Billy? Surely, it's Joe who should be doing the asking?"

Annie sighed. "I know, I know," she said. "But it's all such a mess and anyway, it's all my fault that Billy married Mary in the first place…"

Again, Euan stopped her. "I don't know all that's gone on before," he said. "But you can't take responsibility for three lives and that's not even counting *your own.*"

Annie looked at the brown eyes of Euan MacPherson. "And when did you get so wise?" she asked, feeling the weight of guilt suddenly easing from her shoulders.

"It's not wisdom," he said smiling. "It's just that I think I know you and sometimes you're too helpful for your own good, if you don't mind me saying so."

"Go on," Annie said, sensing there was more to come.

"I don't want to remind you of the way Alex treated you," he said gently. "But you felt responsible for his behaviour too. Am I right?"

Annie's mind mulled over the words. Euan was right. She had blamed herself for Alex's violence. And she blamed herself for Mary's dilemma and for Billy's plight.

"Maybe you should stop blaming yourself, Annie," Euan continued, his voice easing back into her head. "And start loving yourself instead."

"But..."

"But, nothing."

Annie began to feel the weight of duty disappear in the realisation that she wasn't responsible any longer. Not for Mary, nor for Joe and *not* for Billy.

"Thanks Euan," she said, slowly nodding as the sense of freedom spread through her.

Euan MacPherson stood up and extended his hand to her. "Welcome to the rest of your life," he said. "My friend Annie Melville."

Annie took his hand and felt a surge of gratitude towards Euan. "I couldn't have done it without you." Annie smiled. "My friend Euan MacPherson."

Chapter 25

Billy sat perfectly still, the stabbing words of John Anderson bouncing off the impenetrable barrier that surrounded him.

"Call yourself a man," John Anderson continued. "Don't make me laugh." He threw back his head and roared with glee. "Look at him everyone," he sneered. "The great Billy Dawson. A beggar *and* a *coward*!"

The assembled wreckage nudged one another and began pointing and muttering.

"Cast 'im out," shouted one, egged on by his contemporaries.

"Tar an' feather 'im," screamed another.

Billy sat emotionless, his eyes never leaving the form of John Anderson as he strutted and howled before him.

"And he expects a woman like Annie Pepper to *love* him!" he taunted. "*Him*, this woeful wreck who trembles at the mention of war."

"Stop it."

John Anderson turned slowly and leant over Billy's slumped shoulders. "What was that?" he asked scornfully. "Did you say… stop it?" He placed his hands on his hips and laughed louder than ever, accompanied this time by the entire hall of failed humanity, cackling and goading Billy, sensing there was, at last, someone to whom they felt superior.

"Please," Billy murmured. "Stop it!"

But John Anderson was not for stopping. "Pleeeeeasseee," he whined, imitating Billy to perfection. "Pleeeease don't make fun of me," he mimicked. "And who's going to stop me?"

"I am," said Billy, feeling something akin to anger stirring in the depth of his soul.

"Hhhhhaaaaaaaaa," whooped John Anderson. "Did you hear that? Little Billy Dawson's going to stop me." Howls of laughter rang in Billy's ears, led by John Anderson, the man who'd slept with his wife and now… who'd made a fool of him in front of Annie.

Billy pushed his chair back and tried to stand up amidst the raucous howl which surrounded him.

"*Sit down*," shouted John Anderson above the noise, pushing Billy roughly in the chest so that he fell back, missed the chair and landed in a heap on the floor. The laughing grew louder. "Look at him," roared John Anderson, turning to the crowd of tramps, now enjoying the spectacle. "Is Annie Pepper under the table do you think?" he yelled, "Is that what Billy's looking for?"

Billy lay sprawling amongst the dirt and debris of the wooden floor.

Is this what a son of mine has come to! Billy shook his head as the sound of his father's voice filled his head. *Get up and fight*, it continued. *Where's your pride?*

"You're *dead*," screamed Billy, clutching his hands over his ears. "LEAVE ME!"

The sounds of the baying began to lessen as he pulled himself back to his feet and turned to face his adversary.

"And who's going to kill me?" taunted John Anderson. "The coward of Dundee!"

Billy's heart began to pound as he felt a surge of anger rush through him. "I'm no coward," he said slowly and deliberately. "And I won't hear the name Annie Pepper spoken by an adulterer like you. If I've to kill you to stop you, then so be it."

John Anderson's eyes flashed with triumph. "Try away, Billy boy," he said, urging Billy forward. "If you think you're man enough." John Anderson unbuttoned his tunic and, taking it off, handed it to one of the Salvationists to hold.

"Mr Anderson," she began. "What ir you doin'?"

"Hush now, Jean," John said calmly. "We're just about to reclaim a lost soul."

Billy was pulling the heavy army greatcoat from his shoulders, when John Anderson's blow struck him full on the chin. Billy felt his head jerk back and his feet stagger beneath him.

"C'mon, coward," he goaded. "Annie Pepper despises you too."

"STOP SAYING HER NAME!" Billy shouted, dredging every ounce of energy from his depleted system.

"MAKE ME!"

Billy closed his ears to the sounds around him and fixed his eyes on the sneering face of John Anderson. He launched himself over the table and landed on top of John Anderson, knocking him over along with several of the jeering crowd.

"I'll make you alright," Billy screamed. "She's *mine* and don't you ever forget it." Lack of food and sleep had turned Billy's muscles to jelly and it didn't take long for John Anderson to overpower him. The tramps booed at the poor show and, mumbling discontentedly, returned to their seats.

John Anderson extended his hand to Billy. "Let me help you up," he said.

Billy took the hand and grasped it tightly as he hauled his ravaged frame back onto its feet.

"I'm sorry I had to do that," John said quietly. "But I had to know if the man still lived within."

"And does he?" Billy asked, unsure of what was meant.

"He does."

Billy pulled back his shoulders and felt his aching back begin to straighten.

"And, if he'll let me," John added, "I'd like to be his friend."

Billy's eyes were still dull with pain as he tried to understand what was happening to him and the motives of the man in front of him. "I think I'd like that," he said warily, his mind still slow and unsure. But the fire was back in Billy's heart.

"Will you let me help you Billy," John asked. "Me and Josie?"

"Josie?" Billy repeated.

"Josie MacIntyre," John replied. "She's a friend of mine too you know."

Billy nodded slowly.

"C'mon," John said gently. "Let's get out of here."

Despite the lateness of the hour, there was still a glimmer of light in the sky.

"Meet me at the Salvation Army Hall in Victoria Road tomorrow, after the service," John said, looking at the sky. "It'll be a good day tomorrow, Billy, God willing."

Billy watched, as the figure of John Anderson disappeared down Artillery Lane and into Tay Street. The cold night air was making him shiver, but it was a natural shivering and not the uncontrolled shaking he'd known for so long.

Billy's eyes blinked at the moon, waxing in the night sky. "Don't despise me Annie," he whispered. "I love you."

Billy spent the night under the stars on Magdelen Green. He watched as the Fife coastline gradually appeared out of the darkness and took on the colours of the land as it sloped towards the River Tay. The bridge curved to his left and snaked across the river towards the Wormit Halt, its central spans different from the rest, marking the place where it had collapsed into the river one stormy night, taking with it a train and all the souls on board to a watery grave.

Billy remembered his last journey across the bridge, taking him and Joe Cassiday to the battlefields of France. He could see Jock Thomson's grinning face as the coins they had tossed into the river, cleared the girders of the bridge before descending to the waves below.

"It's a good sign," Jock had said. "Means we'll come back safely." Billy smiled ruefully. Joe's coin had hit the girders.

He rolled onto his back, pulling his coat around him and gazed at the dawn. Birds were calling to one another and he could hear the solitary chime of a chapel bell as it called it's congregation to early mass somewhere in the Nethergate. It had been a long time since Billy had attended a church, let alone a Catholic one, but today… today would be different. He brushed the grass from his coat and pushed the straggles of hair behind his ears. His stomach was empty, as usual, but his heart was full of new hope as he made his way towards the sound of the bell.

The interior of the Chapel of St David was still and peaceful. Candles lit images of Christ and the Virgin Mary around its walls and the altar, draped with white and gold, glowed at the end of the aisle. Billy moved slowly towards it, allowing the silence and candlelight to seep into his soul. He sat in the front pew, his hands clasped together and his eyes closed.

"Thank you for my life," he said simply. "And help me to live it again."

There was no more to be said, no more to ask for. Billy opened his eyes. Father O'Brian stood before him.

"Welcome to the House of God," he said. "You're early for mass but if you'd like, I'd be happy to give you Communion."

Billy rose to his feet. "I'm sorry, Father," he began hesitantly. "But I'm not a Catholic."

Father O'Brian smiled. "It matters not to God whether you're a Catholic or not," he said softly. "Only that you come in good faith."

Billy nodded. "I've come in good faith, Father," he said. "And I would like Communion."

The Priest turned to the altar and genuflected, making the sign of the cross as he did so. "Please wait," he said to Billy. "I won't be long."

He returned with a goblet of wine and a bread roll, but instead of standing before Billy, he sat down beside him.

"This is the body of Christ," he said, breaking the roll into two pieces and giving one to Billy. "Eat this in remembrance of him."

Billy took the bread and ate it.

"And this is the blood of Christ," continued the Priest, offering Billy the goblet. "Drink it in remembrance of him."

Billy sipped the red liquid and swallowed its warmth.

"There," said the Priest. "Now you are at one with your God, healing can take place."

Billy felt a stillness inside him that he hadn't felt for longer than he cared to remember. With Annie, beside the river in Ireland was the last time he'd felt still.

"Thank you Father," he said. "You don't know what this has meant to me."

The Priest nodded. "God knows, and that's what matters."

Billy felt tears of gratitude fill his eyes. "May I come back sometime?" he asked.

The Priest clasped Billy's hands in his. "The door is always open," he replied. "To all of God's children."

The summer sun was warming the streets as Billy emerged from the Chapel and made his way through the Sunday morning quiet of the town. Pigeons scattered as he disturbed their morning roosts around the Town House and others, of his ilk, who had spent the night sleeping in corners, watched with bleary eyes as Billy passed them by. It seemed that he was seeing the town for the first time as he took in every detail of the shops and dwellings which lined the Wellgate. His feet made a scuffing sound as he moved over the stone cassies and he hummed a tune to himself as he climbed the steps into Victoria Road. 'I'm going to be alright,' he told himself. 'Alright.'

John Anderson welcomed Billy warmly into the Hall, empty now except for himself and Josie Anderson.

"Hello Billy," Josie said nervously. "John - Captain Anderson - has been telling me about how things are with you."

Billy looked at John Anderson, suddenly suspicious of his motives.

"Calm down, Billy," John said soothingly. "Josie's here to help."

Billy looked at his feet, ashamed of his ingratitude.

"I know," he said. "I know. I just suppose I don't know what to expect any more."

John Anderson put his hand on Billy's shoulder. "Come away man," he said. "Josie deserves your thanks, not your wariness. It's down to her and her belief in you that you're here with us today."

Josie felt herself blush as Billy's eyes found hers and conveyed their unspoken gratitude.

"Your room's still waiting for you," she said. "If you'd like to come back."

Billy couldn't believe his ears. "You mean, you'd have me back, after all that…"

Josie interrupted his words. "After all you've been through," she said. "Yes, Billy, I would. And Mr Campbell at the Mill wants you to know that your job's still there for you, any time you're ready."

Billy felt an overwhelming wave of gratitude surge through him. People who should have hated him were helping him. Neither John Anderson nor Josie MacIntyre had anything to thank him for, and yet…

"Why?" he asked.

"The Lord works in mysterious ways, Billy," said John Anderson. "Let's just say, he's working for you this time."

Billy looked at the two people in front of him. "Then I thank God for friends like you."

"Let's go home, Billy," said Josie. "You look as though you could do with some home cooking."

For the first time in a long time, Billy felt laughter tingle inside him. "And a good scrub," he added.

Chapter 26

Annie awoke to the early light of a Sunday morning and pondered Euan MacPherson's words from the night before. Had she really been so blind as not to see her desperation to help Mary and Joe was really to hide her own need to be loved! She pushed back the bedcovers and swung her legs over the edge of the wooden frame. Lexie needed her love, she told herself, and returned it a hundred-fold.

A picture of her child formed in her head and Annie smiled to herself as she filled the kettle with water from the well. And there was John, her son, in Ireland. Annie tried to picture him, but couldn't. She must write to Bella, find out if the boy in the care of Bella's mistress was indeed her own son. Her's and Billy's.

Annie finished her grooming and put pen to paper. So much had happened to her since Bella's last letter, she hardly knew where to begin, but begin she must. It was a difficult letter to write, bringing back as it did the memories of Alex, but finally, she finished it.

Dear Bella, it read,

I've had terrible unhappiness of late. Alex, my husband, is dead. Don't ask me to explain too much just yet, suffice to say, I'm now a widow. Lexie is fine, but it is more important to me than ever now, to know if the child being brought up by the good Doctor Adams and his wife is the child I bore in the poorhouse. Please write soon and remember my thoughts and love are with you. Ever your friend, Annie."

Annie folded the page into its envelope and sighed deeply, as images of Billy again filled her head. Quickly pulling on her coat, Annie left the house and made her way down to Jessie Grieg's to collect Lexie. Her daughter was laughing, as usual, when she entered the small room. She'd been blessed with a sunny nature and for that, Annie was truly grateful.

"C'mon my wee pet," she said scooping the little girl up into her arms and making for the door before Jessie asked too many questions. "We've to see your Auntie Mary and the new babe before we go home."

"Is she alright, Annie?" asked Jessie. "Mary eh mean?"

Annie nodded. "She's fine Jessie, just a bit tired, but now she's home, I'm sure she'll pick up."

"Sic a shame about that man o' hers?"

"You mean Joe," Annie replied sadly.

Jessie's eyes misted. "I mind when he wiz a Tenter at the mull," she said. "Every wummin in the place had a wee thing about Joe… an' now look at 'um." Jessie hung her head in genuine sadness.

"I know, Jessie," agreed Annie. "But at least he's alive, more than can be said for many another brave lad."

"Aye, aye," Jessie said. "This war's a terrible thing right enough. God help'im."

Annie felt herself beginning to dip back into a well of pity, but managed to pull herself together. "Thanks for minding Lexie," she said. "And I'm sorry I've to leave so soon, but I must see Mary and today's…"

"No need to explain," Jessie hushed, waving her finger in command. "See to your sister, lassie. I'll see you at the mill in the mornin'."

Annie took Lexie's hand and skipped her over the doorstep and onto the landing.

"Thanks Jessie," Annie said. "For everything."

It was only a few minutes' walk to Mary's house and Annie tried to decide whether or not to tell her about Billy as she walked, but failed. As it happened, the decision was made for her.

"It's Annie," she called as she passed the kitchen window. "Can I come in?"

"The very person we wanted to see," Joe said warmly, as he opened the door to Annie and Lexie. "Come away in."

Mary was sitting by the fire rocking her new child in her arms and looking pale and tired.

"Are you alright?" Annie asked anxiously, her eyes ranging over Mary's white skin for a hint of colour.

"She's fine," answered Joe. "Just needs feeding up."

Annie looked back at her sister but Mary just nodded.

"Here," said Annie. "Let me take little Joe for a while."

Mary handed the child over gratefully. "Thanks Annie," she said. "It's just taken it out of me, that's all."

But Annie wasn't so sure. She pulled the shawl clear of the child's face and gazed at him. He was a beautiful child and Annie felt her heart lift at the new life in her arms.

"He's beautiful, Joe," she said. Joe grinned sheepishly and acknowledged the compliment with pride.

"Is Mary alright?" she whispered anxiously, as soon as she was out of earshot of her sister,

"She seems very listless." Joe coughed nervously. "Never better," he replied loudly. "Isn't that right Mary!" Annie felt a wave of concern at Joe's feigned casual manner. "Nothing's going to spoil our happiness Annie," he said. "Everything's going to be fine."

Despite herself, Annie's anxiety grew. "What is it Joe?" she asked worriedly. "Something's wrong and you must tell me what it is!"

Annie heard Mary sigh deeply. "Tell her Joe," she murmured. "She'll find out soon enough anyway."

Annie felt her stomach tighten. "Tell me what Joe?"

Joe ran his fingers through his dark hair. "You'd better sit down."

Annie felt real fear now. "The doctors found something wrong with Mary when she was in hospital."

Annie's nails bit into her palms as she clenched her fists. "What is it?" she asked, trying to anticipate whatever Joe was going to say. "What did they find?"

Joe's shoulders slumped. "What've we done to deserve this?" he cried, his eyes filling with tears.

Annie froze to the spot. "Tell me what it is Joe," she said, her voice taking on a strange calmness.

"It's Mary," he stammered. "She's got TB."

For a moment the world seemed to stop spinning as Annie took in the words.

"TB!" she echoed, her heart pounding in anxiety in her breast. "Are you sure?"

Joe nodded. Mechanically, Annie handed the baby to his father and moved towards Mary. She clutched the white hand in hers, trying to find words that would reassure and comfort her sister, but failed. They both knew the only release from the disease was death.

"It's God's punishment on me," whispered Mary. "No more than I deserve for the terrible things I've done in my life…"

"No, Mary," Annie said softly. "You mustn't think like that. You've done nothing to deserve this, nothing at all."

A wry smile pulled at Mary's lips and she closed her eyes against the tears that were threatening to fall. "Not even Mrs Cook?"

Annie's grip tightened around her sister's hand. "You were frightened Mary," she said. "That's all. There's nothing sinful about being frightened."

Mary nodded in resignation. "Nor in living like this, I suppose. In sin."

Annie drew back in shock at her sister's words. "But you love Joe," she said adamantly. "And he loves you and the baby! How can that be sinful, Mary?"

But Mary's eyes had closed in an exhausted sleep.

"Oh, Joe," Annie whispered, her heart heavy with her sister's pain and shame. "What's to be done?"

But Joe's eyes were bleak with hopelessness. "Nothing," he said simply. We are living in sin. If I was half the man I'm supposed to be, I'd have killed Billy Dawson when I had the chance and…"

"Stop," interrupted Annie anxiously. "You mustn't say such a thing Joe. Whatever Billy's done, he's paying for it now too…" Annie tried to calm herself down. "He's a beggar in the streets Joe," she said slowly. "I've seen him and it scared me."

Joe clenched his fists. "And I'm a cripple," he said bitterly. "More of God's punishment is it?"

Annie pulled Lexie to her. "I don't know any more Joe," she said quietly. "There isn't one of us who's without sin as I can see and if that's God's way, then he's not much of a God."

"I'm sorry, Annie," Joe said woodenly. "I didn't mean to take out my frustrations on you." Pain was etched in his every feature. "I just don't know what to do for the best."

"Just be with her, Joe," said Annie. "She's going to need you to be strong."

Joe nodded. "I'll try," he said. "So help me, I'll make her days with me as happy as I can."

Annie clasped his hand tightly. "And I'll make sure, she doesn't die in sin. Billy's got to see he has to divorce her. Then she'll be free to marry you. I'll see to it." Annie wasn't at all sure how she was going to do this, but she had to try, for Mary's sake.

"She'd like that, Annie," Joe replied. "If only it could be so."

"I'll do what I can." She leant over and kissed Joe on the cheek. "I'll come by tomorrow night and every night that's needed. Isabella will mind Lexie for me."

The door closed behind Annie releasing her back into the outside world. Lexie's little hand slipped into hers as they walked slowly down William Lane and into King Street. Her mind and heart felt somehow numb as if it hadn't yet understood Mary's plight. Her only thought was to find Billy again and get him, somehow, to agree to divorce Mary. Surely, no man would refuse the request of a dying woman, not even Billy.

The thought of returning to the Soup Kitchen filled Annie with dread and asking John Anderson for help felt even worse, but he was her only link with Billy and speak to him she must.

He ushered Annie quickly into his study, in response to her visit, instructing Isabella at the same time to look after Lexie.

"Annie," he called brightly, his usual solemn expression masked by a smile. "The very woman I need to speak to."

"You seem remarkably cheerful for one who should be ashamed of himself," Annie said coldly.

"Ashamed!" John Anderson retorted. "And why should I be ashamed Annie Melville?"

"After what you did to Billy on Saturday night…"

John Anderson held up his hands to still her voice. "Forgive me, Annie," he said placing his hands together in prayer mode in front of him. "I had to do what I did and…" he cupped Annie's face in his hands. "It worked!"

Annie's eyes filled with confusion. "What worked?"

"Billy Dawson," he said enthusiastically. "Is *back*."

Annie shook her head. "Back," she said. "From where?"

John sat Annie down in a chair. "Back from Hell," he said. "A Doctor friend of mine has been working with soldiers sent back from France, usually labelled cowards…"

Annie flinched. "Billy's no coward," she said angrily. "He's sick."

"Exactly," replied John. "The medical term for it is shell-shock. The trembling, the despair, the deep isolation, that's what Billy's been suffering from…"

Annie's eyes widened in amazement. "And, can he get better?"

"Yes, he will get better Annie."

Annie tried to understand but couldn't.

John Anderson pulled a chair over and sat down beside her. "Sometimes, when someone closes down like Billy had, they disappear so far inside themselves no one can get to them. But sometimes, just sometimes, something or someone that they really love, can trigger their emotions to start working again."

Annie still didn't understand.

"Seeing you, Annie," John continued, "Opened a tiny door into Billy's prison and what I did was to make sure that door opened wider by forcing him to react. I had to try to get him jealous and then angry, don't you see? He had to feel again." John sat back with a sigh of satisfaction. "And, Annie, it worked. After you left, Billy and I fought."

"*Fought*?" Annie repeated. "Is he hurt?"

"Calm down," said John. "He's not hurt, Annie, he's on the mend, well on the mend."

Annie thought she understood. "Where is he now?" she asked.

"Where he belongs, with Josie MacIntyre. She's going to look after him till he fully recovered. She's a fine woman."

Annie sat back into the chair, trying to understand all John Anderson had said and also trying to understand the twinge of jealousy she felt that Josie MacIntyre and not she, was with Billy. She pushed the thought from her head.

"Something terrible has happened to Mary," she said.

It was John Anderson's turn to be caught unawares and he visibly flinched and quickly rose from the chair and returned to his desk. "Mary?"

"She has TB, John," Annie announced sadly.

John's brows drew together. "Is it certain?"

Annie nodded. "She feels it's God paying her back for the bad things she's done." Annie hadn't set out to wound John Anderson, but the barb hit home.

"I suppose you blame me for that!" he said quickly, his earlier humour now gone.

Annie shook her head. "I don't blame anyone, not you, not Mary, not anyone, but Mary blames herself and that's the worst thing. She wants to marry Joe and that won't happen 'til Billy divorces her. That's why it's now doubly important that I see Billy. Get him to agree to it, so Mary doesn't die in sin."

John Anderson paced the floor of the small study. "I don't think it's a good idea you see him just now," he said. "He needs to build up to life again slowly and any stress at the moment could put him right back into the blackness."

Annie waited till the pacing stopped.

"He sees me as a friend," John continued. "Will you trust me to speak with him, when the time's right?"

"Have I a choice?" Annie asked.

John Anderson came out from behind the protection of the desk and stood in front of her.

"There's always a choice, Annie," he said. "But I'm asking you not to exercise it and trust me to act when the time is right."

Annie felt a huge weight drop from her shoulders. "You're a good man John Anderson," she said, "I trust you."

Once again, Annie could see why Mary had loved John Anderson. His authority and strength seemed to spread calmness in her, making her feel protected and secure.

"Thank you Annie," he said. "And I'll pray for Mary."

Chapter 27

Billy watched Josie turn the key in the lock. The door swung open into the hallway releasing the familiar smell of lavender.

"Welcome home, Billy," she said, beckoning him into the dimness. "I'll just make us some tea." Josie disappeared into the kitchen and he could hear the water hitting the base of the iron kettle as she filled it at the sink.

He inhaled deeply and stepped over the threshold. After so long living on the streets, the walls seemed to close in on him and he pushed his hands against them as small beads of sweat formed on his brow.

Josie bustled into the hallway on her way to the parlour for no reason other than to find out why Billy hadn't followed her into the kitchen.

"Billy?" she said anxiously, hurrying towards him. "It's alright." She grasped his arm tightly. "Come away," she said softly. "Come and sit down."

Billy allowed her to lead him through into the parlour and lower him shakily into a chair.

"There," she said soothingly. "Everything's alright now. Just sit there a while till I get the tea."

Cautiously, Josie released his arm and disappeared back into the kitchen as Billy tried to steady his breathing. He could smell his unwashed body in the confines of the warm room and felt a wave of nausea as the odour settled on his stomach. Josie pushed open the door with one foot and bore the tray of tea things into the room.

"Now then," she said, switching into her caring mode which had been perfected as she'd nursed her husband in his last months. "I'm sure you'll enjoy this." She rattled the cups and poured the brew into them as Billy grew more and more anxious.

"It's not going to work," he finally blurted out. "I can't do this."

Josie put the teapot down and sat back on her heels on the floor at his feet. "What can't you do, Billy?" she asked evenly.

Billy's lip began to tremble. "Come back here again, like this." He ran his fingers through his lank hair and pulled at the ragged greatcoat which enveloped him. "You'd have been better off leaving me where I belong… on the streets."

Billy closed his eyes and wrapped his arms around himself wanting to shut out the world and Josie MacIntyre.

Josie picked up the cup of tea and began to drink it in silence. She'd been warned by John Anderson to expect things to be difficult and knew it was essential that she persevere.

"You'll feel better after a good wash," she said matter-of-factly. "And some clean clothes."

Billy heard the words through a haze of pity.

"And, you're wrong," she continued. "I wouldn't have been better off leaving you on the streets, because that's *not* where you belong, Billy Dawson."

Billy felt the tension ease in his stomach and sniffed loudly.

"Here," said Josie handing him her handkerchief. "Blow your nose now and drink your tea."

The soft white cotton hankie felt like silk to his hardened hands and he ran his fingers over it in wonderment. He pressed it to his face and smelt the trace of soap it had been washed in. It was as if his senses were wakening up from a deep sleep.

"Will I be alright, Josie?" he asked hoarsely. "I don't know, you see, I feel like a helpless newborn."

Josie clasped her hands together to prevent herself from reaching out to him. "You'll be fine Billy," she whispered. "Just trust me a little, please."

Billy nodded and handed her back the handkerchief. "I think I will have that tea now," he said, a glimmer of hope returning to his weary heart. "If that's alright."

Josie handed him the tea. "Bathtime next," she said smiling. "Then sleep."

Over the weeks that followed, Josie's patience and perseverance worked miracles and every time Billy looked like slipping back into the blackness of fear and panic, Josie would cajole and humour him back into the light. First, the colour returned to his face and then a shine to his hair and his muscles, prematurely wasted through lack of food and exercise, began to rebuild as Josie encouraged him to take long walks in the fresh air.

"You'll soon be able to return to the mill," she said one evening in her matter-of-fact way, after they'd finished their meal. Billy's eyes widened.

"Do you really think so?" he asked quietly, his stomach suddenly alive with butterflies.

"John says Mr Campbell will have you back any time you're ready."

Billy stood up and paced the small kitchen, a thousand 'what if's' flashing through his head. "What if I can't handle it, Josie?" he asked earnestly.

Josie smiled at him. "You will."

"What if Mr Campbell changes his mind once he sees me again?"

"He won't."

Billy ran his fingers through his hair in agitation. "How can you be so sure, Josie?"

Josie clasped her hands in her lap. "Have you looked at yourself recently?" she asked, smiling.

Billy frowned. "Looked at myself?" he echoed. "What for? I know what I look like."

"Do you?" asked Josie, taking his hand and leading him through into her bedroom and the Cheval mirror in the corner. She tilted it slightly and encouraged him to look.

Dark hair streaked with sliver curled around his forehead and the collar of his shirt. Dark brown eyes gazed out at him above a lean jaw and strong mouth. Little lines creased the corners of his eyes and deeper lines were carved into the hollows of his cheeks. Billy felt a surge of embarrassment as he took in, for the first time, the transformation that Josie had accomplished.

"You see?" she said quietly. "You're ready."

"If I am," Billy said softly. "It's down to you and your care. I shan't ever forget what you've done for me."

Josie felt herself colour. "It's only what any good Christian would do," she said. "And anyway, you did it all yourself really, you just needed a little help, that's all."

Billy gazed at the bowed head of Josie, her eyes never meeting his and her hands firmly clasped together and a rush of tenderness filled him. He moved in front of her and tilted her chin with a finger, forcing her to look at him. Her blue eyes were filled with anxiety. She mustn't allow herself to love him again, nor believe he felt anything for her except gratitude and maybe a certain liking. But his nearness threatened to overwhelm her and she quickly turned away.

"I'll tell John Anderson the good news," she called over her shoulder as she hurried from the room and back to the kitchen. "I'm sure he'll be as pleased as I am." She rapidly moved dishes and pots around the little scullery in an effort to calm down and keep herself from exploding into a welter of emotion.

Billy listened to the clatter of cutlery and felt his heart long for Annie. He wished he could love Josie, she would be so easy to be with and he owed her so much, but… Billy cursed himself under his breath.

Josie was right, he was ready to go back to work again and ready to live again as well.

"I'll go and see Mr Campbell tomorrow," he said to Josie's back as she scrubbed the pots at the kitchen sink.

Her small headed bobbed up and down in agreement.

"Thanks for everything, Josie," he added, searching for words to reinstate their friendship.

A soapy hand waved in acknowledgement before returning to the hot water.

"Do you mind if I go and see John Anderson myself?" Billy asked, pulling on his jacket. "Thank him man to man."

Josie shrugged her shoulders, hot tears now joining the water in the sink.

"I'll see you later then," he added gruffly. "I won't be long."

The door closed quietly as Josie's heart broke. She'd taken a gamble and lost and she knew now that Billy Dawson would never love her.

Billy took the short walk up Forfar Road to Janefield Place in the darkness of the late evening tasting the jute in the air and his heart quickened with anticipation and an anxiety to be over his final hurdle back to normality.

"I've come to see John," he told a surprised Isabella as she peered into the gloom of the porch to see who was knocking at their door at that time of night.

"You'd best come in then," she said, not sure how to take Billy. "I've heard a lot about you but I don't think we've ever met."

Billy stepped into the warmth of the hallway and shook her hand. "I'll tell John you're here," she added, releasing her fingers from his strong grip.

John Anderson appeared at the door of his study. "No need, Isabella, I overheard Billy's entrance. Come away in, man."

John's study was dark-brown and warm like a secret hideaway. A paraffin lamp burned on the desk casting long shadows into the corners of the room and competing with the fire for ownership of the communal spaces.

"I see you're better then?" he said, smiling at the change in Billy.

Billy nodded. "She's done a fine job on me," he said. "Josie, I mean."

John laughed. "Oh, I know who you mean alright. I'm sure the woman's an angel."

"Josie said you can see Mr Campbell, about me going back to the mill," Billy began. "Is that right?"

"It is, Billy," replied John. "And are you telling me that's what you want, to get back to work at the mill?"

Billy nodded.

John released an audible sigh of satisfaction. "Well done, man," he said. "I knew you'd pull through."

"I couldn't have done it without you and Josie," Billy replied quietly. "I can't thank you enough for… everything."

"It's Josie you want to be thanking," replied John. "It was her who kept faith in you, when everyone else gave up. If it hadn't been for her insistence… well, you know how much she loves you and you don't need me to tell you that love can move mountains."

John tapped his pipe out in the ashtray. "Can I offer you a whisky?" he continued, not waiting for Billy's agreement. "To celebrate your recovery." He poured two glasses of liquid amber and handed one to Billy.

Billy gazed at the glinting tumbler and was instantly back in the burning kitchen of his home in William Lane where a glass of whiskey had nearly cost him his life.

"I'll decline, if you don't mind," he said. "I don't have much taste for the whisky anymore."

John Anderson replaced the two glasses on the small cabinet beside the decanter. "That's what I wanted to hear," he said. "I'll call Mr Campbell tomorrow, tell him you're ready to return." He clasped Billy's hand in his. "By the way," he said. "There's one more thing I need to speak with you about, if you've got the time right now."

Billy nodded.

"It's about Mary," John Anderson began, conscious of his past involvement with her. "Things haven't gone too well for her lately and I've had Annie come to see me about her."

"Annie!" Billy exclaimed, his heart beginning to race at the mention of her name.

"Yes, Billy," John repeated evenly. "And what she wanted, only you can fulfil."

Billy clenched his fists. "I only wish that it were so," he said. "I've nothing I can offer Annie."

"Mary has TB," John told him gently. "And she's dying Billy."

Billy felt a wave of shock hit him. "TB!" he repeated anxiously. "Are you sure?"

John Anderson shook his head sadly, remembering the lovely Mary he himself had fallen in love with.

"I'm sure."

"Annie doesn't want me to go back to Mary, does she?" Billy asked painfully, aware that he was still her husband, "I couldn't do that… not even for Annie."

"No, Billy," John replied. "It's not that. Mary's in love, but not with you and not, for that matter, with me. She's living with Joe Cassiday and has a child to him."

Billy allowed the revelation to sink into his soul. "I don't understand…" Billy began. "If she's with Joe, what can I do?"

John sighed deeply. "Sometimes I wonder what men have done to God that he's blamed for everything that happens in this life. Mary thinks she's being punished by God for her past and that she's living in sin. She'll die happy, Billy, if she dies as Mrs Joe Cassiday and only you can make sure that happens."

Billy's face was fixed. "You mean, divorce her?"

John nodded. "Divorce her Billy, so she can marry Joe and give her child the future she herself will now never have."

"Is that what Annie wants from me?"

John Anderson nodded again. "Can you see it in your heart to do so?"

"I'll see to it," Billy replied, his thoughts focussed on Annie's wishes. "It's the least I can do for what I put Mary through." Billy felt his eyes sting as he remembered the painful silence of their life together. None of it should have happened, none of it. "Tell Annie, I'll see to it."

John Anderson nodded. "It's been a long road, Billy Dawson, for all of us, but perhaps now, we can see a turning."

The men shook hands warmly. So much water had flowed under the bridge and so much pain that neither of them had the heart for hatred any more.

"Is Mary still at the single-end?" Billy asked.

"With Joe and Nancy and little Joe," replied John. "God go with you."

The door closed behind Billy and the night enveloped him in its cloak of anonymity. He walked up Forfar Road to Clepington Road and down into the Mains of Fintry. Autumn was in the air as the harvest moon lit his way across the fields, shorn of their oats and barley now and being grazed by docile sheep before the winter set in. Billy pulled the collar of his jacket up round his neck and dug his hands into his pockets as he walked, his mind wandering with his steps where it would but always returning to Annie.

He could taste the saltiness of her skin and feel the softness of her lips on his. The sound of the stream babbling through the Den of Mains took him in his imagination back to the day in Ireland when he had first made love to Annie, down by the river beside the flax field. The day had been hot and he had kissed each bead of sweat from her breasts. He'd been the first and he knew it.

A rabbit rustled by him, out foraging, bringing him back to reality.

"I love you Annie Pepper," he called into the night. "I love you."

Mary's Consumption had worsened with the onset of the Autumn weather. Each breath seemed to tear from her lungs and dark circles were a permanent part of her pale features. Joe did what he could to comfort her, but leant more and more on Annie as the weeks went by.

"I can't bear much more of this, Annie," he said late one night as he took Annie to the door of the little house. "There's no betterment to it."

Annie squeezed his arm. "Don't say that Joe, she needs you more than ever now. You must be strong for her sake."

Joe hung his head. "She keeps on about God and how she's in a state of sin and she'll go to Hell when she…" Joe pulled the door closed behind him as tears began to choke his throat.

"Oh, Joe," Annie cried softly, wrapping her arms around his shaking frame. "It's alright, let it go."

Annie held on to Joe while his heart crumbled within him.

Suddenly in the darkness someone spoke. "I've come to help."

Both Joe and Annie jumped at the sound of the deep voice in the shadows.

Billy stepped into the glimmer of light filtering out into the night from the kitchen window. "If you'll let me."

Annie gasped as she realised who had spoken. "*Billy*?"

For a moment each stared at the other, unable to believe what was happening.

"I've spoke with John Anderson," Billy said evenly. "He's told me everything."

Annie moved closer to Joe. "What has he told you?" Annie asked defensively, remembering Billy's temper of old.

"That you want me to divorce Mary so she can marry Joe and be forgiven by God."

Joe's eyes searched Billy's face for any signs of anger but found none.

"Can I see her?" Billy asked cautiously, not knowing if it would make things better or worse.

"She's very ill, Billy," Annie said quickly. "I don't know…"

Billy held up his hand to stop her. "I've changed, Annie," he said softly. "No one goes through what I've gone through without learning some of life's lessons. Please, I think it'll help."

Joe and Annie nodded simultaneously. "Follow me," said Joe. "She's in bed all the time now."

The little procession entered the single-end, Joe leading the way, followed by Annie and Billy.

"Mary," he whispered softly in her ear. "Billy's here to see you."

Mary's eyes flickered open and for a moment Joe thought he saw a faint tinge of colour touch her cheeks.

"Billy, at last," Mary said weakly. "I've prayed and prayed God would send him."

Joe stood back making way for Billy to come closer to her.

"Hello Mary," Billy said softly, tears of guilt and shame forcing their way to the surface. "I'm sorry for all the hurt I've caused you."

Mary shook her head. "It wasn't your fault," she whispered. "I shouldn't have forced you into marrying me, not knowing how you felt about…"

"Sssshhhh, now," said Billy. "Save your strength for your wedding to Joe."

Mary's eyes took on a momentary sparkle. "I love him so much Billy," she murmured. "And we've a lovely baby boy."

"I know, I know," replied Billy. "And as soon as I can arrange a divorce, you and Joe can marry."

It was as if a huge weight had been lifted off Mary's shoulders and an angelic smile spread over her whole face.

"Thank you God," she whispered. "I can come home now." Her hand lay limply in Billy's and her eyes closed.

"Mary," Annie called anxiously. "It's Annie, speak to me, Mary."

Billy gently placed her hand back on the bedcover. "She doesn't hear you Annie," he said, a deep sadness in his voice.

"Mary, Mary," Joe cooed in her ear. "It's Joe, it's alright, we're to be married soon. Billy's going to fix everything…" A huge sob of pain forced Joe to stop. Mary had gone.

"She's dead isn't she?" Annie asked Billy, her voice barely audible.

Billy nodded imperceptibly. "I'm sorry Annie," he said softly. "For everything."

Annie knelt down beside Joe and together they wept for the woman they both loved while Billy slipped unnoticed back into the night.

"Do you think she'll go to heaven?" Joe asked Annie. "Like she wanted to?"

"If there's a God in heaven she will," replied Annie. "And I'm sure there is."

Chapter 28

"Billy!" exclaimed Mr Campbell. "Come away in, it's good to see you."

John Campbell clasped Billy's hand in both of his. "John Anderson said you'd be coming in to see me." He pulled a chair up to his desk and indicated to Billy to sit down. Any nervousness Billy had felt was soon dispelled by the warmth of John Campbell's greeting.

"And when can we expect you back to work?" he asked immediately Billy had settled into the chair.

"Well, whenever you want me, I suppose." Billy grinned. "The quicker I get back to normality, the better."

"How about Monday next?" John Campbell suggested. "I'm sure Jessie Greig will be glad to hand over the reins to you again. She's coped remarkably well, but it takes a man to do a man's job."

"Monday it is then, Mr Campbell."

John Campbell beamed. "Welcome back, Billy."

Josie MacIntyre was watching from the window and saw Billy turn into Morgan Street. She'd encouraged Billy to go back to work, but now that it may be happening, she was acutely aware that his need for her would no longer exist.

"It's only me," Billy called from the hall. "Is there any tea on the go?"

Josie forced a smile to her lips. "Does this mean we're celebrating your return to the big world?" she asked.

Billy dropped his jacket over the back of a chair. "It does, Mrs MacIntyre," he said lightly, "It certainly does. And, now, maybe I'll be able to repay you financially for all your work on my behalf."

The statement felt like a physical blow to Josie. She hadn't done it for money, she'd done it for love.

"There's no charge," she said quickly, turning to fill the kettle and avoid his gaze. "I told you, any good Christian woman would have done the same."

Billy's shoulders dropped at the remark. He'd hoped that by paying Josie money that he could have kept up the pretence to himself that she hadn't done it for love of him.

"Well, thank you anyway," he said feigning brightness. "I'll be starting back to work Monday week, so you'll have me out of your hair before too much longer." He waited for her reaction and it wasn't long in coming. He could hear quiet sobs coming from the kitchen.

"Josie," he called gently. "Are you alright?"

She sniffed loudly. "I don't want you to go," she said. "There's no need to, you can stay here as long as you wish."

Billy sighed. "I can't stay Josie, you know that as well as I do."

Josie swung round and he could see the hurt burning in her eyes. "And why not? Is Annie Melville going to have you back? Is that it?"

Billy felt himself flinch. "No," he said simply, "But if she did want me back, I'd go in a shot."

The remark seemed to freeze Josie in mid-flight. "Maybe you should go now then," she said unhappily. "I think I'd rather be alone."

"Josie," implored Billy. "Please don't do this. I never said I loved you and…"

"And you never said you could," she finished.

Billy sat down at the kitchen table and pushed his fingers through his hair. "You're a lovely lady Josie, and you'll make someone very happy one day, but that someone's just not me… that's all."

Josie dabbed her eyes with the back of her hand and sniffed again. "Then there's no more to be said, Billy Dawson, you're well now and it's time for you to go, that's all."

"Josie," Billy whispered. "Can't we still be friends?"

"No," Josie replied "We can't."

"Can I come back and see you, sometime in the future?"

Josie shook her head. "Go now, please," she said sadly. "I've things to do and I've a pupil arriving soon for an English lesson."

Billy pushed the chair back and stood up. "It's goodbye then, Josie," he said quietly. "And thanks again, for everything."

He was packing his meagre belongings into his army rucksack when Josie came to the door of his room.

"I've changed my mind," she said briskly. "You can stay till you make other arrangements, if you like," she said. "I'm being selfish and stupid and I'm sorry."

Billy frowned. "Even though you know I don't…"

"Don't love me," Josie interrupted. "Yes, even though you don't love me. Please, stay as my friend."

Billy had an almost unbearable urge to kiss her. No one deserved to be loved more than Josie MacIntyre, if only…

"Did I tell you I think you're wonderful?" Billy said, smiling. "My little guardian angel."

Josie smiled too, despite herself. "No you didn't," she said quietly, relieved now that he was still going to be close to her even for just a little while longer.

"Here," said Billy, dumping his rucksack back under the bed. "Let's go out and celebrate. I know there's a war on, but there must be somewhere we can go that's special."

"I've a pupil coming," Josie reminded him.

"Send him away," Billy urged. "We'll go to Broughty Ferry, walk along the beach, just like we did that day last year before the war started."

"But it's freezing and it's going to be dark soon and…"

"Alright, alright," Billy raised his hands in mock defeat. "Then let's have a picnic here instead and be friends."

"Friends," agreed Josie. "And it's your turn to make the tea."

For a moment it seemed, Billy touched happiness, before a knock at the door interrupted his mood.

"I've come fir my lesson, Mrs MacIntyre," said a small voice.

Billy heard Josie mumble some reason for sending him away and made his way into the kitchen.

"Cheese sandwiches do you?" he called through to Josie.

"Cheese will be fine," she replied. "And we can pretend we're sitting on the sands at Broughty Ferry."

Billy brought through the food and Josie poured the tea.

Her blond hair hung in tiny curls over her forehead and around the nape of her neck as she leant over the teacups, her delicate hands arranging them on the table. From somewhere deep within him, Billy suddenly felt a longing to hold her. She handed him his tea.

"I almost lost you," he said. "Didn't I?"

Josie's eyes held his. "Would it have mattered?" she asked softly.

"Yes," said Billy, swallowing hard. "I think it would."

Josie blushed and spooned sugar into her tea. "Here's to the future," she said, raising the cup to her lips. "Whatever it brings."

"To the future," answered Billy.

Bella's letter arrived on the morning of Mary's funeral.

Annie, my dearest friend, it began,

Such news, as you're never goin ti beleev. I've found out that young Master Adams ***is*** *your own born son Annie, I swear it's the truth. I asked Cook where he come from and she told me the nuns brought him in the ded of nite, sed he was a gift from God and that the mother was sickly and couldn't look after him. Annie, they brought him the same day as you bore him. He's your babe, for certain.*

Annie crushed the letter to her breast and tried to understand the confusion in her soul. Her son was alive! Billy's son! A wave of regret swept over her, a sorrow she felt too heavy to bear.

"Now's the time to tell Billy," she decided to her reflection in the mirror, once Mary was laid to rest and she could see clearly.

The knocker on the door clattered against its metal plate.

"Coming," Annie called, taking a deep breath and pulling back her shoulders. "Joe!" she exclaimed at the sight of the pale face in front of her. "Come in, please." She ushered him into the kitchen and sat him down at the table. "Where's Nancy," she asked. "And little Joe?"

"Mrs Ogilvie," he muttered, pain etched into every line of his handsome face. "She's minding them till the funeral's…" His voice tailed off like a kite drifting off into the air.

Annie sat down beside him and took his hands in hers. "Oh, Joe," she whispered. "You mustn't take on so, you'll make yourself ill."

"I can't cope Annie," he replied, his voice barely audible. "Mary was my strength and support, mine and the babes', and now…" His eyes met hers begging for an answer. "I don't know what to do, Annie."

Annie felt herself take his pain onto her shoulders. "I'll help," she said, not thinking it through to the end. "You can depend on me."

Joe's eyes filled with tears. "Do you mean that, Annie?" he asked. "Really mean it?"

Euan MacPherson's words suddenly sprang into her mind and she became aware that she was doing it again, taking on the cares of the world, shouldering responsibility for things that weren't of her doing.

"This isn't the time to talk of this Joe," she said kindly. "We must lay Mary to rest first and then decide what's best."

Joe nodded sadly. "You're right Annie," he said wearily. "Mary must be laid to rest with her God."

The funeral was short and sparsely attended. Annie and Joe, John Anderson and Isabella, her arm around Lexie's small shoulders, Jessie Greig and Joe's brother Charlie and two of the neighbours from William Lane. She had hoped Billy would have come, but she didn't see him. Not, that is, until she and Joe turned to go back to William Lane to collect the children and it was Joe who saw him first.

"Isn't that Billy over there?" he asked Annie, pointing with one of his crutches to the tall figure standing beneath a leafless willow tree.

Annie felt her throat tighten and she caught her breath as his form filled her eyes. "It is Joe," she said almost to herself. "And I must speak with him."

She heard Joe sniff in an effort to stem the flow of tears that had relentlessly flowed down his cheeks during the burial of Mary.

"I'll see you back at William Lane," she said. "If that's alright."

Joe nodded lamely. "Charlie'll walk back with me."

His brother nodded to Annie and put his arm around Joe. "C'mon boyo," he said. "We'll take it slow."

Annie watched as the two men moved slowly down the cemetery path, Joe's crutches scraping into the hard earth.

Billy watched the scene from the shelter of the tree, a panorama of memories drifting in and out of his head in the silence of that dead place. He saw Annie walk towards him and felt a sudden fear. He didn't know why he'd come to the funeral, he hadn't loved Mary for a long time, if ever, and he knew Annie cared nothing for him, and yet… he was here.

"Can I speak with you Billy," she began. "Please?"

Billy nodded silently.

Annie gazed at her shoes, not knowing where to start, but knowing she had to start somewhere to bridge the gulf of time that was between them.

"Thanks for what you did," she said. "For Mary, I mean, and Joe."

Billy acknowledged the gratitude with his eyes.

"Will you walk with me to William Lane?" she asked quietly. "I've things to say to you that can be said now… now that Mary's at peace."

Billy looked over his shoulder to the gates of the cemetery. "I can't Annie," he said. "Josie's waiting."

Annie raised her eyes and looked past him. The slim figure of Josie MacIntyre, a black bonnet tied beneath her chin and her coat turned up against the chill, was standing by the railings that flanked the iron gates.

For an eternity neither of them spoke while each tried to quell the trembling inside them, Billy's of long standing and Annie's newly formed.

"Is it serious?" Annie asked, already knowing the answer.

Billy nodded. "She's a wonderful woman Annie, and I don't deserve her, but…"

Annie felt the last of her emotions drain out of her. "I see," she said.

"What did you want to say to me?" he asked, uncomfortable now in her presence.

"Nothing," Annie answered. "It'll keep." She indicated Josie's anxious form. "You'd better not keep the future Mrs Dawson waiting," she said. "And thanks again, Billy… for everything."

"It wasn't meant to be like this, Annie," he said sadly. "Not like this at all."

Annie felt a wry smile pull at her lips. "No, Billy," she replied, her eyes levelling with his. "It wasn't." She watched his tallness stride through the grass between the headstones till he reached Josie MacIntyre and she could watch no more.

The sky was darkening. It would rain soon on the emptiness of her soul. She gazed at the brightness of the headstone, new and still alien to its surroundings.

"Mary," she whispered. "Say hello to Mammy and Daddy for me and tell them I'm going back to Ireland soon to find my son." She bent down and patted the earth covering her sister. "Nobody could play the banjo like you Mary," she said. "And I'll tell Lexie all about you when she's bigger… and my son John too… when I see him."

"Are you alright, Annie?" the gentle Scottish lilt of Euan MacPherson's voice sounded at her side.

"Sergeant MacPherson," she said, startled. "I didn't hear you… how long have you…"

Euan put his finger to his lips. "Hush now, Annie. Not long." He helped her to her feet. "It's a sad day, Annie," he sighed. "A sad day."

Annie nodded silently.

"Can I see that you get home alright?" he asked gently. "I'm off duty now and if there's anything I can do to help…"

"You sound like me," she said, glad he was there. "Always taking the cares of the world on your shoulders." He linked his arm in hers. "And wasn't it you who told me to stop worrying about everyone else and look after myself?" she added, allowing him to lead her away from the graveside.

"Ach, what do I know," he said, sheepishly. "A simple bobby like me."

"More than most," said Annie, feeling the warmth from his body by her side. "More than most."

THE END

Printed in Great Britain
by Amazon.co.uk, Ltd.,
Marston Gate.